FOREST PARK

A Rick Conwright, PI Mystery

Peter Swan

Copyright © 2015 Peter Swan
All rights reserved.

ISBN: 1515204383
ISBN 13: 9781515204381

This is a fictional work. The characters, events and most of the specific places and businesses in this story are not real and are not intended to refer to or resemble actual persons, entities or places.

To the oppressed, displaced refugees of this world

Tuesday, April 7th afternoon

A light rain was falling. That was helpful. Pulling the hood of his parka up and around his face would seem natural. Under the parka, he carried a large, empty daypack. He had parked his car where the shoulder widened out some eight-hundred feet from the house. He confirmed that there were no sight-lines from the neighboring homes once he reached the driveway. The truck was gone, confirming that the homeowner was still at work. He jogged to the wooded area behind the house and tried the back door. It was locked so he moved to a window beside the door. He peered in and saw that the door opened into a small room with cupboards, a utility sink, and a water heater.

He had brought a glass cutter and used it to tap out a crude semi-circle. His gloved hand could just reach the bolt latch on the inside of the door. Seconds later, he was inside.

He walked quickly through the rooms on the ground floor. He saw no computer. Upstairs, in what must have been an unused bedroom, he found a desk and a laptop computer. He turned on the computer and was relieved to discover it was not password-protected. He scanned the documents file and slowed when the listing reached a document named "The Past Perfect Murder". He opened the file and had only to read the first few pages. He loaded the laptop into his day pack.

He reasoned there had to be field notes or written statements. The drawers in the desk proved to hold only bills to be paid and customer information for the homeowner's business. An unlocked file cabinet had old tax returns, nursery catalogues, and car servicing records. The field notes must be hidden and he did not have a lot of time left to search. If such notes existed, he believed they would be in that room. There was a small bookshelf containing paperback novels and hard-cover books on landscaping and sylviculture. He checked behind the books and found nothing. He tried to imagine where the man could have hidden a tablet or a small notebook, yet still have it readily available when he needed to refer to it. He looked behind the frame of the only wall-hung picture in the room, an enlarged photo of a hummingbird. Nothing. A banjo clock on the wall had a compartment at the bottom but, it too, was empty other than a winding key.

He swept the room with his eyes one last time. His gaze fell on a narrow table against the far wall. He lifted a brass table lamp with a hexagonal base. The bottom felt pad had been removed and inside the cavity he found a spiral-bound four-by-six notebook.

There was not time to read through the little book. Reading the first page was enough for him to know. He added the notebook to the daypack and hurried through the back door.

1

Thursday, April 9th late afternoon

Yesterday, the killer had observed a man resembling Westlake taking his dog on a late-afternoon walk into Forest Park. The dog, a German shepherd with a muzzle that was starting to gray, was running free, but did not stray far from his master. Today, the killer walked five hundred yards down the trail, then veered off fifteen feet and hid behind the mossy hulk of a long-fallen fir. He found himself in a natural blind concealed by the log and by the scented boughs of saplings. If Westlake was consistent in the timing of his dog-walking excursions, he guessed his target should appear in about fifteen minutes. He drew the Walther PP380 from the pocket of his cargo pants and slipped off the safety. Laying the gun on the needle-covered ground, he pulled on latex gloves. Finally, he pulled a nylon stocking over his head. He willed himself to stay calm as he awaited Westlake's arrival.

It had not been difficult to locate his victim. Westlake was in the residential listings of the phone book. Two days earlier, he had taken Westlake's laptop. What he saw there, confirmed his worst fears. Westlake was a serious threat.

It would have to look like a simple robbery that took a violent turn. Westlake's living near the edge of the huge wilderness that was Portland's Forest Park made his job easier. The fact that homeless persons were known to camp in the park could support a random-killing theory.

He would take Westlake's wallet and jewelry, if he had any, to anchor the robbery illusion. In a moment of inspiration, the killer had entered the only nearby cocktail lounge, The Skyliner. He had scooped up a matchbook at the unattended hostess station and quickly departed. Using a ballpoint pen, he printed the name "Carolyn" on the inside of the cover. He would leave this in one of Westlake's pockets to further confuse matters.

Just then he heard striding footfalls on the trail of packed dirt. He also heard a voice saying "stay close, Wolfgang, or else I'll have to use the leash." He peered over the log and saw Westlake and the German shepherd moving down the path. He let them get a good fifty yards ahead, then jammed the gun in his pants at the small of his back. He crept back to the trail and fell in behind Westlake. A minute later, he had closed the gap between them. He was confident that no one on the road above would hear the sound of his gun.

Westlake sensed his presence and looked over his shoulder. Glimpsing the stocking mask, Westlake spun around.

"Who are ..? What's this!"

The killer pulled the Walther and fired twice. Westlake fell heavily to the ground. He studied the body and felt along the jawline. There was no pulse. He could see both rounds had hit Westlake in the upper torso and blood was starting to spread on the front of Westlake's denim shirt. The dog, who had been exploring in the undergrowth fifty feet away came back and started sniffing the body and whimpering. The murderer ran back to where he had fired, searching quickly but finding only one of the two cartridge cases. He picked it up and headed back to the body to search his victim's pockets.

Just as he reached the dead man, the dog charged him with an enraged growl. He raised his leg to fend off the leaping dog. The shepherd's jaws closed on his thigh before he could shake it off. The dog charged again. He thought of shooting him, but did not have time to draw his weapon. With desperation, he kicked out and landed a crushing blow to the dog's right foreleg. It howled in pain and limped off into the forest. He dropped his pants long enough to see some blood and several puncture wounds. He grimaced at the pain, but thought iodine and a bandage would be all he needed once his business there was finished.

He had seen no others on the trail, but the killer knew he had to hurry. He was damp with sweat from the adrenaline rush. He took Westlake's wallet and keys and found a Rolex on his wrist. He removed the watch and planted the matchbook. He could not see any cell phone. Careful not to break any branches as he moved, he dragged the body ten yards into the forest. He found a small windfall branch and used it to sweep any footprints off the trail as he headed back to the road.

2

Friday, April 17th early afternoon

My girlfriend, Angie, and I were finally talking seriously about combining our households. Angie stayed over several nights a week on the houseboat that also doubled as my office. But she needed her own home office and, cozy and fun as my place was, it was a bit of a tight space for two. Angie's apartment was close to downtown, but it too was not large enough. Portland's residential housing market was recovering nicely and we wanted to get in before homes became too pricey. My private investigation business was doing quite well thanks to the successful and well-publicized outcomes of the Langlow kidnapping case and the Caughlin murder case. And my half interest in a twelve-unit apartment complex gave me a nice cushion in case the PI business slowed down. At the same time, Angie Richards' career as a TV newscaster at a leading Portland station had earned her a raise and some well-earned attention in the area. All this, meant we could think seriously about buying a more conventional home. I no longer liked the idea of having my professional office in the same place as my residence. I had already had some threatening intruders confront me at the houseboat. I had no intention of mixing that kind of "work" with my and Angie's new residence-to-be.

For several months we had been discussing our future and this was a next step to a more permanent arrangement. We knew our love for each other was far more than a physical infatuation. Our personalities and strengths and hopes had been challenged and tested. They had held up very well and given us reason to see an enduring future together.

Jim Blanchard was a fellow player on our City League volleyball team. He was a realtor and we both liked him. We had asked Jim to keep his eyes open for us, especially for homes along Alameda Avenue between forty-fifth and fiftieth. If we could find such a place, the price – even today -- would likely be a stretch. That meant we were hoping to find a well-built house with a good floor plan that nevertheless needed some sprucing up and a modernized kitchen. You might say we were looking for a quality fixer-upper.

I was almost finished with my report to a client on a car-repair insurance scam. There was nothing I had to take care of on the weekend and Angie was free after her mid-day newscast. We decided Saturday afternoon would be a good time for our first house-hunting meeting with Jim followed by Angie and I cruising some neighborhoods. The weather report for tomorrow was promising and we were excited to start the process.

It was right after lunch when my phone rang and a man asked if he could see me about handling a case. He insisted on meeting right away, so I gave him directions to the marina. I added that my boat was the second one from the north end of the float. I called Angie and Jim and explained that there was a slight possibility that I would have to postpone our initial meeting. Forty-five minutes later, a tall, slender man in his middle fifties knocked on my door. He introduced himself as Melvin, "call me Mel", Westlake. I showed him to the office, put my nearly-completed insurance report aside, and offered a pop or a beer. He declined and got right down to business.

"Mr. Conwright, my brother Brian was murdered eight days ago."

That opening took the smile off my face. Whatever he wanted me to do, it would not be a straightforward job. "That's terrible. I'm so sorry. How do you think I can help you?"

With a little snort of disgust, he said "the police think it was a robbery gone bad. Brian lived very close to the West edge of Forest Park and his body was found near one of the trails in the park. His watch and wallet were missing and he'd been shot twice in the chest. The coroner found the bullets in his body and, in his pocket, a matchbook from a nearby cocktail lounge with a woman's name, Carolyn, printed inside."

"Do you know if he's been seeing anyone named Carolyn?"

"Not that I know of. Brian and his wife have separated. But, given that he and his wife have not yet filed for divorce, I doubt he's seriously dating. I do think he's seen a little of an old friend named Carla, but that's it."

"What was the name of the cocktail lounge?"

"I think the homicide detective who spoke to me said it was 'The Skyliner'."

"Would your brother have been one to frequent such a place? Maybe make it his 'local'?"

"I suppose he might have, but he was not really a bar kind of guy. Besides he didn't smoke so the matchbook doesn't make much sense to me."

"Have the detectives turned up anything else?

"I don't think so. They were fairly good about touching base with me in the first few days. Except for a little blood where the body was found, they don't even seem to have any forensic evidence like the cops on TV always find. Of course they've interviewed his immediate neighbors, but they tell me no one saw anyone strange or out of the ordinary. The police detective also told me there have been no charges on his credit card so far. But I've heard nothing in the last few days and I get the impression that I won't be 'in the loop' going forward."

"Did your brother often enter the park?"

"Well, I'd guess he walked his dog there quite a bit, but he worked hard at his job and I doubt he did a lot of hiking on the weekends."

"You say he worked hard. What was his occupation?"

"He was an arborist. He worked out of his home."

"Tell me more about the wife"

"They've been estranged for almost a year. I don't think there were any big fights or hostility, but I haven't sensed they were making much progress toward reconciliation. I have a feeling it would've ended in a divorce."

"I gather you're frustrated with the police. Are you asking me to try to find who killed him?"

"Yes! I'm afraid they're going to let it stand as an unsolved crime. I'm worried they'll think it was just some unidentifiable homeless guy who had a gun and panicked before my brother handed over his money."

It is true that some of the homeless camp out in the park, but I doubted the police would write it off that easily. Mel Westlake seemed a little impatient, but it did sound as though he wanted my help. "Do you have reason to think it *wasn't* just a hold-up that got out of control?"

"No, not when you put it that way," he said with a resigned sigh. "But Brian was my kid brother. I've always tried to be there for him. He was a nice, steady kind of guy ... he wouldn't hurt a soul and I find it hard to believe he could've made a mortal enemy. And he was a calm person ... I can't see him doing anything to panic a would-be robber. I *do* want to get justice for him ... to bring his murderer to account! I've read about your cases in the papers and heard about them on television. You're the person I want digging into his death!"

"Well, I could spend days, even weeks, on this and perhaps only match what the homicide detectives can discover. And my fees could pile up."

Westlake gave me a determined look. "Listen, I own several Burgerville restaurants. I'm not stinking rich, but I'm comfortably well off. If you take the case, you won't have to worry about getting paid!"

"I'm sorry. I didn't mean it that way ... I was trying to say it could be time-consuming and, despite your present frustration with the police, there might be a whole lot of overlap by the time it's done."

"No offense taken. I get your point. But the police work, shall we say, for the larger community. I want someone to work on behalf of my brother!"

"Alright. I'll take your case." I handed him my standard engagement contract.

He hurriedly scanned it, initialed the places indicated and added his signature at the bottom. "Thank you, Mr. Conwright"

"You can call me Rick."

"Okay, Rick. Can you start tomorrow?"

I could see he was anxious that I get right into it, but I was going to protect Angie's and my first foray into the housing market. "I can get started for a few hours in the morning, but I'm quite tied up the rest of the day. Tomorrow, I will check out his house and the place where his body was found and then talk with his wife. I'll go on from there on Sunday."

He handed me his business card. "You don't have to send me written progress reports, but I will greatly appreciate it if you can just call me as often as you have something worthwhile to report."

"I'll do that. Do you have keys to his house? Would you give me the name and phone number of his wife?"

"Brian wanted me to have an extra set of keys so I do have them. He handed me two keys and wrote down the address of his brother's house and the wife's information. He had come in looking stressed and weary, but he left the boat with a look of relief and strode down the float toward the marina gate.

3

Saturday, April 18th morning

My relationship with the Portland Police Bureau detectives is mixed at best. I guess it's safe to say at least one of the lieutenants thinks I'm a loose cannon when I'm working an investigation. It is true that a couple of times I have not waited for the police to work through their procedures or to make a decision about a person of interest. But it's also true that in those cases I have been the first to identify the real perpetrators and to set up their capture. When I worked for The Oregonian as an investigative reporter, I enjoyed a good deal of autonomy and was able to probe successfully into several explosive situations. But, yes, it was that same determined probing that eventually got me fired and stressed my then marriage. My wife felt I was obsessed with a particular developer who, I was convinced, was corrupting local politicians. The developer was influential and contended I was harassing him. I never quite found the smoking gun I was hunting for and the paper finally had had enough.

Anyway, I may be seen as a bit of a "cowboy" by some in PPB, but I have a success record they can't argue with. Another big plus is my long-standing friendship with homicide detective Paul DeNoli. I first encountered Paul when he came under Internal Affairs scrutiny for fatally shooting one of two men escaping the scene of a liquor store robbery. The robbers would not surrender and a shootout ensued. Both men had been firing at the police. One of them had, unknown to Paul, emptied his magazine and dropped his gun just as Paul's bullet hit him. I was covering the event as part of a story on armed robberies. I finally tracked down a witness who was able to corroborate Paul's contention that he had no way of knowing the dead man's gun was empty or that he was attempting to leave at the moment Paul fired. This witness saved Paul's career and Paul went on to win his detective's badge a year later. He has been my point of contact with PPB and my source of information about police procedure ever since. And, when I'm on a case that also involves law enforcement, he has usually been able to facilitate our working together.

I called Paul to tell him I had been retained on the Westlake killing and to ask if he was handling it.

"No," Paul said, "that case has been assigned to Dan Niemus. Do you know him?"

"I think I've heard his name, but I've never met the man. I'll give him a call."

"Good idea, but be warned. He's pretty territorial ... even with the rest of us. This Westlake is the guy who got robbed and killed in Forest Park?"

"That's right. I've been hired by his brother. He seems to want 'double coverage' ... doesn't want it to fall into the unsolved file."

"Well, don't play that up to Niemus. I'm sure they've already rousted the park people and are in full investigation mode. Anyway, good luck!"

I asked Paul if he could transfer my call and I caught Niemus at his desk even though it was Saturday. I introduced myself and started to explain how I came to be involved.

"Yeah, I've spoken with the brother. Told him I'd try to keep him in the picture. What the hell does he want you to do?"

Was I sensing some insecurity and defensiveness? Or was Niemus just an overworked detective who didn't want me trampling on his leads or prematurely contacting persons of interest?

"Of course he wants the murderer to be caught," I replied. "I guess he thinks an additional pair of eyes can't hurt ... maybe a different perspective, someone to scratch around the edges, kind of a complementary effort. And, of course, if I turn up anything fresh, I'd let you know."

"I don't like this much, Conwright! You could screw up our investigation even if you didn't mean to. Why don't you just tell the brother he can consult with you after we report progress to him?"

"Detective Niemus, I'll be straight with you. Mr. Westlake wants me to actively investigate. But I'm a professional. I won't leak information that has to be kept from the public. And, by sharing information and ideas, we could work well together without compromising the efforts of you and your team."

"I'm sorry Conwright. Maybe I didn't make myself clear. I don't need to share information or 'ideas' with you. I want you to keep your Goddamn distance and not meddle in our investigation!"

This guy must never have enrolled in Public Relations 101! "I'm sorry that's your attitude. You might want to talk with Paul DeNoli. He'll tell you I've worked with PPB before and haven't screwed up any of its cases."

Not a great beginning for sure, but I had touched base and made an effort to set up some cooperative effort.

My first stop after ending the call to Niemus was Brian Westlake's home on Forest Lane. It had a second story at one end, and a green aluminum roof punctuated by a brick chimney. It was set on a fairly large lot with evergreen trees and an outbuilding in the rear. I entered and started taking pictures as I moved from room to room. The furnishings were modest and free of dust. I guessed they were purchased in the late nineties. A copy of The Oregonian for the day Westlake died lay on a small pine table next to an easy chair. The chair faced a relatively small flat-screen TV. The dining room featured an attractive corner cabinet with some china and a silver coffee pot. There were no dirty dishes in the kitchen and the appliances were fairly new. There was a pet dish and a bag of dog food near the back door. I noticed a semi-circle of glass had been cut out of a window next to the door and wondered if that meant someone had broken in.

An upstairs bedroom had been turned into an office of sorts. If there were any items or documents that would shed light on Westlake's business activity I would probably find them there. I decided to check the master bedroom next and then return to the office. The clothes in his closet were plain, but of nice quality ... mostly from Eddie Bauer or Land's End. I searched the boxes on the shelves, but found nothing untoward and nothing to shed any light on his personal life. There were no porn magazines or racy videos stashed under the bed or the mattress. The medicine cabinet revealed no drugs, prescription or otherwise.

I returned to the office and began a fast review of his bank statements, his appointments book, the desk calendar, and a small stack of bills. The house was not a crime scene so I decided to take a folder marked "contracts", his appointments book and his calendar with me for some follow-up later. The most interesting thing I found was a series of deposits of twelve-hundred and fifty dollars each month for the last four months. The amounts did not appear on his books as revenue. Could he have been blackmailing someone? Someone who wanted to stop the blackmail by killing Westlake? The amounts seemed too small and the timing too regular, but it was worth running down.

From the house, I went to the workshop. The second key on the ring his brother had given me unlocked the door. His stake-bed truck, a 2006 Chevy, was parked beside the workshop. It had several ladders on side racks and, under a tarp on the bed, I saw a set of lineman's climbers with a safety harness and various picks and shovels. On each door was a sign "Brian Westlake, Certified Arborist /Landscaping" with his phone number. The workshop held no sealed boxes or, if there had been such, the police had taken them. On the shelves were the usual things: tools, gas cans, some fishing tackle, a Christmas tree stand, and half-empty paint cans. Under the plastic-roofed shelter just outside, I saw a stump grinder and a Ditch Witch chained to the framing.

I took photos of the equipment and headed on foot for Forest Park. As his brother had said, the park boundary was no more than a quarter of a mile down the road. The packed-gravel Lane ended at a gate where it widened a little so hikers could park their cars. It was there that a trail began. The path dropped gradually for several hundred yards as it headed for a trail junction and then became steeper. There was no longer any crime-scene tape so I had to approximate where the shooting took place. Despite his orneriness, Niemus had told me the body was found on the right side of the trail and about six-hundred-and-fifty trail-yards from the gate. I paced what I hoped was that distance and stopped to look around. The forest was still, with the morning sun filtering through the boughs of tall firs. The undergrowth was not overly dense: saplings, Oregon grape, some salal, and I thought I saw some wild strawberry vines growing on a carpet of needles. I wasn't really expecting to find a red-hot clue, but I never like to start work without a first-hand impression of the place where the trouble occurred.

I had called Westlake's estranged wife, Sandra, earlier and she was expecting me when I rolled in around eleven. She had moved to a community, Milwaukie, just southeast of Portland. She lived in an apartment in an eight-unit complex on Wake Street. There was no real landscaping, but the building itself had been freshly painted a dusty rose. I introduced myself and stated again that her brother-in-law had retained me. She was probably in her early forties, but looked to be closer to fifty. Her dark brown hair had strands of gray and unbecoming red-framed glasses gave her a somewhat severe appearance. I offered my condolences on her husband's tragic death and accepted a cup of coffee. She asked me what I would like to know.

"Anything and everything you can tell me about Mr. Westlake. Let's start by my asking if you can think of anyone who would want him dead?"

"I thought this was just supposed to be a robbery by a stranger that turned violent."

"Yes, it could turn out that that is how it happened. But I want to consider every angle and every scenario."

"Well, the answer is 'no'. I can't think of a single person who would have any reason to kill Brian!"

"And no one with a grudge against him?"

"Well, there was a sad thing that happened almost four years ago. We had been invited by a friend, Jeff, who owns a ski boat to go to Haag Lake. There were six of us and we all took a turn skiing. After a while, Jeff asked Brian if he wanted to drive the boat. A few minutes later, a young girl being towed behind another boat swung so close it seemed she would be right in front of our boat. Brian made a sharp turn, but the girl got clipped by our propeller. She was hospitalized for over a week and ended up with a disfigured left leg. Her father sued Jeff and Brian. He didn't win, but he was very angry and spiteful to Brian."

"Has he acted out in any way or threatened Brian since the trial?"

"No, but shortly after the trial he wrote us a very ugly letter. His letter claimed Brian was drunk and should be in jail. Said he wasn't watching out for others on the lake. The Sheriff investigated, of course, and said it wasn't our boat's fault. Brian had had *one* beer at our picnic hours before this happened and he passed the Sheriff's breathalyzer test with no problem!"

She said she had kept the letter and I asked her for a copy.

When she returned with the copy, I continued, "Forgive me for asking, but could there have been another woman?"

"No, I would've known. Brian was a straight-forward person. He could not have kept a secret like that from me. It's true we had grown distant and weren't communicating well. And I was the one who wanted a change, but it wasn't because he was unfaithful."

"Did he have a partner or any employees?"

"Yes, he had one employee, Cliff Gaston. Cliff did not want to work full time. He is a veteran and is pretty moody … maybe he has PTSD … I'm not sure. But Brian seemed to get along with him and it was good to have someone to help with the bigger jobs.

"How about friends I could talk to?"

"Well, we didn't have many close friends. Some back in Indiana, but not so many here. Brian was pretty private. But his best buddy, is … was – that's hard for me to say …" and I saw some moisture behind those red glasses "… Gary Stratley was his best friend. Gary owns a nursery in Tigard. I'm sure Gary would be glad to help you."

"Thanks, I'll be sure to talk with Mr. Stratley. Anything else you think I should know? Any habits or hobbies for Mr. Westlake?"

"Oh, Brian loved birds. He wasn't one of those birdwatchers who take trips to jungles or keep journals or anything like that. But he could identify quite a lot of them and, since he was up in trees a lot, he would even photograph them sometimes."

"He'd take a camera up a tree with him?"

"No. But he had a good cell phone and it was always with him."

"I understand his watch was taken. Was there an inscription on it?"

"No, no inscription. Brian really did like that watch. I gave it to him for his birthday five years ago. It was a very nice Rolex. Kind of a splurge, but it was a gift he really loved."

"I saw a dog's dish in his house. Did he have a dog?"

"Oh, yes. Brian had Wolfgang for over eight years … got him as a puppy. He's a German shepherd and was very devoted to Brian. I told that detective about his injury, but he didn't seem very interested."

"What do you mean by 'injury'?"

"Well, right after Brian's death, I got a call from Brian's next-door neighbor. Of course she knew Wolfgang and she said he turned up the next morning apparently in great pain. I came right over and the poor dog couldn't even put any weight on his right foreleg. I took him to our vet and he told me the leg was broken. When the vet released him a couple of days later, I took Wolfgang over to Mel. Dogs aren't allowed here so that was all I could do."

"I understand. Could you give me the information on your vet?"

She jotted down the name and address.

"I found some entries in his bank records. It seems he was depositing twelve-hundred-fifty dollars each month. Do you happen to know what that was all about?"

"Well, I can guess. Brian inherited a building lot in Gresham from an elderly cousin. He had no use for it. A few months ago, he told me he had been able to sell it. I think he sold it to an individual and Brian financed it himself. Those could be the monthly payments."

I wrote that information in my note book and I was about to leave when I stopped and asked one more question.

"Did your husband have any life insurance?"

"Yes, two policies, and one is rather large. I suppose if we'd divorced that might have changed. Since we have no children, I am the sole beneficiary."

"May I ask how large were the benefits?"

"I have cooperated with you, Mr. Conwright, but I don't think that's any of your business."

On that note, we parted. I left thinking I would sooner or later have to ask her what she was doing on that fatal afternoon. For now, I headed for our meeting with our potential realtor, Jim Blanchard.

4

Sunday, April 19th morning

Clifford Gaston lived in a mobile-home park in Aloha. The outside of his butter-cup yellow double-wide was clean and tidy. Two nice rose bushes, one on either side, flanked the stepping stones that led to his door. He greeted me with a day's growth on his rounded face, his shirttail out and a Seattle Mariners cap on his head. After some small talk about the Mariners' prospects, I asked him if he minded if I recorded our interview. He minded. Instead, I opened my notebook and asked my first question.

"Were you working with Brian on any jobs shortly before his death?"

"Well, there was a two-day job just a few days before. The first day, Brian was getting rid of most of the limbs and he didn't need me to help. The next day he would go up almost to the top for the last of the limbs and I had to be there to handle the safety ropes for him. Then we would bring the trunk down in three foot chunks. That's the dangerous part and we had to work as a team".

"Can you think of anyone who might have wanted Brian dead?"

"No way, man. He was a mellow guy. Honest too!"

"You liked him?"

"Yeah, sure. He was fair to me. A good boss."

"No disagreements? Arguments?"

"What! You thinking I had anything to do with his death!"

He half rose from his chair and gave me a glare that would laser the hide off a croc. I replied in a soft voice, "I hear you can have a temper sometimes."

My frank and calm statement seemed to cool him down. "Yeah, well, okay. Sometimes things get kind of crazy for me. I've been in a couple of fights since I've been back. But nothing ever with Brian! In fact, he kind of helped me get past those moments a couple of times when other people were involved."

"Is it okay if I ask you where you were from late afternoon into the evening on April ninth?"

"Yeah, you can ask! I was at a veterans group-counseling meeting at the VA hospital from six to nine. I guess I got on MAX to go downtown around five. Check it out, man! The counselor's name is Nelson ... or maybe it's Nielsen ... "

"Thanks, Cliff, for helping me on that. I hope everyone is as understanding as you've been. And the rest of us owe you veterans big time. But you know I have to ask questions if I'm going to figure out who killed Brian."

We shook hands and I took my leave. Yes, I would have to check with the VA about the counseling session, but Cliff Gaston slid quite a ways lower on my "persons of interest" list.

My next project was to check with Paul DeNoli to make sure Brian Westlake did not have any kind of a criminal record. Paul was not too thrilled about doing a little work on a Sunday, but he had the password to access the Law Enforcement Data System from home. He called me back ten minutes later to say both Westlake brothers were totally clean beyond a very few traffic tickets.

From my office, I ran a credit check on Brian and it showed no collection actions, no defaults, and a good payment history. I could not reach the State Consumer Protection staff on the weekend so my questions about customer complaints would have to wait.

I drove back to Forest Lane. The houses were not so densely spaced in this almost-rural part of the city, so I decided to contact only those in the closest two homes in either direction from Westlake's house.

One family was not home. The other three had similar comments. Brian Westlake was pleasant enough, but quiet; kept mostly to himself; and he seemed to love his dog. No one had anything negative to say about him and no one had any reason to believe he had enemies.

I was already west of the Willamette river so I decided to see if I could catch up with Brian's best friend, Gary Stratley. I took Skyline through the big cemetery on the hilltop, then Barnes Road until I reached Highway 217. Even on a Sunday 217 had plenty of traffic, probably a lot of it going to or from the huge mall at Washington Square. From 217 I picked up U.S. 99 West and was soon in Tigard. On the way, I called Mr. Stratley as I waited for a light to change. He had gone to early church and had just arrived home when I caught him. He sounded eager to help and gave me directions to get through a tricky intersection.

I parked at the curb and saw a split-level brick-faced house with a shake roof on what appeared to be a sizable fall-away lot. At the door, a ruddy cheeked man with a full head of dark hair and a wiry six-foot frame shook my hand. He still wore a sport coat and tie from attending church. He had the presence of mind to ask to see my private investigator's license. Once that was taken care of, he removed his tie and walked me downstairs to his den. We sat in comfortable chairs and he said how shocked he was that something so awful happened to a close friend. I, in turn, explained how and why I was working for Mel Westlake.

"So anything I can learn about Brian, his habits, his interests, whether he seemed worried or stressed in the last weeks ... anything you can offer would be helpful."

"Well, I can assure you Brian was not into anything crooked or anything that would have caused him to cross paths with any criminal element. He was pretty darn ethical and even a little righteous occasionally. And he was a hard worker. He got a lot of repeat business from his larger clients like city parks and golf courses. And of course he did projects for individual homeowners too."

"This separation from his wife ... could that play into this?"

"I don't see how. It was an amicable separation. There was no bad blood. I think they gave it a good run for almost six years and then Sandra just decided she wanted a change ... or at least wanted some time to try living apart."

"And Brian had no secret vices? Gambling maybe? Other mens' wives?"

"No, he was totally straight in that regard. He often played in our friendly poker games, but we only played nine or ten times a year and the big loser never lost more than twenty-five dollars ... pretty harmless! And if there were anything else that could've led him into trouble, I believe I would have known."

"Okay. Did he seem stressed or anxious in the last few weeks of his life? Any changes in his attitude or personality?"

"No, I wouldn't say that. He pretty much kept on an even keel."

I gave him my card and asked him to call me if he thought of anything else. We were climbing the stairs when he stopped and tapped me on the shoulder. "Wait a minute. There *was* something that was a little unusual. I used to tease him about being up in a tree and gazing down to see some gal nude sunbathing in her back yard. It was kind of a running gag between us. Sometimes he'd come up with a whopper about some babe in a pool just to keep it going. But a day or two before he was killed, he was over at my place to discuss a particular tree that one of Brian's clients wanted to add to his property. When we had finished that business, he said the day before he had seen the oddest thing when he was high up in the branches. A man ran out into the back yard next door to where Brian was working and another man in a white jumpsuit followed him. They were arguing and the white-suited guy seemed pretty aggressive. Then Jumpsuit waved something orange at the other guy and they disappeared from Brian's view heading back toward the house."

"Did he say what happened after that?"

"I asked Brian and he said there was no more noise and he wasn't finished up in the tree so he just kept working. When he finally came down, the house looked normal and there was no one outside and no vehicle in the driveway. He figured it was just a neighborhood row of some kind and took no action ... but he did mention it to me. He was pretty casual about it ... more in the nature of 'you never know what you'll see when you're up in a tree'."

Before going back to the houseboat, I thought it worth trying to reach the vet to whom Sandra had taken Brian's injured dog. I got lucky. Instead of an answering machine, I got Dr. Asad Humet himself. He said a customer with a sick goat had taken him out on a house call and he had just returned to his office to do the paperwork. He said he would be there another half-hour or so and that he would be glad to talk with me.

Dr. Humet was considerably shorter than my six-foot-two and slight of build. His broad smile beneath a trim mustache welcomed me as he answered my knock. We went directly to his office and I explained in a little more detail why I wanted to talk with him.

"I had no idea Mr. Westlake had been murdered!" he exclaimed, wide-eyed. "Mrs. Westlake seemed distraught, but I assumed it was because of Wolfgang. Mr. Westlake was the one who brought the dog in normally, so I hardly knew his wife and I didn't want to be nosy. All she told me was that someone may have kicked or attacked the dog."

"So his foreleg was broken?"

"Yes. Fortunately it was broken in a way that I could stabilize it and did not have to put him down. She was very relieved at that."

"Since you now know what happened and why I'm involved, did you notice anything else about the dog that might shed some light on this killing?"

"As a matter of fact I did. I had to anesthetize Wolfgang to work on the leg. I wondered, if he had been attacked, might he have fought back? I checked his mouth and found a few blue denim threads between his teeth. I even thought I saw a little dried blood on the threads. I removed them and put them in a little plastic jar. My thinking was if someone had been abusing Wolfgang and had been bitten in return, the threads might help in identifying the culprit. In my book, anybody who is cruel to animals ought to be jailed. Now I suppose 'culprit' could even be 'murderer'."

"Saving those threads was very good thinking on your part, Dr. Humet! Would you be willing to give them to me?"

"Yes, I will do that. You can do more with them than I ever could! I thought about giving them to Mrs. Westlake, but I never got around to it."

I asked Humet to sign a chain-of-custody document that I hastily drew up. I intended to give the threads to DeNoli or Niemus. If the dark blotches really were blood, they might provide some DNA for analysis.

"Tell me, did the police ever talk to you?"

"No. No one from the police has contacted me."

I thanked the doctor and drove home. It was past lunchtime and I was hungry but, after lunch, there was something I needed to check. I knocked off a roast-beef-and-cream-cheese bagel sandwich and then moved down the hall to my office. I opened Westlake's appointments book and paged back two weeks. I jotted down the clients' names, their addresses and home phone numbers, and the nature of each job. The comment made by Gary Stratley about what Westlake had seen from up in the tree was a tenuous lead. But, tenuous or not, it was more intriguing at the moment than Sandra Westlake's being an insurance beneficiary or whether the father of the injured water skier had an alibi. I could always follow up with them later.

Most of Westlake's jobs had been pruning or improving the health of a tree or spraying. But two jobs during that period had involved felling tall trees. And one of those had been just four days before he was killed. I decided to visit those two sites to see if one of them could have been where Westlake saw that strange behavior in the neighbor's back yard. If either of the sites looked as though it could have been that place, I would contact the homeowner.

My first stop was an address on Nevada Street close to the appealing "downtown" of Multnomah Village. The house's siding had been stained to give it a woodsy feel. There was one fir tree left standing on the rear of the property and homes were relatively close on either side. I rang the doorbell. I heard a woman's voice behind the door asking what I wanted. I told her I was a private investigator working on a case and hoped to ask just a few questions about the arborist who had done a job for her. That apparently reassured her enough to let me in. She was a rather plump middle-aged woman with merry brown eyes. "That arborist I spoke of, Brian Westlake, was murdered about ten days ago."

"Oh my God," she exclaimed and put her hands to her face.

"I'm just trying to trace what he did and where he was on the last few days of his life. I know he felled a tree for you folks and just wondered if anything unusual happened during that process."

"He did a wonderful job of it! It was over sixty feet tall and we worried about it falling on the house in a wind storm. In any case, he dropped the branches and the trunk very neatly and the only damage was to one of my rose bushes."

"So just a normal day or days in the neighborhood, then?"

"Well, not normal in the rest of the neighborhood, no! The first day he was here was the day Denise's husband disappeared!"

"Who is Denise and what do you mean 'disappeared'?"

"Just that. Denise is our neighbor. She was spending the day shopping with her sister. Brad – he's her husband -- was planning a lazy day around the house. When Denise got home, Brad was nowhere to be seen.

Denise has been worried sick. She reported it to the police and they are doing what they do when a person has gone missing, but they have nothing to tell her!"

"I see. Yes, that certainly was *not* a normal day. I think I had better talk to her. Can you tell me her last name?"

"Lunberg"

"One last thing. Would you mind showing me where the tree stood?"

She led me to their back yard and pointed to a newly re-turfed circle. The center of the circle was about twenty-five feet from their house. I walked over to the fence and she confirmed that it ran between their property and the Lunbergs'. As I peered over the fence, it looked to be between fifty and sixty feet from where the tree had stood to the middle of the Lunberg's back yard. I hated to intrude upon an anxious woman, but it was time to contact Mrs. Lunberg.

5

Sunday, April 19th afternoon

I rang the doorbell at the house next door. I heard footsteps approaching the door and then stopping. I guessed Mrs. Lunberg was studying me through the security peep-hole. A voice asked what I wanted. I identified myself and stated, in general terms, why I wished to speak with her. I also said I would place my license where she could see it through the nearest window. We went through that process and that seemed to reassure her somewhat. Seconds later, the door was opened by a blond woman in her mid-to-late thirties. She wore a soft-green sweater over forest-green slacks. There were dark circles under her brown eyes and despite her nice features, she looked haggard. She ushered me into a Berber-carpeted living room where she gestured for me to sit on an ultra-suede couch. I expressed my concern and sympathy over her missing husband. After some awkward moments for both of us, she relaxed a little and I told her of Westlake's death. I said I wanted to understand everything he had experienced in his last few days on earth. I acknowledged that her husband's vanishing was probably a separate and unrelated situation, but said that I needed more information to be sure.

"I know nothing at all about Brad's disappearance, but I'll help you if I can."

"I understand you were shopping that day. Can you remember when you left and when you got home? Whether you two spoke on your cells while you were away?"

"Well, I left fairly early, about a quarter to ten, I think. Brad had a nasty cold and decided to stay home from work. And, no, we did not call each other. Not calling would be pretty normal unless there was some change of plan or Brad wanted me to pick up something at the grocery store. I got back home after three … probably three-thirty."

"Were you with anyone?"

"Yes, my sister, Madeline Teller. We met at Nordstroms, shopped a while, then had lunch and saw that movie about Steven Hawking … I'm not very good about titles. "

"And nothing was amiss inside when you got home?"

"No. Although a floor lamp wouldn't turn on and I could see the bulb was gone. I remember thinking it was not like either of us to remove a burned-out bulb and not replace it. Are you wondering if there was an intruder?" A shadow of fear passed over her face as she asked the question.

"I'm just trying to get the scene in my mind," I equivocated. "Do you have a supply of replacement bulbs?"

"Yes we do. I checked and we had two extras in a cupboard in the garage."

"Your neighbor said your husband's car was still in the garage."

"Yes it was."

"What did your husband do?"

"He was a real estate agent with Saltzman Realty."

"Has he always been in real estate?"

"No. He used to work for the Bureau of Alcohol, Tobacco, & Firearms. It's a federal agency. He was a field agent in Phoenix."

"Do you mind if I ask why he left?"

"That's okay. He worked undercover sometimes and that was dangerous. We were planning to get married and he didn't want to continue in that role. He wasn't interested in a desk job there … he loves meeting people and getting out. So we decided to make a clean break and move to Portland and let him start a new career."

"How long ago was that?"

"Almost eight years ago."

"Please don't think me insensitive, but can you think of any reason he would want to leave his life here?

Her eyes teared up, but she calmed herself and answered. "No! No reason! We were very happily married and our eighth anniversary was just three days after I last saw Brad. And we had bought airline tickets and put a sizable payment down to reserve a cruise in the Caribbean this summer."

"I assume you have reported Mr. Lunberg's absence to the police?"

"Yes, of course! But they haven't learned anything. They've been monitoring charges on our credit card and there have been no charges other than those I've made. They've checked hospitals and emergency rooms and the coroner's office and found no trace. I'm relieved to hear *that*, but I'm nearly mad with worry for him!"

"Did you find any messages left on your home phone while you were shopping?"

"No. I think the police officer I talked to asked that same question."

"Would you mind if I talked to your neighbors just to see if anyone saw or heard something out of the ordinary?"

"That would be okay. But tell me: you're taking such an interest in my problem; do you see some connection to the murder case you're working on?"

"I accepted that case only two days ago and I'm just getting started. The closeness in time of the two events might mean something or it could be a total coincidence. But I try to learn everything I can and, once in a while, a linkage jumps out at me and I can start to connect the dots."

I gave Denise Lunberg my card and asked her to call if anything came to mind. I started my canvass of the neighbors as the sun sank a little lower and a chill breeze made me turn up the collar on my jacket. The first two neighbors were aware of the situation, but weren't home at the relevant time ... one retired couple visiting friends all day and the other couple, both at work. At the third house, the couple had been home, but saw nothing unusual. I crossed the street and the older, single woman in that house *had* noticed something.

"Yes, I remember this white van backed into their driveway. Then a man in coveralls or a jumpsuit got out. He went to their door and went inside."

"What color was the jump suit?"

"It was white."

"Okay. Sorry for the interruption. Please continue."

"The van had 'Armstrong Appliances' on its side so I was wondering whether the Lunbergs needed a repair or were getting something new. I kind of went back to my window from time to time and, after a few minutes, the man came out and unloaded a large carton and wheeled it up to the front porch on a hand truck. Then he took it inside. About forty-five minutes later, he came out wheeling a big water heater. So I figured they'd replaced their water heater. Not very exciting, but since you asked ..."

"Did he bring out the carton you saw also?"

"Yes, I think he did. He put everything back in the truck and drove away."

Thank goodness for the neighborhood busybody, I thought. But she was right: nothing very exciting.

I went back to Mrs. Lunberg and asked one question. "Did you need to have your water heater replaced?"

"Why no! What a strange question. We had a new one installed when we bought the house, but that was only five years ago. It works fine."

"This is kind of a silly request, but would you mind just taking a look to be sure?"

Shaking her head in bafflement, she walked down the hall to the utility room and showed me the water heater. "That's it. The one we've always had."

I thanked her and left hurriedly to avoid the question she was very likely going to ask. I needed to give this some thought and to check one thing out.

As soon as I got to the houseboat, I Googled "Portland Beaverton Tigard appliance dealers". I could not find an Armstrong Appliances, but I did see Armstad Appliances. I called them and they said they never had an order from or made a delivery to the Lunberg household.

DeNoli was at the annual hunting and fishing show when I reached him on his cell phone.

"Paul, you know I'm working on the Westlake murder. By the way, you were spot-on about Niemus. He told me to butt out and wasn't the least interested in sharing any information or ideas. But that's not why I called you."

'So what's on your mind, Rick?"

"I talked to Westlake's best buddy and he told me something that seemed a little odd, but not significant at the time. It seems Westlake told him that the day before – that'd be three days before he was killed -- he had been working high in a tree and saw – in the back yard of the next house – two guys having a heated argument. One of the guys was wearing a white jump suit and was pretty aggressive. Then Jumpsuit waved something orange at the other guy and they disappeared from view. After that, everything was quiet and normal so Westlake kept on working up in the tree and did nothing about it.

"Well, you know me. Nothing useful had turned up so I thought maybe I'll just check with the people he did jobs for in the last couple of weeks. And I started with jobs where he had been felling or pruning tall trees. The first place I hit, the lady of the house shows me where her tree used to be and sure enough you could see into the next yard from up in the tree. Then she mentions that the man next door has been missing for over a week! That leads me to talk to her neighbor. The wife tells me he was home when she left to go for a day's shopping and not there when she returned. She said her husband is still missing and she has reported a missing person.

"I decided to canvass a few of the neighbors and the lady across the street says she saw a van pull into the driveway with 'Armstrong Appliances' on its side. A guy in a white jump suit goes inside for a few minutes then comes out and hauls a large carton from the truck back into the house. After almost an hour, he comes out hauling a large water heater. So I go back to the wife and ask have they ordered a new water heater. She's surprised and says 'no'. I find no Armstrong Appliances in the phone book, but I do find an Armstad Appliances. I call them and they say there was no such order. Something doesn't smell right!"

Paul had been listening patiently. Now he said, "I agree. Come in tomorrow morning and let's kick this around. It's hard to believe that any of this ties to your case with the arborist, but I'm thinking I'd better talk with Missing Persons. Until we have a body, I can't really open a homicide file. But maybe you can do a little investigating and see if there's a connection."

6

Monday, April 20th morning

I was about to head downtown when Angie called sounding a little excited.

"Rick! I just got a call from the manager at one of the network TV stations in Denver. They have an anchor slot opening. He said they had heard of my work here and want me to send them a resume and some on-screen minutes from my broadcasts."

I was a little stunned. I knew Angie was ambitious and was quite possibly in line to anchor the evening news desk here in Portland. But the idea of having her half a continent away was not in our house-hunting plan, not to mention our romantic game plan. It took me a second to find my voice.

"Well, that's great! Are you going to send a resume?"

"I think I might. I probably won't have a chance, but it would be nice to see where I stand. You're not happy with that are you?"

"Not ecstatic, no. What about us, our own plans?"

"I won't jeopardize that, lover, but it would be worth thinking it through … how we could work it out if I got an offer."

I didn't want to splash cold water on her obvious excitement and she was right: we should at least explore that scenario. "Yeah, we should think about it. I suppose the station manager is in a hurry?"

"Yes, he sounded that way."

"Then you should send him the resume and the video. Let's talk it over tonight. Are you coming over?"

"Yes. I don't have to cover for anyone at six and I don't have to be back to the studio until ten for the eleven o'clock news. Rick, don't be glum! However this develops, we'll work it out!"

I was still reeling from this new development as I left the houseboat. I had made a morning appointment to speak with Madeline Teller. We met at a Starbucks not far from her home. She confirmed the day of lunching, shopping and watching "The Theory of Everything" with Denise. She seemed comfortable and at ease. No looking away, or hesitating, or fidgeting. Denise

Lunberg would seem to be in the clear for the time of her husband's disappearance.

Sandra Westlake had given me the name of the angry father whose daughter was injured in the water-skiing accident. His name was Ron DelGriggio. She called the attorney who had defended the lawsuit and asked if he could find the man's work phone number and business address. He could. She passed it on to me. DelGriggio was not eager to talk to me, but finally relented. We set up a ten o'clock meeting in his office.

He was an insurance broker and his office was on Hawthorne on the East side. Out in the avenues, Hawthorne is one of the liveliest streets in Portland with hundreds of small retail shops, many restaurants, bakeries, and low-rise apartment buildings. I parked on a side street and hoofed it a block-and-a-half to his office. It was a small suite on the ground floor of a two story building.

"You said it was about Brian Westlake and that he had been murdered. Why do you need to talk to me? I haven't seen the man for over two years!"

"I've learned about your daughter, Mr. DelGriggio. I'm very sorry about what happened. I've also learned that you considered Westlake to blame and that you sent a letter to him that could be considered threatening."

"Are you the police! You said you were a private investigator!"

"That's exactly what I am. I do not work for the police."

"But you think I could've killed Westlake? The police have never even questioned me!"

"Look, I've just started my investigation. I don't have a list of suspects or anything of the kind. But he *was* murdered and I'd like to eliminate you from my consideration. If you can tell me where you were from late afternoon into early evening on the ninth, that should clear it up."

He half rose from his chair, his jowly cheeks flushed and his fists clenched. "You have your nerve coming in here with your suspicions! I ought to send you on your way."

"As I said, sir, I have no suspicions … I'm just doing my job to understand the possibilities."

"Alright." He let out a big breath. "I was in Chicago at an insurance convention. That would be easy to check. Stayed at the Hilton downtown. I flew home that day and my Delta flight arrived in late afternoon. I don't remember exactly when, but it was probably a little after six when I got out of the garage and started for home. Are you satisfied!"

"Could you give me your flight number?"

"No, Goddammit, I can't! I didn't *save* the itinerary!"

"After sending that letter, were you ever again in contact with Mr. Westlake?"

"No, no! I kind of lost it with that letter, but I never followed through in any way."

"Thank you for your time," I said, closing my notebook and letting myself out.

I reached the Portland Police Bureau building – officially known as the Justice Center – at eleven. Paul DeNoli met me in the lobby and we went to the homicide division's office on the thirteenth floor. The detectives' squad room was almost empty. We picked up mugs of the strong brew they call coffee and got right down to the business at hand.

"I'm guessing Westlake saw the guy who 'disappeared' Lunberg," I said. So maybe this guy thinks Westlake would be an incriminating witness and he has to take him out."

"Maybe, but how does he even know Weslake observed him?"

"Maybe Brian is making noise up in the tree .. using a saw or whatever. Or maybe Jumpsuit just happens to look up and sees this guy up there pointing something that is shiny in the reflected light. Is it a camera? A cell phone? Binoculars? Whatever it is, Jumpsuit knows he's in trouble!"

"Right, but how does he know the identity of this 'man in the tree'?"

"That's easy. Westlake's truck is sitting on the driveway right next door. And each door panel has a sign with his name and profession. So now Jumpsuit has a name. Brian is listed, along with his address, in the residential section of the phone book."

"I can see that it *could* have happened that way. But wait! Let's not jump to conclusions. What's the crime here with Lunberg?" DeNoli asked with a frown. "Kidnapping? If so, how? Murder? Where's the body?"

"Okay. I concede we don't know enough yet. But what we do know suggests a criminal scheme of some kind. Can you check to see if any white delivery vans were stolen in the previous few days?"

"Yeah. I can do that right now." He punched in the number for a colleague in Property Crimes and explained what we wanted to know. I was getting one side of the conversation.

"Yeah. Okay, the day before. That's interesting; a little CYA for the code violation. …. Uh huh, still in the lot … Yeah, don't release it yet! I want the criminalists to go over it."

"Ask him if there was a sign saying Armstrong Appliances on the side," I injected.

"What about any signage on the van? None?" A shrug in my direction. "Okay. Thanks, Bill."

He hung up and turned to me. "Yes, such a vehicle *was* reported stolen a day before Lunberg goes missing. It's been recovered and they've notified the owner, but the van's still in the impound lot. They'll hold it until I can get a forensics team on it. He says no signs. Someone on the team will call me later today with their early findings. I'll let you know what they say. Oh, and the owner said the right front headlight was out and he was just about to replace it when the van was stolen."

"So, Paul, back to your questions about how could the perp have taken Lunberg from the house, dead or alive. I've been thinking about that myself. He goes to a lot of trouble to create the illusion of delivering a water heater that was never delivered. Why was that? Could he have quieted Lunberg down with a tranquilizer or tased him and then gagged him? Once he was silenced and immobilized – or dead – could he have somehow stuffed him inside that water heater?"

"What have you been smoking, Rick!"

"No, think about it! A good magician sets the stage so the audience 'sees' what they expect to see. In this case, there did happen to be an audience: the nosy lady across the street. He commits the crime and walks away right under the neighbors' noses making it look like a perfectly normal happening."

"Okay, I guess that *is* a possibility. I'm still officially not engaged in this so you talk to some appliance people. See if it could be done. But even if you're right and he got him out that way, where's Lunberg or his body now?"

"Listen, this guy's a planner. He would've had that covered somehow. If Lunberg's dead, he dumps him off a boat in the river. Or buries him out in the forest somewhere. Or ... you remember that case where the perp had to make an incriminating car disappear? He took it to a chop shop. In a few hours, there was nothing left to connect it to him."

"But your water heater has a body in it!"

"Right. But the idea's still there. What about a scrap yard with one of those giant compactors?"

"Whew! Okay, that's another thing you can check out."

"And I will. Here's something you can do. Denise Lunberg told me her husband retired from being an ATF field agent based out of Phoenix. Could you use your 'law enforcement' connections to get a line on what he did, when he did it, and could he have made enemies? She also said he worked undercover sometimes."

"The feds can be damned tight-lipped, but I'll give it a shot. Do they know he's missing?"

"His wife didn't say, but somehow I doubt it. Maybe you can play that card to get some cooperation."

It was almost noon so we decided to grab some lunch. The sun was out so we walked down to the food carts at Third and Oak. This once novel means of getting a fast meal was now almost ubiquitous in Portland with large "pods" of carts in eight or more places around town. As we walked, Paul asked me about Angie.

"Funny you should mention that. She's just been contacted about an anchor job at a major Denver station. "

"Holy shit! Is she interested?"

"I think she's going to send a resume and some cuts from her newscasts, but she's saying it's just to see what will happen."

"Where does that leave you?"

"Well, I'm glad she's getting noticed and building her reputation, but – beyond that – I'm kind of on my heels. She just heard this morning so we haven't had time to seriously discuss it yet. She's excited I think, but she tells me not to worry."

On that sobering note, we reached the line of a dozen or more carts and the tempting aromas hit us. I got a burrito and Paul chose a Thai curry at a different cart. We waited a few minutes for our food to be ready and then headed for Pioneer Square to sit on the amphitheater-like steps and eat our lunches.

I needed to talk to the real estate broker for whom Brad Lunberg had worked. I wanted to get a better idea about the man and see if he had conceivably made any lethal enemies. The broker had heard earlier from Denise and asked if Brad had been located. I told him the search was ongoing. I asked him about possible threats or persons who could be thought of as enemies. The answers I got led nowhere. Brad had a good personality, never had a client problem, and was a successful agent.

I went back to the houseboat and found the name of the woman at Armstad Appliances to whom I had spoken before. She transferred me to one of their senior repair persons. I'm sure the poor guy had never been asked a question like this before. After a few words of explanation, I asked him "Would it be possible to stuff a human body into a water heater?"

"Christ on a crutch! So this is a murder case! And you think that could have happened?"

"No, not at this point. But, if it *were* possible, it could fit what few facts we presently have."

Seconds went by and I heard some "hmmm-ing" and mumbling. Finally, he said, "Yes, if it were an eighty-two gallon tank or bigger and if the top had been cut off and the upper internal piping removed, I think there would be enough space. You'd have to re-attach the top to make it look normal, but that could be easily enough done … at least to pass muster at a distance. The body could not be that of a real big person but, say, one-hundred seventy or less pounds, no taller than five-ten or five-eleven … it could be done. Might need a little pushing and shoving, but yes … possible"

"Would it be difficult to get ahold of a water heater for that purpose without leaving a paper trail?"

"Not especially. You could pay cash at a used appliance outlet, or maybe even find one in a scrap-metal yard."

"Would a lot of specialized tools be needed?"

"Well, nothing exotic. Some good wrenches, a portable spot welder, a hacksaw, that sort of thing."

I thanked him for his help and asked him to keep my questions to himself. I told him that my investigation was very preliminary and speculative and that there was no pending police investigation.

Back in my office, I picked up the folder with "contracts" written on the tab that I had removed from Brian's home office. I found a contract about his work for a golf course and one for the recent purchase of a chipper. The third one down was for the installment sale of an undeveloped lot in Gresham. The buyer paid five thousand dollars up front with monthly payments of twelve-hundred-fifty dollars. Sandra's guess was correct and I was happy to see that Brian Westlake was not blackmailing anyone!

I still had the better part of an hour to kill so I finished the report on the car-repair insurance scam. That taken care of, I called Angie on her cell and said I would be a little late and would probably get home around seven fifteen. She said she would use her own key if she got there ahead of me.

I waited until almost five for my next project. I intended to do a little experiment to check DelGriggio's story. At Portland International airport, I was fortunate to get a helpful ticket agent at the counter and persuaded him to find out when the late-afternoon Delta flight from Chicago arrived on April ninth. He had to access a data base that was not familiar to him and it took several minutes. Luckily, there were plenty of other agents to help travelers and no one behind me seemed unhappy about the time it took.

He finally found the information and looked up with a smile and said, "The flight arrived at the gate at five-thirty-nine."

I thanked him for his trouble, walked to my car in short-term parking, and timed my departure for six-ten sharp. Traffic was fairly heavy with many of the weekday commuters still on the road. I headed for Westlake's home in Portland's West Hills. I was going against the homeward-bound traffic as I came toward downtown and made pretty good time, but picked up the last of the evening rush hour crossing through the heart of the city. It was slow going until I climbed onto Cornell Road. The entire trip took fifty-one minutes. If my trip was representative, DeGriggio could not have arrived at Westlake's home until after seven.

Would Westlake have walked his dog in the near darkness? And, if he did, would he have chosen to enter the urban wilderness of Forest Park? And could DelGriggio have arrived, staked out Westlake's home, and been ready to stalk him on that tight a schedule? I very much doubted it. Angry and sometimes threatening as he may have been, I did not consider DeGriggio a very plausible suspect.

Angie had already arrived when I got back to the houseboat. She had dinner going on the stove. I wrapped her in my arms and kissed her. Our kiss lasted a good while. She gave me a final squeeze and pulled away to rescue the vegetables. I went to wash up and saw, as I passed, that the phone's message light was on. I listened to DeNoli telling me to call him at home. He picked up on the second ring.

"Rick, the criminalists gave us this much right away. No fingerprints so he must have been wearing gloves or else did a thorough wipe-job. But there were traces of adhesive on the sides of the van. They'll be analyzing the samples in due course, but they found a partial pattern that suggested vinyl signs could've been attached that way."

"That sounds like it could be the mystery delivery truck alright."

"Yeah, and they tested the lights and both headlights worked."

"So maybe the guy didn't want to risk getting stopped for a one-eye and replaced the bulb himself."

"Makes sense," admitted DeNoli.

I told Paul that my contact at the appliance store said it was possible to cram a man's body into an eighty-two gallon water heater after some simple alterations to the tank. To tidy up some loose ends, I informed him that Denise Lunberg had an alibi for the time her husband went missing. I added that though Ron DelGriggio could not be ruled out entirely, the timing made it pretty unlikely he could've been involved in Westlake's death. I closed the call and helped Angie get our food to the table.

7

Monday, April 20th evening – Tuesday, April 21st morning.

Angie had prepared flank steak, baked potatoes and a Waldorf salad for our dinner. We generally make dinner together when she is over, but I got a pass tonight to simulate the trip that Mr. DelGriggio might have made from the airport.

Angie is just under five-six with natural blond shoulder-length locks, sky-blue eyes, and curves to match. And, she has a mind that can chase me out of the park when it comes to scrabble, world affairs, or literature. Angie is not only the love of my life, but a real pro in the journalism field. She has determination, smarts, and a knack for getting people to speak freely. The fact that she is drop-dead beautiful probably doesn't hurt her career either. She had been a competitive tennis player at Whitman College and still plays a mean game. She isn't pushy and is always respectful of her superiors, yet has plenty of ambition to succeed in her chosen career. She is a great teaser and her gentle sense of humor can always make me chuckle.

Angie had been engaged her senior year in college and that came to a tragic end when her finance was killed in an auto accident. This left her cautious about entering into deep, new relationships. We had dated casually, then more seriously, and we were now what my friend, Julio, calls "an item". From hiking trips in the Columbia Gorge to my getting to know her parents in Boise to meeting her close friends to going to station parties and getting acquainted with her colleagues, we are starting to twine our lives ever more together.

I opened a bottle of ancient-vines Zinfandel and we touched glasses and started our meal. The offer from Denver came up soon after we sat down at the dining table.

"Suppose – just suppose – that I were to take that job. Would you come to Colorado with me?"

"If it meant not losing what we have together, I would. But I have no idea what prospects I'd have there. I don't have any business contacts in Denver. My reputation as a PI is strictly local to Portland. I wouldn't have Julio's bunch to help out and I wouldn't have Paul DeNoli as my liaison to law enforcement. I'm not saying I could not start over, but I don't like the idea that you might have to support me for a while."

"That sounds more like temporary male pride, honey!"

"Just saying. It wouldn't be a simple transition professionally."

"How about another newspaper? Or an existing firm of private investigators that wanted to expand?"

"Yes, a newspaper is a possibility. But most of them are letting good people go … scaling back … relying more on national news services for investigative stories. I'd have to check on larger PI firms, but I've been on my own for a while and don't know how well I'd fit in someone else's shop. Does that all sound selfish?"

Angie looked into my eyes before answering. "No-o-o. But I can tell it would be uncomfortable for you."

"I guess we could try my 'commuting' on weekends and such. Some couples try those arrangements, but I haven't thought many of them work out."

"I agree. Besides, I want to be with you more often than just weekends."

"If an offer came through, couldn't you use it to leverage a bigger role here," I asked.

"Yes, I might be able to do that. God knows it happens quite often."

"I'll get on the internet about private investigation firms and see who the players are in the Denver area." Angie looked pleased at that and I changed the subject a little.

"I admit it was a quick little sampling on Saturday, but was Alameda Avenue still your favorite neighborhood?"

"Yeah, I think so. There're probably better values in places like the Clinton neighborhood and I thought those homes on the 'Terrace' streets in the northwest hills looked really interesting. And they were close to downtown."

"That's true. Everything up there ... Monte Vista Terrace, MacLean Boulevard ... is very appealing. The houses are newer too. I'll tell Jim Blanchard we're still excited about the idea, but active searching's on hold for a while."

"That's probably best for now."

On that bitter-sweet and wistful note, we finished our dinner and cleared the table.

Angie got delayed at the studio with a brief team meeting after her eleven o'clock newscast and it was after midnight when she got back to the houseboat. By then I was dead to the world and she crawled into bed without awakening me. The next morning, I made omelets for our breakfast and Angie left a little before ten.

First on my list was to see Julio Mendez. Julio owns a thriving messenger service in Portland. He started with a few young men and women on bicycles and, as his business grew, he added two vans and some motorbikes. I initially met him when I was still an investigative reporter for The Oregonian. I was doing a series on juvenile delinquents and the risks of recidivism as the kids moved into adulthood. Julio had done a little time in "juvie" for stealing a car with another boy. They had just wanted to joyride the car and they abandoned it, undamaged, the next day. But the time behind bars was an eye-opener for this intelligent young man. He saw others heading in directions that could only mean criminal futures. Julio served his short sentence and promptly found himself a job. With this modest self-support in hand, he enrolled at Portland Community College.

Three years later, he had earned his Associate of Arts degree and took out a Small Business Administration loan to start his business. He hired young Latinos and Latinas. Many of them had juvenile records, but he selected only those who had convinced him of their desire to rise above their troubled beginnings. I was so impressed with Julio and his young employees that I stayed in touch with him. A few years later, Julio founded a charity that gave educational grants primarily to young persons of South or Central American heritage. I did a follow-on story for the paper that featured Julio and his efforts.

Our relationship soon grew into a real friendship. Not only did Angie and I enjoy socializing with Maria and Julio, but I also developed a professional relationship with Julio and his employees. When I needed help digging into factual things or needed some surveillance work, I used Julio's young men and women. Julio made it clear early on that they could not be directly exposed to danger and that nothing they did could be deemed unlawful. We were all content with those conditions. That arrangement allowed me to scale up my efforts with street-savvy helpers when I was busy without having to employ full-time assistants. I paid them half again what Julio was able to pay and, in return, had my own squad of "Baker Street irregulars". And Julio's people seemed to enjoy the challenge. Julio himself had also played important roles in some of those investigative adventures. In cases where Julio and his team had been involved, I told their story to my clients and that almost always led to nice donations to his charity.

I drove to Julio's small building near Seventeenth and Morrison. On the street level he had his office, a storeroom, and a garage for the bikes and vans. Upstairs, he and Maria had fashioned a comfortable home. Maria, who doubled as bookkeeper for their business, was on the phone in the office and waved as I entered. Julio slid out from under one of the vans when he heard our voices. He grabbed a rag to wipe his hands.

"I was just in the middle of an oil change, Rick. Como estas?"

"Doing okay, amigo."

I told him about the feeler Angie received from the Denver station. His dark brows furrowed and his great smile vanished.

"What does that mean for you guys?"

"Right now, it's nothing more than they asked her to send a resume and some clips from her newscasts. If it goes further than that, we'll have to see how we can work it out."

"Well, damn! We want the best for her, but you two have to stay here!"

"I hope that's how it will work out, but we'll see. Listen Julio, I've got a new case and I could use some help from your people. If you can spare one or two of them for half a day, they can do some digging for me."

"Today's already planned, but tomorrow afternoon, I could spare a couple. What will they be digging for?"

"I'm interested in a mystery person who stole a delivery van and may have used it to do something much worse. The owner of the van told the police its front-right headlight was burned out. When the cops found it, both headlights worked. That tells me this guy didn't want to risk a traffic stop so he had to buy a replacement bulb. I'm hoping we can check all the auto parts stores like Napa and Schucks and O'Reilly's to see who bought a bulb for a 2010 Ford delivery van on the fourth or fifth of April. If they get a hit, they should see if anyone in the store can give a description and a name. The guy probably paid cash and didn't give a name or gave a phony one, but even the description would be helpful."

"Sure. We can do that. Miguel and Theresa helped last time and liked it. I'll see if they want another job. They're both out on a run right now, but I'll ask them as soon as they get back. If they can't do it, I'll ask the others. I'll call you on your cell to confirm"

"Great, Julio. Thanks. I've got to get a move on, but we'll be in touch."

Yesterday, DeNoli and I had been trying to figure out – if Lunberg was indeed dead -- how the killer could have disposed of the body. Unless the killer owned a boat in the Portland area, I thought dumping a body in either of the big rivers would have been logistically complicated. Burying a body in the forest somewhere would have been hard work for a lone man digging a grave, but could be done. But then he would still have needed to dispose of the water heater. Having access to a vat of highly corrosive acid would suffice for both body and metal, but that seemed very unlikely. My thoughts kept coming back to the possibility of using a scrap yard. A legitimate scrap yard might very well disassemble the heater to separate copper components and insulation, thus finding the body. Were there operations that were not so particular and would follow instructions to crush the heater as is?

That was a question I needed to ask Richie B. I would hesitate to call Richard Bonaface a friend or even an associate, but we do have a sort of alliance. Richie B. is a minor player in the Portland underworld. He owns a strip club on Eighty-Second Avenue and I suspect he has a little action in the numbers racket and maybe even in fencing low-end stolen goods. Richie had been involved – in several ways – with the goings on that led to my brother-in-law, Vince Langlow's kidnapping. Information from Richie B. had helped me solve that case and was very useful again in the Caughlin murder case.

Yes, Richie was a guy with plenty of rough edges, but he also had a big streak of decency. If I didn't push too hard, I could usually count on him to do the right thing. It was still before noon. Richie would not show up at his club until late afternoon so I drove over to his Tudor-framed house on the lower slopes of Mt. Tabor on Portland's east side. Near the top of the "mountain" were two sizable reservoirs for Portland drinking water. They were open to the air and the city had just lost a long-running dispute with the EPA over whether they had to be covered. From what I had heard, the city was going to decommission them and build new, covered ones.

Richie was home and personally answered the doorbell. "Oh Christ, Conwright. What troubles do you bring to my door today?"

"And good morning to you too, Richie! How about letting me in?"

"Okay, okay."

With his swarthy face and solid frame, he might have been mistaken for a retired boxer or the manager of a baseball team. He motioned to the stairs leading to his basement office. His wife did not appear to be home, but I remembered Richie always "talked business" downstairs. Perhaps there was a household understanding that life upstairs would be insulated from what went on below. Once in the office, he dropped, with a sigh, into his oversized desk chair and pointed me to a chair.

"So what do you need?" Richie was not one for a lot of introductory pleasantries.

"Let's say I'm involved in a murder case and that case seems to have spilled over into another case where a guy has gone missing … vanished from his own home, car still in the garage, no note to the wife, et cetera. I have good reason to believe he – or more likely his body – was cleverly taken from the house inside a metal container. I don't have a lead yet on who 'disappeared' him and the police don't have a body so they're not in it yet."

"Sorry, Conwright, I don't know any magicians doing corpse disposal."

"Yeah, yeah. Here's what I'm thinking. Could he have used a scrap yard? One where they could be persuaded not to look for anything to recycle and just send the container straight to the crusher?"

"Oh, shit, Conwright! I don't deal in scrap or bodies!"

"I'm sure you don't, but if you made a couple of calls, and if there were such an operation, you might be able to tell me where to look. I'd appreciate that."

"Sure! And have it be known it was me who fingered them? Not a good way to get along in my social circles!"

"Listen, Richie. There's no reason to think the Wise Guys are in any way involved. And you know I can't go in with a search warrant. Whatever I did would be very low profile … I'd have a cover story. Besides, if it went down the way I said, there'd be no physical evidence to get the yard in trouble, anyway. I'm looking for the murderer, not some yard man who took a couple of hundred bucks to speed things up a bit and wasn't told why!"

Richie lit a cigarette, took a deep draw and studied an old Rocky Marciano fight poster framed on the wall. The seconds ticked by. Finally, he shot a long plume of smoke from his nostrils and leaned forward, forearms on the desk.

"Yeah, murder is over the line. Too many trigger-happy fuck-ups out there these days. Doesn't sound like this would help you much, but I'll ask around. See if there's any such place. I'll let you know."

I thought the killings I was working on involved much more planning than a job done by a trigger-happy mug, but I kept that thought to myself. Richie wasn't much for thank-yous or hand shaking, so we both stood.

"You have my cell number," I said. "Say hello to Crusher for me."

Crusher was Richie B's towering bouncer/enforcer at the club. He had helped me out of a serious jam as I was rescuing my brother-in-law from a demented kidnapper. They say you never know who your friends are until you really need one.

Coming back from the Mt. Tabor area, I stopped at Millennium Records to see if they had a Cal Tjader disc I liked. They wouldn't sell used disks unless they were of very good quality. It was my lucky day and I found one. The temptation to linger in this rambling store with ramps and steps defining several levels was always strong, but I cruised back to the cashier and saved treasure hunting for another day. Driving home, I heard my ring tone. It was DeNoli. I said I was driving and would call him back in twenty minutes.

Just as you enter my living room, I have an enunciator from an old cargo ship. An enunciator stood on a ship's bridge and was used to transmit and confirm orders to the engine room. I had hunted for years to find one and consider it my favorite piece of "furniture". As I entered, I saw a finger smudge on its gleaming brass case and pulled out my handkerchief to polish it away.

The arrow on the round dial pointed to "Slow Ahead". I thought about a decent man killed while walking his dog and a missing former federal agent. It was time for "Full Ahead".

8

Tuesday, April 21ˢᵗ afternoon

I hung up my jacket, made a ham sandwich, and touched Paul DeNoli's name on my phone.

"Rick, I got a call back from the forensics people. They found two six-foot-long two-by-twelves in the back of the van. They waited until they could reach the owner to see if they were his. He said they were not. A lone man could probably have boosted a water heater into the van without needing a ramp. But, if there were an extra hundred-and-seventy pounds involved, he'd have to have wheeled it up a ramp. I think we can assume he needed those boards to carry out his delivery-man act."

"That makes sense. Did the criminalists get anything useful off of the boards?"

"A little dirt and one oily smudge. Probably came from a truck bed but, on the face of it, nothing unique as an identifier. They also found a hair on the headrest. I'll have them get elimination samples from the owner and whoever else he had driving the van."

Those were some more little pieces for our puzzle. Not especially helpful right now, but at least the new information did not refute my theory of how the body could have left the house.

DeNoli continued, "And, I got through to the Deputy AIC in the ATF Phoenix field office ... a man named Stan Madruga. They did not know about Lunberg's disappearance. They didn't sound too interested since he retired over eight years ago. Madruga did say there was a time when Lunberg was being harassed, practically stalked, by a woman who had been employed by an IT contractor they used. Apparently they had dated a few times and Lunberg lost interest. Madruga thought the lady's elevator didn't go all the way to the top floor. The contractor soon after fired her and ATF thinks Lunberg finally had to get a restraining order to keep her away. Madruga said they would interview her if they could find her, but I'm guessing that's about as far as they'll go at this point."

"Were you able to find out what kinds of cases he was involved in?"

"Yeah, they said he was one of their best undercover guys and he gave some key evidence in three pretty important ones over the years."

"Did he say when these cases went to trial and whether they got convictions?"

"It sounds like two of them were earlier in his career and the last one was about eleven or twelve years ago ... that would be four or five years before he retired. My contact said all the cases ended up in convictions and all the defendants did serious prison time."

"Could you call him back and get the names of the people who were convicted, where they were sent, when they got out, and where they are now?"

"I think I see where you're going with this. He'll probably tell us the facts of record but, if they've passed the term of supervised release, the feds probably won't know where they are living now. Do you really think this is a 'pay back' kind of thing?"

"Your guess is as good as mine, but we might as well explore it and see if anything fits."

I ended that call and sat on my aft deck eating the sandwich. I watched a blue heron roosting on the aft bulwark of the boat on my left. He was patiently looking for his own lunch. It was then that Richie B called back.

"I got you something. Don't go shooting off your mouth to the cops unless this really leads you somewhere, okay? Scrappy Jack's out in Banks is an outfit that might not be too particular taking stuff in. And you didn't hear that from me!"

"It's a start. You came through, Richie. I won't forget it."

I had been thinking how to probe for information at a scrap yard and decided that if Angie would be willing to help, she might have the most success. She was going to have a seat on the evening news desk today, so I knew I could reach her at the studio. She told me about a breaking story from the Philippines where a ferry was sinking and they were trying to rescue survivors in the cold light of dawn. When she finished, I explained the angle where I needed her help.

"Do you think you could use a cover story ... maybe getting background for a feature on recycling? You'd only need to ask for a tour, keep your eyes open and try to chat up whoever was showing you around. You might have to go to a larger yard first -- like Schnitzers – just to get a feel for what goes on. Then visit this place that I've heard might bend procedures if there were a little sweetener. *That's* where you might pick up something interesting."

"Is this a place your pal Richie B. knew about?"

Angie is such an intuitive news hawk she can always sniff the beginnings of a story. Plus, she already knew I was wondering about a linkage between Westlake's murder and the disappearance of Lunberg.

"No comment on that, sweetheart. If DeNoli and I ever get this sorted out, you know you'll have a story, but it's early days. Besides, we PIs are almost as secretive about our sources as you reporters!"

Although it had not always been this way, we were now comfortable enough in our relationship that we respected the ethics of each other's professions. On the other hand, in private, we had enough trust to share ideas on stories or cases.

"Alright, I can do that. I have some time tomorrow in the morning. Give me the addresses and I'll take care of it. So, best case, you hope we'd learn that someone did drop off a water heater during that window of time and arranged for it to go straight to the compactor?"

"Exactly. No one would come right out and say that, but you never know what they might let slip or infer … especially if you get them talking about process or start-to-finish time."

"Got it. I'll have to tell my boss, but I'll just say that it's early fieldwork for an idea I might develop later. He cuts me a lot of slack in that regard. He might wonder if I'm helping you again, but he won't push it."

"Thanks, Angie! We may be sniffing down the wrong trail or you might run into tight-lipped types, but it's worth a try."

After we ended our call, I went back to the office and dug out Dan Niemus's business card. He was at his desk and, somewhat to my surprise, accepted my call.

"Detective Niemus, I'm just checking to see if you've got any suspects in Brian Westlake's killing."

"No. There's a guy who's been known to camp in the park not too far from where we found the body, but we don't have anything to put him together with Westlake. We talked to him twice. He was sent briefly to the psychiatric unit about three years ago for making a disturbance and pushing people in Pioneer Square. And he panhandles with some regularity but, like I said, no connections we can see to the dead man."

It was interesting to me that Niemus was even that forthcoming. It sounded like he had no leads at all. I waited to see if he was going to ask if I had turned anything up.

"Don't suppose you've found any smoking Colt 45s either, huh?"

I certainly didn't have anything hard to give him. At this early stage, I was not ready to share my nascent idea built on Westlake being an eye-witness to Lunberg having an argument with a bogus delivery man.

"No, I haven't."

"Are you still on it?"

"Yeah, still poking around. So you still favor a random mugging?"

There were a few seconds hesitation before he answered, "That's still my best bet. We're going to talk to the wife again. Even though they'd separated, she had a big insurance policy on him."

"Did Paul DeNoli pass on the threads from Westlake's dog's teeth?"

"Yeah. I have them. We've sent them to the lab. When we catch the guy and *if* the lab people can find any DNA, they could be very useful."

I waited a beat. Nothing. I guessed that was as close as Niemus would get to thanking me for turning up the threads.

I called Mel Westlake and reassured him that I found nothing regarding Brian's social or work relationships that could have resulted in any malice toward him. I confirmed that I had again talked with Niemus and that he did not seem to have any promising leads. Mel asked if I had any 'outside-of-the-box' ideas. I told him about the mysterious disappearance of a man – who might well have had enemies – from a house next door to where Brian had been working on the same day. I cautioned that that may have been a total coincidence, but said I was gathering more information because I could imagine a link. He asked why I could imagine that. I reminded Mel that, as Brian himself had mentioned to Stratley, he may have seen something while up in a tree ... something that I speculated could have been incriminating.

I had not yet called the VA hospital about Cliff Gaston's alibi. The receptionist transferred my call to the counselor who ran the session. I explained who I was and why I was calling. I told him that Gaston had invited me to call and confirm. Even then, he was reluctant to even give me a "yes" or "no" as to whether Gaston had been there on the day in question. He said he would try to reach Gaston and call me back if Gaston gave *him* approval. Ten minutes later, he called to say, yes, Gaston had been in the session the entire time. I scratched that little inquiry off my list.

There was a nice elderly man, John, whose houseboat was eight places further to the south from my berth. He was sharp despite being a little hard of hearing and tottering a bit when he walked. We talked Ducks football occasionally. He was a big fan. He knew all the current information about the players and he enthusiastically shared that with me. On a far more sobering level, he had been taken hostage for a few minutes last year. A killer had come to the marina to stop me from testifying in a federal smuggling case. I overpowered him and took his weapon but, before I could summon the police, he grabbed John as a hostage and got away. I would not shoot while he had John in front of him and my shots, after he pulled John into his car, missed his tires. I gave chase and found John, whom he had pushed out the car door, crawling – bloody and dazed – on the shoulder. I took John to the ER and we became even better friends for having gone through that terrible experience together.

John's old floating home needed painting on the weather side and I had offered to do it. The week before, I stripped the old paint off and it was now time for a good primer coat. I would have to wait for DeNoli to learn more from ATF and for Angie to try to glean information from Scrappy Jack's. I changed clothes and headed for John's houseboat.

9

Wednesday, April 22nd morning

Angie had contacted the yard manager by phone to set up her visit to Schnitzer Steel's facility. She used a story about educating herself for a possible TV news segment on recycling. She had to pull out the stops to convince them to give her a tour. The massive scrap yard off Burgard Road was not far from where the Willamette River joins the Columbia. They received Angie politely, gave her a hard hat and turned her over to a young woman wearing boots, Carhartts, and a glow vest along with her bright orange hard hat.

"I'm Jamie," she said and shook Angie's hand. "We'll be able to walk most places and I'll try to explain as we go. Just stay close: there're big pieces of equipment here and the operators are not used to watching out for visitors."

The "tour" took thirty-five minutes. Angie had taken notes as they walked. She left with a fair sense of the weighing, sorting, stock-piling, transporting, shredding and loading that took place in this large yard.

Banks is a very small town twenty-five miles west of downtown Portland. Angie drove toward the coast on Highway 26. At the fork where the Wilson River highway peeled off toward Tillamook, she turned left. A few minutes later, she drove into the parking lot at Scrappy Jack's.

Angie walked up to a mobile home that had been converted to an office. A corpulent man, with deep-set black eyes and a cigarette in his mouth, looked up from a ledger he was studying. Mute, he gave her a questioning look. Angie gave him her best smile and a cheery "good morning". That still did not elicit a response. She gave him her name and the call letters of the station where she worked. That provoked his first words.

"What do you want with us?"

She gave him the pitch that she was considering producing a television segment on the role of scrap metal in recycling. It might even be expanded to the role recycling played in the conservation of resources and increasing industrial efficiency, she suggested.

"Can't you do your research at a library or on the internet?"

"Good point. I've already done a little, but I need to see real yards to determine whether there are good visuals. You know, interesting stories about the job, video of the operations to show the viewers how the process really works. And there's no better way for me to start learning about a new field than to see it first-hand."

"What do you mean by 'first-hand'?"

"If you could give me a tour of your operation here, explain how you handle the material, give me a look at your machines in operation, that sort of thing. I'm sure at this stage I don't need more than, say, twenty or twenty-five minutes."

"I donno. We're not really looking for publicity."

"Well, gee. This is just preliminary. If I do produce such a segment and you don't want the company name mentioned, that's okay. Think of it as a public service."

He was realizing that this woman was going to persist until she got her little tour. "Well, I guess it can't hurt," he said with a scowl. "I'll get Mark to show you around."

He got on an amplified speaker system and summoned "Mark" to the office. Mark turned out to be as skinny as the man at the desk was over-weight. He was twenty at the most and had the cocky self-assurance of young manhood. He listened to his instructions -- emphasizing "stay with her and make it fast" – but never took his eyes off Angie. She followed him through a gate into the yard itself. Mark wore just a cap that had "Brunswick" on the front and did not offer Angie a hard hat. Angie saw lots of oily engine blocks, slabs of corrugated steel, and old washing machines and dishwashers. Once away from the office, Mark seemed quite eager to talk to the beautiful woman now close beside him.

"So do you take all kinds of metals here?" she asked.

"Pretty much. Nobody brings us silver or gold, of course, and we don't resell zinc. But everything else that's a metal we take."

"Does everything get sorted before it gets compacted?"

"Well, steel's steel so there's not much to sort out, even with different gauges. I think we separated a special kind of alloy once, but I never did know who we shipped it to. Basically magnets are used to sort ferrous metal from non-ferrous."

"And the cranes and dozers just push everything straight to some sort of a compactor when it comes in?"

"Not really. We have backlogs. It would probably sit in a pile for five to ten days before it gets crushed."

"So you decide what goes next?" She could see he liked the idea that she thought he made those kinds of decisions.

"Yeah, sometimes."

"And the people who sell you stuff don't care when it gets crushed?"

"Oh, I had one guy came in couple of weeks ago. He wanted his stuff at the front of the line. It was kind of stupid, I thought. All he had was an old water heater. It might've had a little copper inside, but not a big loss for us if we missed it."

"That's weird! At another yard I visited, the same thing happened. They said that man was tall with a wild red beard and drove a Chevy pickup."

"Not the same guy. This shmuck had black hair and a weird ear ... and I wouldn't say he was tall. Besides, the vehicle he unloaded was a van for an appliance store."

"I hope he tipped you well, anyway!"

"Ah, well I'm not sure that's any of your business."

"Right. Sorry to seem nosy. It's not important for my treatment of the recycling issue anyway."

A break horn sounded and the machines shut down for a few minutes. Mark used the stoppage as a moment for Angie to get a close look at the bailer. This machine compacted various chunks and pieces into solid volumes looking like gray hay-bales. It operated in a different – and simpler -- way than the giant, twenty-five-hundred horsepower "mega-shredder" she had seen at Schnitzer's, but it got the job done. They finished her tour by going to the last set of scales and the crawler-grapples that moved the bales of squashed metal to a loading dock. Angie told Mark it was all very interesting and thanked him for showing her around. She said that, if they decided to produce the segment and include some camera work at Scrappy Jack's, she would be in touch.

Angie left the yard and stopped for one of the legendary burgers at the Helvetia Tavern. As soon as her order was taken, she used her cell to call Rick.

Paul DeNoli called around ten-thirty. He had talked again to Stan Madruga in ATF's Phoenix field office. Paul learned that the names of the four men convicted in Lunberg's last undercover case were Ignacio Garcia, Michael Jacobson, Sean McNair, and Darius Roberts. They had all received maximum sentences of ten years to be served at the medium-security federal prison in Arizona. Garcia had died of lung cancer while still in prison. Jacobson, McNair and Roberts were released in 2010 and paroled into three years of "supervised release". Those three had served eight-and-a-half years inside after time off for good behavior. Jacobson's last known address was in Carver, Oregon. They had no current address for NcNair. Roberts had been arrested in February of this year on federal drug charges and has been in prison ever since.

"So, if you're thinking of a vendetta killing of some kind, looks as though it's going to be either Jacobson or McNair," DeNoli said."Right. I'll start with the low-hanging fruit and see if Jacobson will talk to me."

I looked in the phone book for greater Portland and there Jacobson was with an address in Carver. I wanted to talk to him directly and not over the phone.

Assuming he was working, that meant an early evening visit. I sat in my office chair and gave some thought on how to question Jacobson if he were willing to talk.

It was late morning when Angie called. She gave me a fast summary of scrap metal operations and then cut to the chase with her visit to Scrappy Jack's.

"So this young guy, Mark, had actually dealt with a man in your time-frame who wanted to have a water heater smashed up right away!"

"Maybe you hit the bull's eye right there, Angie! So how did he pull it off?"

"He 'tipped' him something, but Mark wouldn't tell me how much. He said the guy just emphasized that he wanted it sent to the compactor right away."

"Did you get a look at the compacting machine?"

"Yes. They call it a bailer, but that's what it does. It wasn't running because they were on break, but I got up close. It would have no trouble swallowing a large water heater … or even an entire car, well maybe only half a car but, anyway, it was a powerful big thing. But they would put several items in the maw at once because everything gets reduced in volume so much and the bales seem to be more or less a standardized size."

"Do you think this Mark is the key man for such goings on?"

"Oh, I'm not too sure about that. I think he's probably the low man on the totem pole out there. But he's moxie enough that he would know how to pick up some quick money if the opportunity was there. Maybe everyone on the staff turns an eye from time to time." She chuckled and added, "It didn't strike me as a high-class operation. Or is that an oxymoron when referring to scrap yards?"

"Har, Har. Did you by any chance get a description of the guy who dropped off the water heater?"

"Hey, I'm earning points for my PI badge, lover! Think I'd forget that? I told him a little fable about a similar incident with a tall, red-bearded man. He said, no, no. His guy was medium height with black hair, clean shaven and a 'weird ear'. And, he drove an appliance van."

"I'll be damned! Nice work! Now we have something to work with."

I figured if I was going to Carver anyway, I might as well eat dinner at the Stone Cliff Inn. I asked Angie if she wanted to join me. She thought it was a nice idea. She would take her own car so she could return to the studio for the eleven PM newscast and I could move on to seeing Jacobson.

I drove through Oregon City and headed East on Clackamas River Drive. It's a pretty drive: the road passes meadows and forests as its sweeping curves follow the river. When I reached Carver, I did a one-eighty to climb the steep private road up to the restaurant. The building perches high above the river and features massive stone work and large timbered beams. It has a great deck for summer-time eating and drinking, but at quarter to six on an April afternoon, we chose indoors. I ordered a flatiron steak and Angie had poached salmon. Part way through our meal, the conversation drifted around to Angie's career.

"If you had the evening news co-anchor job here, would you stay in Portland?"

"Yes, I would. The two metro markets are about the same size. And *you're* here!"

"I think you're next in line, but I don't know when there might be a vacancy. Is Sonja likely to leave?"

"I agree that I should be next in line. Marilyn has seniority on me by almost four months, but she hasn't produced much. And she seems a little languid for the most important air time. As for Sonja, she's pregnant and she hinted to someone that it's twins. Sonja's damn impressive, but I can't see her trying to mother two babies at once and still do the news. So things might change five months from now. If I'm right, Sonja might resign or ask to be shifted to a back-up slot."

"And they let you produce your own special on extending the streetcar line last year."

"Yes, but I had to beg and beg."

"Maybe so, but it was quite a success wasn't it?"

"Yeah. Everyone said it was good and the station manager was glad they let me do it. But more specials are not a given and it's not in my contract that I can do more of them."

On that note, we split a fudge sundae. Then we split the check and headed for our cars.

10

Wednesday, April 22nd evening

M ichael Jacobson lived in a plain one-story house on a street that could have used some pot-hole repairs. His and all his neighbors' homes were nevertheless well maintained and had well-kept lawns. A forest began where the street ended a block past his house. It was dark by the time I arrived on his porch and used the brass knocker. The door opened and I saw a man almost my height with blond hair in a ponytail. He wore jeans and a fleece pull-over. If he was surprised to see a stranger on his doorstep at seven in the evening, he didn't show it.

"Yes?"

"I'm Rick Conwright. I'm not handing out religious literature or anything," I said with a smile and handed him my business card. "If it's not inconvenient, I'd like to speak with you about some of your colleagues back in the day."

He gave me a long look that was half annoyance and half curiosity. Finally, he nodded and said, "Alright, come on in."

He ushered me into his living room to the left of the small foyer. The room was nicely carpeted and he gestured toward two captain's chairs on either side of a real, wood-burning fireplace.

"What did you mean by 'colleagues', Mr. Conwright?"

"I suppose you could say the men who were your associates in the gun modification business."

"What do you know about that?"

"I know you were convicted and did federal time."

"So now, twelve years later, you come to my door to ask questions? I'd like to know why you have to invade my privacy like this." He said it calmly and without rancor, but his piercing gray-blue eyes suggested I had better have a good reason for my intrusion.

"I've been hired by the brother of a man who was shot to death. I'm trying to find out who killed him. The police aren't making much progress and the brother wants me to have a go at it. The more I've looked at it, the more I think it could be connected to another man's disappearance or death."

"Okay, but how does that tie into me or my 'colleagues' as you put it?"

"The man who vanished was a retired ATF agent. He worked undercover and was a witness against you in your trial."

"Jeb Furman!"

"That may've been his work name; I don't know. Would this be the man you knew as Jeb?" I showed him the picture of Brad Lunberg that his wife had given me.

"Yes. That's him." Again, he seemed strangely calm. "What was the connection to your guy?"

"I prefer to hold that back for now. The ATF man went missing on April seventh. My client's brother was killed on the ninth."

"And you want to know if I killed those men?"

"You make progress in my business by eliminating possibilities, Mr. Jacobson. The sooner innocent people convince me they couldn't have done it, the sooner I cross them off the list of 'possibles' and move on."

"Well, at least you're honest about what you're after. Of course, the real culprit could lie to you."

"Yes, that could certainly happen. But remember I said 'convince me'. I'd look for corroboration."

"Alright. Let me tell you my story. I didn't have a sick child who needed surgery that I couldn't afford, or anything as heart-rending as the guy in 'Breaking Bad'. But I had run up way too much credit card debt and I was starting to drink heavily. I had worked for a gunsmith and knew a fair amount about guns. You might say I fell in with bad company and the temptation of some fast money was more than I could resist. Some of my 'colleagues' were already career criminals. I was just a new initiate. I'm not claiming that I was unjustly convicted. Only that I wanted to get out of that life and be a normal person. I never used drugs in or out prison and I never joined a gang."

"In the joint," he continued, "I eventually became sort of a trustee. They used a few prisoners to do the landscaping work. I'm not saying it was like a fancy resort or anything. But they had some lawn, an irrigation system, some shrubs and a few ornamental trees. There were even a few rhodies in front of the public entrance. There was another con who had worked in a nursery and I worked mostly with him. He taught me a lot. So, I get out and look around in the landscaping field. With this kind of business, I can make an honest living. I like doing it and I've become that 'normal person'."

"What were your feelings about 'Jeb'?"

"Oh, there was some anger at the time. Sure ... a guy who worked shoulder-to-shoulder with us and was lying to us the whole time. I always thought he seemed too eager to know everything we were doing even when he was the new kid on the block. And when the prosecutor asked for the maximum sentence and I saw Jeb as the key witness, I suppose I hated him, yeah. But I didn't kid myself. I was among the law-breakers and he was – sneaky or not – on the side trying to stop us.

Anyway, life is too short for me to carry a grudge over all these years. If I had run into him on the street, I might've glared at him or made a shitty remark, but I would not have swung at him let alone tried to kill him!"

"So then, Mr. Jacobson, do you want to tell me where you were from mid-afternoon through early evening on the ninth?"

He turned on his cell phone to check the calendar. "The ninth was a Thursday, right?"

"Yeah."

"Okay, we had a big job at McMenamin's Edgefield property. It started on that first Thursday and went on for eight days. We didn't work Easter Sunday, of course. I didn't go out on the Saturday before Easter because I was sick, but I was out there every other day. I could give you names of the guys on the crew so you could check."

"But the early evening on the ninth?"

"Oh, yeah. That would be the second Thursday and that's when some friends and I play our monthly poker game. We played at Tom Radley's house. We started with a little supper at six and played until eleven-thirty. Call him if you want; he's in the phone book."

"That's very helpful. Thanks. What can you tell me about Sean McNair?"

"Well, old Sean he had quite a temper. He was smart though. To the extent we had financial records,

Sean did them. He seemed a little unstable to me, but he and I never got cross-wise."

"So how do you think he felt about Jeb?"

"He was surprised and angry that we got maximum sentences. He felt Jeb had betrayed us – and he *had*, I suppose. Sean had a lot of names for him and 'fucking traitor' was probably the nicest."

"Do you think he carried that anger over all those years you guys were inside?"

"I couldn't really say. But I think, before we got caught, he'd met a girl and they were getting serious. Of course she didn't know we were modifying and selling military-type guns in that building. Her father owned a string of car washes. Sean told me they planned to get married and he was going to use his share of the payment for the last batch of guns to buy into the family business. He already had a sheet, but I think, like me, he wanted to go straight. So it seemed like he figured Jeb cost him everything: a new life and his marriage to this girl."

"Can you tell me anything else about him? Occupational skills besides guns? Sports he was good at?"

"You don't know how to reach him, do you?"

"No. He seems to have gone off the grid."

"He told me he grew up in the San Francisco area. I think he said his dad was a professional diver and worked in the Bay. I got the impression he was close to his old man. As for jobs, I know he worked as a bartender and an appliance repairman. And he seemed to know a lot about meat-cutting, but he never said he actually worked as a butcher or a meat packer."

"How about hobbies? Interests?"

"He did have a hobby for sure. He liked model airplanes. He even got permission from the warden to build a few and they let him fly them in the yard once in a while."

"hmm ...*that's* an interesting hobby! Anything else you can remember about him?"

"He never talked about playing sports. I'd say he was strong, but not especially athletic if you know what I mean. He did go nuts for the New Jersey Devils though."

"You mean the hockey team?"

"Yeah. Maybe he lived there once or something. But if one of their games was on TV in the common room, he was sure to be there."

"Did he ever use an alias or a different name?"

"None I ever heard. He did have a nick-name, but he didn't like it much so we never used it in front of him. He was missing the earlobe on his left ear. I don't know whether he'd been in a knife fight or what, but it wasn't there. So some people called him 'short ear' or 'short-ear Sean'"

That seemed about the most I was going to get from this pretty- decent-sounding guy.

"I appreciate your talking with me, Mr. Jacobson. Could you give me those names from the crew that worked the Edgefield job with you?"

"Yeah, sure." He wrote some first names, Rafael, Dillon, and Cisco, and the name of the company, Green Valley Landscaping, on a scrap of paper. "You going to hunt Sean down?"

"Well I do want to talk to him, but it seems he'll be damn hard to find. Do you mind if I ask if he's been in touch with you since you've been out?"

"Yeah, two or three times. All in the first couple of months after we were released. Actually, I got out about ten days before him for some reason. He wanted to know how I was making the adjustment, whether I'd found a job, whether I was getting any nookie, that sort of thing. After those first few times, nothing."

"Did he still seem angry about the ATF guy?"

"It didn't come up. He didn't sound super happy, but nothing specific ... maybe he was just a little depressed."

I felt like there were one or two more questions that I should have asked, but nothing clicked. I checked my notes and they looked complete. I again thanked Jacobson and took my leave. So Sean McNair knew how to repair – and possibly disassemble – appliances.

11

Thursday, April 23rd morning

DeNoli had to testify in a trial and expected to be the first witness on the stand that morning. He thought, even allowing for his cross-examination, he would be back in his office by eleven-thirty. I asked him if I could come to the Justice Center to work a little more on the ATF man's case. He was fine with that and said he would call me when he was excused from being a witness.

While waiting for DeNoli to be available, I called Tom Radley. He was at work, but his wife gave me the work number. He confirmed the poker game and said that Jacobson arrived on time for supper and stayed until they quit a little after eleven-thirty. When I called Green Valley Landscaping, I was told Cisco had injured himself and was going to be out all week. The other two workers were on a job, but the office thought Dillon had a cell phone and gave me that number. Dillon answered and I explained that Mike Jacobson had asked me to verify that he was at work on Thursday the ninth of April. Dillon said he thought so, but wasn't sure. He passed the phone to Rafael. Rafael was positive that Jacobson had been there because, as he said, "my old Honda Civic was out of commission until I could work on it on the weekend" and that Mike had given him a ride to and from work.

It was eleven forty-five when Paul and I met in a more private nook off the homicide detectives' squad room. I gave Paul my conclusion that – if the killer had been one of the ex-cons – they could not have learned Lunberg's real name and current address without access to ATF's records.

"There has to have been a leak, Paul. Can you call Madruga so we can ask him where and how that kind of information is stored?"

We discussed how we could tactfully raise the question of a leak and jotted down a few key questions. Paul used his cell to call Phoenix ATF and asked the receptionist to connect him to Madruga. While we waited, he conferenced my cell phone into the connection.

"Stan, it's Paul DeNoli again ... yeah, some more questions. I have a PI with me on the line. He's a trusted friend. He's working a closely related case and we're coordinating our efforts at this early stage."

I said hello and introduced myself. Paul continued, "Am I right that the real names of your undercover guys can't be publicly connected to their work names?"

"Definitely! Any lists or links would be secret and held very securely."

"Stan," I asked, "how many of your people might've had access to those files over the last four years?"

"Before the files were sent to our Arizona archives, six or fewer. Of course, the U.S. Attorney's Office would've had some access during the trial and the sentencing. After they were sent to archives, perhaps a few more, different, people might see them. The Human Resources material should still be in our offices here. Those HR files would not have work names or case references, but they would have retirement information and last-known addresses."

"Do the archives folks maintain an access log?"

"Yes, they do, Rick. I think they keep it in hardcopy and maybe digitally as well".

"Same for your HR files?"

"Yes."

"Could you find out for us who accessed Lunberg's files in the last four years?"

"Well, I suppose I could, but where are you going with this? You think one of our people could've dropped the dime on Lunberg!"

DeNoli replied, "Right now, we don't think anything. But – if this *was* done by one of those ex-cons -- they couldn't have located him without knowing his real name and address. If everything at your end checks out, our ideas about who did what may be wrong. But if something were amiss inside your shop, you would want to know about it, right?"

"Sure, but I'm not comfortable with you questioning any of our employees."

"I'd be discreet. And if it looks airtight at your end, I'll purge my files of any such conversations," I told him.

DeNoli added, "We at PPB Homicide don't have a body so my investigation is strictly informal and off the record at this point."

Madruga heaved a sigh of resignation. "Okay. Against my better judgment, I'll check with the archivist and HR and see what the logs show. I'll call you back later today."

DeNoli and I went to the building cafeteria and had lunch. Paul wolfed down his meal because he had one new issue to check out for the prosecutor in the trial. I read The Oregonian as I ate my hamburger and soup and ambled back to Paul's cubicle about twenty minutes later. Paul had just finished his work for the trial when Stan Madruga called back.

"Okay. I have something for you regarding that case file and Lunberg's HR file. In the archives, only one person besides our research statistician got that file. And the only person other than our Benefits Coordinator to access his HR file was that same person. Although it's not quite as clear cut as that. This guy requested that HR provide him with the addresses of all the Phoenix field agents who had retired in the last ten years. Of course that included Lunberg."

"That's clever or maybe it's just quite a coincidence," I said.

"Yeah, maybe. Anyway, the guy's name is Del Fulton. He used to be a manager in Procurement."

"Can you tell us anything about him?"

"Hefty retired last month. That is Del's nickname … he's a little on the heavy side. He went out early. There was some talk that he was under investigation by Internal Affairs, but that's all I know and all I could say in any case. I remember he seemed resentful about not getting promoted. In fact, instead of a promotion, he got transferred from Enforcement to Procurement. Less stress, but not a plum for your retirement resume. I didn't run into him too often, but some folks here thought he seemed a little 'strung out' occasionally."

"Can you give us an address or phone number?"

"The phone number is unlisted and we don't give out phone numbers anyway, so no I can't. And – you'll understand this given your theory – since he used to work in Firearms Enforcement, I can't give even you the address. If Paul DeNoli gets officially involved, that might change, but today that's the best I can do."

"I appreciate what you've given me, but Phoenix is a big area. I'm going to be looking for the proverbial 'needle' there. Can you at least tell me anything about his interests or hangouts?"

"I really don't know much personal stuff. I remember he was always talking about his German shorthair ... I think the dog won some ribbons in hunting-dog competitions. He was divorced. That's all I can think of."

"Thanks. Everything helps. How about the statistician's name?"

"He's a very straight guy and will probably try to be helpful. But, If I give you his name, you can't contact him at work and the archivist and I are *not* how you got his name."

"Fair enough," I said.

"His name is Billy Barnstable."

When I got back to the houseboat, there was a message to call Julio. He picked up right away and told me that Theresa had hit pay dirt. She had found a Napa outlet where, in the relevant window of time, a man had paid cash for a single head lamp. Julio passed on the description she had gotten from one of the clerks. It was very general, but depicted a middle-age, medium-height person wearing jeans and a polo shirt with dark brown hair. If we ever identified "Jumpsuit", we could show the clerk a photo of him in hopes of establishing a better connection to the disappearance.

There was a weak link in my theory about Lunberg's disappearance – and I was more and more convinced that his "disappearance" was actually his death. The weak link was how could NcNair or Jacobson have done it if they did not know his real name and address. A possible answer to that riddle lay in Phoenix. I wanted to probe "Hefty" Fulton; in person if possible, otherwise through friends and associates.

I called Mel Westlake, gave him a general update, and asked him if he would authorize me going to Phoenix for a couple of days. He did not sound quite ready to give his okay, so I said I was at a bottle-neck where it would be hard to close in on the suspect unless I could get certain information. I added that I believed that information could best be developed through a trip to Phoenix. I also told him that, if the information showed what I expected it to show, my friend at PPB would most probably be ready to open an official file on the retired ATF man. Mel thought it over for a few seconds and then gave me his approval. He and I had previously discussed my theory about how the disappearance could very well be tied to his brother's death. Mel 'got it' and continued to let me pursue that seemingly unrelated event as a means to the end of identifying his brother's killer.

I was able to get on a late-afternoon flight. In Phoenix, I rented a car and checked into an inexpensive hotel. My plan was to interview Barnstable, the statistician, in the morning. Not only was he in the phone directory, but I guessed he would be friendlier and might even know something helpful about Lunberg or Fulton. I promised an early breakfast in return for a short interview. As Madruga had forecast, he was willing to help and agreed to the breakfast.

12

Friday, April 24th morning

Barnstable told me to call him "Billy". I gave him my card and said I was investigating the killing of my client's brother. I told him that in the course of my work, the trail I was following crossed over to the mysterious disappearance of a former ATF agent. I did not offer my theory of a vendetta by ex-convicts, but merely stated that there might be some relevant information in the ATF archives. We were both piling into huevos rancheros when I eased into my questions.

"So tell me, Billy, what exactly are your duties in relation to the archives?"

"Well, I'm certainly not the Records Librarian! But I do periodically – say every three months -- access files in the archives to gather data on gun types, registration, locations and purposes of illegal buyers, networks of buyers, and syndicate members -- if identified. And I also harvest any new data about cigarette smuggling or imported spirits."

"And once you acquire and update that type of information, do you process it further?"

"Oh, yes. I do statistical studies to look for connections that were not obvious during prosecution and to recognize trends. At the end of the year, I write and compile an annual report. It is used in budgeting, staffing, projections of future violations, improving enforcement procedures ... that sort of thing."

I could see he was proud of his work. "Do you ever access the files in between those routine updating sessions?"

"Not often, but occasionally one of the agents will want to check something. They could do it themselves, but if it involves massaging the data, they ask me to do it for them or with them."

"And have you had such requests in the last four years?"

"Sure. Not many, but probably ten or twelve over that time period."

"Do you remember getting into a file involving Agent Brad Lunberg?"

"Normally I wouldn't remember individual's names, but that one is vaguely familiar. I think that was the one where something a year or two earlier had been mischaracterized or improperly recorded. If I'm remembering the correct incident, I did look at that file, found the mistake and corrected my own data base."

"Did you know Lunberg?"

"No, not at all. I kind of stay in my little corner and don't meet many of the field agents."

"You talked about an 'improper recording '. Was it something scandalous or incriminating?"

"If it had been, I probably couldn't tell you about it. But no, nothing of that nature. Could've been a mistake made in haste or based on a misunderstanding of the classification codes, but nothing at all sinister. It was somewhat important to my calculations and overall analysis, but only for that rather abstract reason."

We finished the last of our coffee and the waiter, a woman who seemed so weary at that early hour that I wondered if she was just finishing the night shift, gave me the check.

I returned to the hotel and opened my laptop. It was time to track down Mr. Fulton. I did not have much to work with: he seemed to some to be "flakey" and "strung out" so maybe he was some kind of an addict. DeNoli had checked the Pima County and Maricopa County conviction and arrest records before I left, but there was no sheet for Fulton. That figured, because I could not believe he would have kept his job if there had been a conviction. Arrests, of course, were a different matter, but Paul found nothing there either. That left me with his hunting dog.

I played around with my browser until I hit a Phoenix-based web-site for German-shorthair owners. I was able to log on without needing a password. I trolled under a chat tab and saw a thread where one of the contributors used the handle "Hefty". That looked hopeful.

I found the organization's address and the web-master's phone number on its home page. I called and gave the web-master a story that I was an investigator working for an attorney handling a decedent's estate. I said the executor had identified Del Fulton as a beneficiary, but we had no address or phone number through which to contact him. The man accepted my story and tacitly indicated that Del Fulton was one of their members. But he said they were not really a formal club so he had no roster and, therefore, no address or phone number. He explained that all communications were done by e-mail or through the web-site. Given that Fulton's number was unlisted, I was not altogether surprised there was no phone information. But I was disappointed about no address.

The web-master, wanting to help a fellow dog lover get an inheritance, suddenly exclaimed, "Wait a minute! We just recently billed our members for their share of this year's user fees for the properties where we hold the trials. Let me look for the check he used in paying that bill." There was a pause of almost a minute. "Ah, I have it." He read me Fulton's address off the face of the check. It was time to knock on Hefty Fulton's door.

Fulton lived in a westerly suburb called Avondale. His home was a ranch-style house that looked to have been built in the sixties. It was sited close to the curving street with a desert-style front yard featuring succulents and cacti. The back yard was fenced and I heard a dog barking back there. I rang the bell. Nothing. I rang a second time and a man with an unkempt blend of black and gray hair answered. He wore shorts and a polo shirt, tight over his extended belly. He packed a good two-hundred pounds on his medium-height frame.

"Yes?"

"Are you Del Fulton?" I asked.

"What do you want?"

"I'm Rick Conwright. I'm looking for Del Fulton."

He stared at me somewhat sullenly. "Oka-a-ay. That's me."

I told him I was a private investigator working on a murder case in Portland, Oregon. He did not budge from blocking the door.

"If I could come in, I would be happy to explain."

He grunted and nodded. I followed him to a living room. It was a good while since the room had been straightened. I saw magazines and newspapers scattered on the carpet, a jacket over a chair back, and unemptied ash trays. There was some dust on a credenza along with bottles of tequila and bourbon. Okay, so he lived alone and was a slob. He dropped into an easy chair and looked at me questioningly. Without being bid to, I settled onto a couch and pulled out my notebook.

"Like I said, I'm working on a murder in the Portland area. There may well be some connection to things in the Phoenix area. My question to you is why did you access ATF files pertaining to Brad Lunberg?"

Fulton's jaw tightened and his eyes jerked to a television that had been muted.

"What the hell! You've been hacking into federal files? I ought to report you right now!"

"Suit yourself, Mr. Fulton. I'm not working as any kind of a federal investigator. But you *were* an ATF employee at the time and now you're enjoying a federal pension. Perhaps you'd rather not draw attention to that access."

I was banking on my letting him know I was not feeling threatened and was throwing a threat back at him. I hoped that would calm him down and get me a little cooperation.

"I had every right to access files on a need-to-know basis," he said more calmly.

"Perhaps you did, sir. But you *did* access the ones I'm asking about. What was your need to know?"

"You think I'm going to tell a civilian something that's a matter of Enforcement security?"

I took that as an implied admission that he had accessed the files. It was time for me to bluff a little.

"So why didn't you follow procedure and give your reason when you logged in?"

" I ... I don't remember what I said. Hell, that was almost three years ago!"

"Well, you could clear this up right now by remembering what you were after even though you didn't log it in."

I saw tiny rivulets of perspiration forming below his sideburns.

"I still don't see what your questions could have to do with some murder up in Oregon!"

"Believe me, I wouldn't have traveled all the way to Phoenix if I didn't have a lead that connected it up!"

"So I have to trust you, a total stranger!"

"Think about it. I can go through channels and the agency will probably shine a bright light on the matter. I came here to ask you, in the privacy of your home, to see if you can help my investigation ... so I can get the information I need in an informal way."

He looked deflated and there were new rivulets on his forehead.

"Listen, Lunberg had worked undercover on a pretty big bust. It involved altering AK47s so they fired like machine guns. Strictly illegal. The deal, of course, was that when the sale was consummated, the gunrunners got the guns and the guys who did the modification got the money. But there were rumors that most or all of the money was never recovered. The rumors were that almost two-hundred thousand dollars was missing. I'd been transferred from Enforcement to the shit-hole of Procurement. I thought that if I poked around and could find the money, I'd be a hero and get back to Enforcement. But it wasn't my case, so I had to study the case file to know where to begin."

"This was a sanctioned look or just freelancing for yourself?"

"Not sanctioned, no. But I wouldn't have kept the money! If I'd located it, I would have just turned it over and hoped to be rewarded with a transfer back. Besides, if the money was all intact – in federal hands - there was no reason for me to make the effort. Don't you see, I had to look at the file to even know *that*!"

"And how about your going after Lunberg's home address?"

"Oh, Christ, Conwright! That's entirely unrelated!"

"But it was within days of your looking at that case file."

"So what! Some of the retired guys were griping that once they were out the door, the agency ignored them ... they became forgotten men. I had this idea to send all the retirees Christmas cards. I thought it would make me look like an 'idea man' with the best interests of ATF at heart."

"Whose 'idea' was it to look for the money? Who wanted you to look at those files?"

Fulton again broke eye contact and looked away.

"No one! No one asked me to. It was my own idea. I thought I could work it alone."

"How did you know that Lunberg was working that particular case?"

"I didn't!" He paused to wipe his brow. "I'd just heard the rumors about the money. I knew of the case, but not which agents were working it."

That sounded like pure bullshit to me, so I wanted to push him harder. "You retired early. Why was that?"

"That's personal. That can't possibly have any relevance for your investigation!"

"Have you had any contacts, directly or indirectly, with the men who were convicted in that case?"

He lurched out of his chair and threw his arm dramatically toward the door. "That's it, Conwright! I've had enough of your insulting questions! Get the hell out of my house!"

You could say that I didn't get any information that was directly useful. I didn't get a confession or the name of the person who put him up to it. But, between his improbable explanations, his obvious anxiety, and the way my last question had pushed his buttons, I now believed he was the guy who leaked Lunberg's information. I closed my notebook and headed for the door.

At the hotel, I used the "business services" computer to see if I could get on an evening flight back to Portland. There were two seats available and I took one of them. Then I called Madruga. I said I had just one question to ask him. Was Fulton the kind of person who would want to send Christmas cards to all the retired Phoenix field agents? That drew a guffaw and a quick answer. "Hardly!" he said then added, "He wasn't a warm and fuzzy guy by any means!"

I was finishing my cannelloni dinner at one of the restaurants at Sky Harbor International when my cell phone chirped. It was Angie.

"Hi, Lover. Are you still in Phoenix?"

"Yeah, but I'm catching an evening flight so I'll be back late tonight."

"Did you find out what you went down there for?"

"Yes and no. I didn't find the old 'smoking gun', but my working theory is still intact. What's up with you?"

"Well, some news about Denver. They want me to come there for an interview. It looks like the salary could be about eight thousand more than I'm making now. They even hinted they would green light a month devoted to putting a special together. I'd be the reporter and would have a strong say in the production! Of course, everything would depend on a good interview."

"That's exciting! They obviously are keen on you for their new anchor. When are you going to do the interview?"

"They're saying next Wednesday. Are you still okay with me doing this?"

"Sure, Angie. If you're the front-runner, you'll sail through any interview. If you really want it, you should go. Then we'll have to really plan how we can work out our lives together. Can we talk some more about it tomorrow night?"

"Yes, of course. I have the six o'clock news tomorrow, but I'm not doing the late news so I'll come over right after the broadcast. Right now, I've got to get to the studio for the eleven o'clock. Don't fret, Rick. I love you and I'm not going to lose you!"

With that mixed message in my head, I entered the concourse and walked toward the gate for my Portland plane.

13

Saturday, April 25th afternoon

I could not sleep on the plane and was pretty zonked when I finally climbed into bed. I slept in and cooked ham and scrambled eggs for a late-morning breakfast. Spring is the most unpredictable season in western Oregon. It must drive the weather forecasters crazy. Crocus and tulips and daffodils manage to sprout and bloom, but there's still a fair amount of rain. The old joke goes that we have gorgeous summers, pleasant autumns, mild winters, and – every three or four years – we have a spring! Joke or not, every time I had a few hours free to work on my boat or old John's, it seemed to rain. The modest aft deck was the only part of my houseboat that was not fiber-glass. The manufacturer had laid teak there. It was a nice touch, but it meant every couple of years it had to be sanded and recoated with marine varnish. I was on my hands and knees with an electric sander when a call came in on my cell. It was the FBI.

After the caller introduced himself as Agent Donaldson, he got right down to business. Weekend or not, fibbies are serious dudes.

"Mr. Conwright, I'm calling because your name came up in the course of my investigation. I'm working on the Lunberg case and this morning I was interviewing Delwin Fulton. He told me you had talked with him yesterday ... harassed him, as he put it. Anyway, he had your business card and that's how I got your name."

"Yes, I talked with Fulton yesterday. Is there some way I can help you?"

"You can start by telling me your interest in Lunberg."

I told Donaldson about Westlake's murder and that I had reason to believe that he had been an eyewitness to the beginning of whatever happened to Lunberg.

"That makes me think Mr. Westlake was killed to keep him quiet. Killed by the same person behind Lunberg's disappearance."

"An eye witness to what," Donaldson asked.

"I've learned from his best friend that Westlake saw a man in white coveralls confronting Lunberg in his backyard. There were angry words. This was the same morning Lunberg disappeared. Westlake was probably the last person to see him other than his killer or abductor."

"Well, I guess that sort of explains why you were questioning Fulton. He's a prickly guy to begin with and he's got a few skeletons in his own closet as well. But how'd you get onto him?"

"I imagine the same way you did. I was interested in who had file information about Lunberg and the cases he worked. Especially the ones where he was working undercover and not using his own name."

"And how did you find that out?"

"I'm a private investigator, Agent Donaldson."

"Okay, I'll leave that alone for now. Anyway, I called to tell you we're working the Lunberg case and we don't want you getting in our way."

I'd seen that movie before, with Niemus. But Donaldson sounded more reasonable than Niemus. I decided to not get into an argument with him. "I did not think Fulton was leveling with me about why he accessed those records. He got very nervous and his reasons were hard to take seriously. Can you tell me about those skeletons?"

"We had pretty much the same reaction to his story. This part is strictly off the record and confidential, okay?"

"Fine. My only interest in Fulton, if he was the leak, is to find out who put him up to it"

Donaldson seemed content with that. "We started sniffing around with the Phoenix police. Fulton doesn't have a sheet, but some years ago, a girl working for an escort service called in a complaint. Apparently he swung at her after a 'date' got out of hand. He broke her nose, bloodied her face and loosened a tooth. I guess the locals were willing to take it on. Then she calls back two days later and withdraws her complaint and says she's won't testify in any trial."

"Predictable, I suppose, given her occupation. But he was a federal employee and if that little escapade became known to ATF, they'd probably can him."

"Yes, I think I can see where you're going with that. But you're barking up the wrong tree, Conwright. We have a person of interest who's becoming more interesting all the time and our scenario for her doesn't need to connect up through Mr. Fulton."

"I'm guessing you're referring to the woman who was stalking Lunberg and against whom he got a restraining order?"

"Ah, you *do* know things! You understand I can't affirm that to you. But if there were such a woman, imagine she had her driver's license suspended and her credit cards revoked. So she has no job, no credit, and no wheels. A diligent investigation would've checked bus tickets to Portland. If such a woman arrived in Portland before Lunberg vanished … *comprender?*"

I decided Agent Donaldson was a pretty good guy after all and certainly was not the lock-lipped type you might expect.

"But how would 'such a woman' know how to find Lunberg? Even know what *city* he'd gone to?"

"Well, if you knew what skills and what job assignments such a woman had, getting into ATF records would not have been too hard."

"I know she worked for some kind of an IT contractor that did work that ATF out-sourced."

"Again, you know quite a lot!"

"There's a homicide detective in the Portland Police Bureau. Our cases have overlapped in the past with considerable success. There's overlap again with Lunberg."

"I get the picture," Donaldson said. "So if the contractor was supporting IT stuff and the hypothetical woman was a clever programmer …"

"Aha! I can see that, but wouldn't it be harder for a woman to dispose of a man's body?"

"Be careful there, friend. No stereotypical assumptions!"

"Okay, put the effort thing aside. But, in my investigation, I have a couple of witnesses who saw a *man* doing things that fit right into my scenario. Besides, if this woman is infatuated with Lunberg, is she going to turn around and kill him?"

"Well, first of all, this woman would be tall, say five-eight or five-nine. Second, he broke off their relationship in no uncertain terms. Don't underestimate a woman scorned, Conwright."

"Now who's stereotyping, Agent Donaldson? Besides, if she's that unbalanced, would she be able to plan such a perfect vanishing act? Would she transfer vitriol born out of unrequited love to my man Westlake even if she thought he'd noticed something?"

"We've been studying the court records in Arizona from the show-cause hearing where Lunberg got that restraining order. I don't think she's playing with a full deck of cards. That said, I have to admit that right now I don't have enough to say she's good for the Lunberg thing."

"What about her movements? Can you place her in the city in time to get Lunberg? Can you place her at his home?"

"Well, the perp wouldn't have *had* to take him from his home. Lunberg could've gone out for a walk to Multnomah Village to get some hamburger buns or something. We're working on those issues. A fellow agent is grilling the woman as we speak. Her story so far is that she hoped to get a job with her brother-in-law who creates and manages web-sites for small businesses. She tells us that she was going to stay with her sister and her husband for a few days until the job thing worked out. It turns out that they expected her a week later and were off on a cruise to Alaska when she arrived. She didn't know how to reach them, so she stayed in a cheap motel until they got back."

"And that part checks out?"

"Yeah, the sister says that was the plan though she doesn't know why the lady arrived a week early. She thinks maybe it was just a communication screw up."

"Sounds like you have nothing very specific on her movements during the days she was at the motel."

"That's more or less right, but our investigation about her is ongoing and I can't comment further. Listen, Conwright, you know you can't be a player on our team, but I can see how you and your police-detective pal can be helpful. And, within limits, I might be able to help you with your Westlake problem. I just got back from Phoenix this morning. Could we three get together this evening?"

That night was when Angie and I were going to talk about the Denver situation. I wasn't going to postpone that. "I'm okay with that idea, but I've got a commitment tonight that I can't break. How about tomorrow?"

"That'd work for me. Say, ten in the morning at the FBI office on Southwest First? I'll tell security to let you in. And you'll have to identify yourselves again to enter our suite."

"Yes, I can do that. I'll be there and I'll call my friend in PPB, Paul DeNoli, to see if he's agreeable."

We ended the call and I stood there gazing at the river. It was glassy smooth in the low afternoon sun. Ross Island mostly blocked the view west to the Portland hills, but there was plenty of weekend activity on the river. I saw a small fleet of hopeful people fishing for steelhead, and a few power-boaters with their partying guests. Just coming into view heading north was a tug moving with a deep rumble as it pushed a heavily loaded gravel barge. I never tire of that always-changing panorama. But it was time to get back to my aft deck. I pulled on a paper mask and started the sander.

I was just sweeping and vacuuming up the last of the sanding dust when I heard a shout from the bow. It was Paul DeNoli. I yelled for him to come aft. He gave me a man-hug and surveyed my work.

"This is why I'm glad I don't own a boat," he said. "Too much elbow grease!"

Although we're good friends, we don't too often see each other on weekends. "What brings you my way on a Saturday, Paul?"

"I was jumping today and over on the east side, so I thought I'd see how you were doing on Lunberg. You look like you need a beer!"

I got the hint. "Two cold ones coming up! I'll fill you in on my trip to Phoenix."

By "jumping" Paul meant he had been on an outing with his sky-diving club. He is all business when working a case, but he has his wild side when it comes to recreation. I've told him more than once what a crazy-ass hobby sky-diving is, but his wife seems to accept it and he won't give it up. We replaced the two canvas chairs that belong on the deck and I went to the galley for the beer. We settled in the chairs and cracked the ice-cold, Portland-brewed Henry's.

I told Paul how helpful Stan Madruga had been and my impressions of Barnstable and Fulton. When I got to the part about Agent Donaldson, Paul sighed and said now everything was going to get a lot harder. I said that Donaldson seemed pretty decent and that I thought we could have a fruitful relationship with him.

"When pigs have wings," Paul offered.

Then I mentioned the invitation to get together on Sunday morning.

"Rick, they'll just suck us dry of what you've discovered and then slam the door in our faces! But I will go to that meeting with you. So they're still apeshit over this woman who used to stalk Lunberg?"

"Yeah, that seems to be their focus. It turns out she's moved to Portland and got here a little before Lunberg disappeared."

"I'll grant you that's an intriguing coincidence, but I just don't see a woman for this."

"I agree with you, but I can't rule her out yet. You heard anything new from our friend, Niemus?"

"Yeah, as a matter of fact, I have. He thinks he may have a suspect. He doesn't have enough to arrest him for murder, but it's plausible, I guess."

"What's he got?"

"Seems there's been a string of burglaries on Forest Lane and 53rd Avenue and they've caught the perp. There were signs that Westlake's home had been broken into and searched, and the estranged wife says Westlake's laptop is missing. In the other burglaries, only valuables – watches, jewels, guns – were taken. And, other than the Rolex he was wearing and maybe the laptop, Westlake didn't have that kind of stuff in his house. Niemus sees it this way: there were no lights on so the thief enters the house but, before he's through searching, Westlake and his dog return and surprise him. The guy panics and shoots Westlake and then takes the body to the Park."

"So this burglar carries a gun and uses it?"

"So Niemus thinks. The guy denies ever entering Westlake's house and agrees to let them search his house, but they can't find any gun."

"It's hard to believe how dumb some of these guys are! If he *did* have a gun, he could've just told Westlake to back off and let him get away. Even if he's later caught and identified, burglary one with a weapon is better than murder two! But how does Niemus think he got the body from the house to the forest? There was still some light and your criminalists didn't find any blood or drag marks."

"Niemus thinks the thief found another way to transport it. He says one of Westlake's neighbors has a big wheelbarrow by the side of his house. And the criminalists *did* find some tread prints that match the wheelbarrow at the very beginning of the trail."

"That's worth checking out. Can you give me the neighbor's name?

"I think Niemus said it was Dunthorpe. I didn't hear a first name."

"What about the dog bite? Did this thief have a bite?"

"Apparently not, but nearly three weeks have gone by. Niemus seems to think it had healed by the time they caught him. Oh, before I forget, Niemus also said the widow had taken out a large insurance policy about a month before Westlake was killed. "

"That's another thing I'll look into after we get through with the Fibbies tomorrow."

Paul took off and I started barbequing steaks for Angie's and my dinner. Angie arrived a little after seven-thirty. I wrapped her in my arms and our kiss lingered. We almost didn't make it to the table, but we were both ravenous so our more romantic moments were put on hold. I put the Cal Tjader disc in the CD player and opened a bottle of Beaujolais.

Half way through our dinner, Angie raised her glass at me.

"To us!" she said. "Rick, I know you're sort of glum tonight, but we'll figure this out!"

"I hope so. I'm sorry if I seem glum. I love you, Angie. And I believe you love me. For each of us, that's a gift ... a second chance on the roulette wheel of life and happiness. I don't want us to stress that gift, to make us tense and cautious with each other."

I reached across the table and took her hand.

"I don't want that either, Rick. But, right now, my professional side wants to test this a little further. I mean even if I receive a firm offer, that's something I can use to bargain with at the Portland end. I could certainly be patient and wait my turn here, but don't you think I should get as much information about that job as I can before we make our final decision?"

"Yes, of course. That makes sense. Even if you got the job and I had to pull up stakes and follow you four or five months later, we could pull it off. It's just ... I don't know, this is all pretty fast ... things just don't seem quite so solid to me."

That was an admission I hated to make. The very saying of it, I thought, might weaken or introduce doubt into our relationship. But we had grown to be totally honest with each other, so I blurted it out.

Then I added, "but I like that you want it to be 'our' decision!"

She looked back at me with a slight sadness in her eyes. "I understand ... and I *do* want it to be *our* decision. I may know how to play the career game, but what we have together is more important!"

"Okay, then. You go ahead and have the interview and then we'll decide on everything."

Angie nodded and then surprised me. "Do you want to have children, Rick," she asked with a smile.

That was a question that we had skirted around with generalizations and light-hearted banter. Now I saw Angie was asking for straight talk.

"You know, I'd like nothing better. Justine didn't seem to want kids. That was a shame. I realize it's hard work and a huge responsibility, but I think parenthood can bring great joy."

"Do you think we could swing it with our careers? Both of our jobs put pressure on us from time to time."

"That's true. I like the work I do, and I know you love your work. But I think we'd be great parents! I'm confident we can figure out how to put any kids first and still do our work well."

"That's the way I feel too. Both of us have jobs that can be exciting and get us all jazzed up, but I know we're smart enough to keep the right balance."

I had some crème brulee in the freezer for dessert. It was quickly forgotten when Angie took my hand and led me to the bedroom.

14

Sunday, April 26th morning

I had set an alarm for seven-forty-five. When its insistent beeping woke me, Angie's warm curves were spooned against my body. I switched the alarm off and lay back in bed. Angie's eyes fluttered and she touched my cheek. I figured she wanted to go back to sleep after I got up so I kissed her gently on the forehead and whispered that I was off to meet with the FBI. She mumbled something that sounded like "tell 'em you're Portland's best detective" and was asleep in seconds.

At the entrance to the building, I flashed my driver's license and DeNoli showed his creds through the glass of the heavy doors. The security guard studied them, checked his watch and looked at his clipboard. Satisfied, he let us into the lobby. With a cheerful "good morning" he walked us to the elevator bay and keyed one of the cars into operation set for the correct floor. The ID process was repeated before we were allowed to enter the FBI offices. Donaldson must have been alerted by the "officer of the watch", because he quickly appeared and took us back to his office.

Paul introduced himself and confirmed that the Lunberg case had been transferred from Missing Persons to Homicide and that he was handling it. I gave Donaldson a more detailed version of what I had sketched for him yesterday, with Paul chiming in occasionally. Donaldson took careful notes and wanted names and addresses of the people I had spoken with. DeNoli said his people had checked all the uniform supply and laundry places serving the greater Portland area. They had not turned up anyone who remembered selling a single white coverall, new or used in the last few months. Then, Paul said, they had broadened the search to include auto-supply stores and janitor-supply outlets. They found only one sale of a white jumpsuit. That suit was bought by a wealthy family's chauffeur who had an airtight alibi for the day Lunberg disappeared. I said the lack of a local sale might mean that the killer was from out of town or that he had a job where he already owned a jumpsuit.

Despite the feds' primary focus on the female stalker, it was clear that Donaldson was interested in what I had turned up. He said the FBI would start to check street cams between the Lunberg home and Scrappy Jack's and from there to where the abandoned van was found. I reminded him that the forensic report on the van stated it had a tinted windshield. That made me doubt the cameras would have captured a facial image even if they had caught the van. Donaldson invited Paul to stay in touch, but implied that the murder of an ATF agent would be a federal crime and within his jurisdiction, not PPB's. I was not so sure that would be the case years after the agent had retired, but I kept my mouth shut.

We broke up the meeting a little after noon. A light rain had started to fall and I was glad I had laid plastic over my newly-sanded-but-not-yet-varnished deck. I picked up a foot-long ham-and-salami and six napkins at a Subway and ate as I drove. My first stop was to see Sandra Westlake. She offered me an iced-tea I accepted and flipped open my notebook.

"Ms. Westlake, you told me there were two policies on Brian's life and that you were the beneficiary of both. But I did not understand that, shortly before his death, it was you who took out the second, good-sized policy."

She looked a little surprised I knew that, but she answered with composure. "Yes, that's true."

"May I ask why?"

"I suppose so. Brian had told me a month or so earlier that he had a little episode of dizziness when he was up in a tree. He said it had not happened again and that he wasn't going to worry about it. Even though we were separated, Brian was always very thoughtful of my situation. He urged me to consider another policy. I would have to pay the premium, but it made sense to me. It's what they call term insurance so it's not too expensive. And it has – I think they call it a rider – that adds accidental death."

"Did he ever see a doctor about that 'episode'?"

"I don't think so. At least not that I know of."

"Do you know which doctor he would see, if he did see one?"

"Yes. Dr. John Clark has been our doctor for years."

I jotted the name in my notebook and thanked her for her time. I made a note to ask Mel Westlake and Gary Stratley if Westlake had ever mentioned the dizziness to them. I doubted he had and I tended to believe Ms. Westlake's explanation, but I always look for corroboration.

My next stop was Westlake's neighbor with the wheelbarrow. The house was actually two lots down from Westlake's place. I could see the wheelbarrow upside down next to the house. I rang the bell. A slender, balding, bespectacled man in a faded cardigan sweater and house slippers answered the door. I gave him my card and said I'd like a word about his wheelbarrow.

"Ah, yes," he said. "A police detective was asking about that too."

"Did you have any reason to think it was taken or used by someone else on April ninth?"

"Well, I couldn't be sure, but when the detective asked me about it, we went to look. It was where I usually leave it, but I generally turn it over. When we saw it, it was right-side-up. Of course, the children down the street play hide-and-seek all over the neighborhood. I heard them playing the day before the detective talked to me. For all I know, one of them may've been hiding under it and just flipped it over when he ran for 'home'."

"I see. Tell me, do you ever take your wheelbarrow into the park?"

The poor guy looked quite uncomfortable all of a sudden. He turned and motioned me to follow him off the porch and into his entry-way. "I ah ... I do take my garden cuttings and grass clippings down there. I don't go very far in ... just a hundred feet or so. There's a little flat area just off the trail. I know we're not supposed to use the park for a dump, but stuff like that decomposes ... "

He let the sentence die. His cheeks reddened.

"Would I be correct in guessing that you did not mention your dumping to the detective?"

"Well, no, I don't believe I did."

So much for the theory about the wheelbarrow being used to transport the body, I thought. I knew I should tell Niemus, but I thought it could very well wait until Monday.

I was half-way back to the houseboat when my cell chirped. I used my Blue Tooth to answer it hands-free. It was Sandra Westlake.

"I know we were talking only an hour ago," she began," but I just found something you might want to see. I was over at our old house. I went there intending to start sorting things out, to get ready to pack things into boxes. I was even going to make a first pass at choosing what would go into an estate sale. I don't want to move back there and I've got to get the place ready to go on the market."

I wondered when she would get to the point.

"Have you let the police know about whatever it is you found?"

"No. If you think it is relevant, of course I will. But they don't seem to have any real ideas so I thought of you first. In any case, I know I'll have to sell Brian's truck too. It won't bring much, I suppose, but I have no use for it."

Come on lady, I thought. Tell me what you found!

"I decided to start off with the truck. So I was vacuuming the truck cab and found Brian's cell phone in between the driver's seat and the center console. It must have slipped down there and – black phone against black upholstery – I guess Brian didn't notice it. The detective, that Mr. Niemus, had asked me if Brian had a cell phone last week. I said he did, but I did not know where it might be."

She sounded hesitant and stopped talking.

"Alright. Please go on," I said.

"I don't know exactly why, but I looked to see if he had saved any photos. There were a couple of bird pictures and a restored car he must have seen somewhere and an old photo of me. But there was also a video and Brian doesn't usually use the video feature. This video was taken looking down at two men in a fenced yard. It looked fairly close up. One man was wearing some kind of a white suit. I think Brian must have taken it while he was up in a tree."

"Could you see the faces of the men?"

"One of them better than the other, but yes. I don't know what to make of it. Brian was not one to snoop."

"Did the men look normal, happy?"

"It's hard for me to be sure, but I thought the man in the white outfit looked mad and it looked like the other man might've been worried … maybe even frightened. Do you think I should take the phone to the detective?"

"I do. But I'd like to see it first. And, if you wish, I'll take it to the police for you."

She sounded relieved and readily agreed that I could take the phone to the police. I said I would turn around and drive right over to pick it up.

When I arrived, she showed me the narrow slot beside the seat where she had found the phone. When I looked at the video, I thought we finally had some hard evidence to add to our stockpile of coincidences and hunches. And, we had an image of the mysterious person in the white jumpsuit! I wrote out another chain-of-custody document. Sandra Westlake signed and dated it and handed me the phone.

I called DeNoli. He said he had been washing windows, but had been chased inside by the rain. We agreed to meet at the Veritable Quandary on First Street. The Quandary is a lively cocktail lounge/restaurant with an "Olde English" ambiance. On a late weekday afternoon, it would be crowded with young professionals and plenty noisy, but Sunday was a quieter day.

I was the last to arrive. I spotted DeNoli and waved. Paul had found us a table in a corner that offered some privacy. We ordered beers and, as soon as the waiter left, I showed Paul the phone. I explained why it had turned up so much after the fact. We studied the video.

"Holy shit, Rick! You've hit pay dirt here. Does Niemus know?"

"No, Westlake's estranged wife just found it this afternoon. You can tell him if you think it's appropriate. It seems more relevant to the case of the ATF man so I'm just turning it over to you. Do you think your lab guys can enlarge the pictures? Get better resolution?"

"I'll certainly ask them to try. My guess is he already had it on maximum magnification. But in the lab, they can play with the pixels and do amazing things. It looks like at one point he got a pretty fair profile shot."

"Yes it does and I think I can see something wrong with that guy's ear. It doesn't look quite right. We need that enlargement!"

"Why are you so excited about his ear?"

"When I was talking with Jacobson, the ex-con who lives in Carver, he said McNair had a somewhat deformed ear … maybe from a knife fight or something. Anyway, he told me that McNair's nickname was 'short ear'!"

"This is getting better and better. I'll have the lab put a priority on it. And I'll make sure Donaldson sees it too."

"Yeah. I don't give a rat's ass about telling Niemus right away, but I agree you should deal Donaldson in."

"So where in hell is NcNair?" Paul asked.

"That's the big question. We know he seems to be off the grid. My guess is he bought himself a new identity, new credit cards, the whole shebang. If he's the doer for Lunberg, he'll be very careful and not stick his neck out. Even if he didn't eliminate Lunberg, he must have his reasons for dropping out of sight."

"Whatever. Now we need to find this monkey!"

With that, we finished our beers and called it a day.

15

Monday, April 27th morning – Tuesday, April 28th afternoon

I took Angie to breakfast at the Chart House. It is on Terwilliger Boulevard as it wends its way up the ridge toward the Oregon Health Sciences University campus. After rain on the weekend, the sky was clear and Mt. Hood looked like a giant snow cone rising out of Portland's east hills. The Chart House has terrific Eggs Benedict and that is what we ordered. I told Angie there was a good chance I would be in the San Francisco Bay Area for the next few days trying to track down my leading suspect in the Lunberg case. I was sorry that I could not be around to take her to the airport for her Denver trip. She said that was no problem and gave me a hug. We would stay in touch by cell phone. Angie had driven her car from my place to the restaurant so, after our meal, we parted right there in the parking lot.

Back on the houseboat, I called Donaldson. I asked if he would find out to which office McNair had reported during his supervised release. I also wanted his address during that three-year period. Finally, I asked him if he could send me the booking photo of McNair. He said he would check and call me back. As for the photo, he said he would send it to DeNoli and it was up to him whether to send it on to me. I asked him if we could photo-shop it to remove the ID placard and make it look like a more normal photo. Obviously wanting to distance himself from our plans, he said what DeNoli did with the photo was DeNoli's business.

Then I sat at my desk and reviewed my progress on the Westlake case. I was more and more convinced that Sean McNair was the key to unraveling DeNoli's and Donaldson's cases concerning Lunberg. Once we had proved McNair was guilty of killing Lunberg, the case for Westlake's death was stronger. The first problem was finding McNair with or without a new identity. I thought the best place to begin was the Bay Area where he had grown up. If that failed and if the FBI could not find him, all bets were off. My gut told me it was worth a trip to California. If the FBI wanted to get there ahead of me or alongside me, fine. If not, I wanted to give it a shot by myself. If I found him, perhaps I could shake Donaldson loose from his focus on the woman stalker. If it reached a point where law enforcement action was needed, I hoped Paul would come through to enlist help from the FBI or the local California cops. I called and told him of my inclination to make a trip to the Bay Area. He was dealing with a new homicide that had been dumped on his desk Monday morning. Nevertheless, he agreed to help how and when he could.

Donaldson called back to say that McNair had been reporting to the San Francisco probation office. He gave me an address for McNair in San Leandro, a community about half-way down the south lobe of San Francisco Bay on the east side.

I called my client, Mel Westlake, and informed him about the cell-phone picture his brother had taken. I also brought him up to speed with Niemus' theory about the neighborhood thief and why I was skeptical about it. I mentioned that the FBI was focusing hard on a woman that had been stalking the retired ATF man, but that Agent Donaldson was beginning to take an interest in my theory about the ex-con. There was no doubt sending me to the Bay Area for two or three days would entail considerable cost but, I told him, I believed it was a necessary next step. I added that if I could not find McNair, it might be a waste of his good money. And, even if I found him, getting evidence to convict him for Brian's death might not be easy. To his credit, Mel said to go ahead. He would continue to finance my efforts. With that taken care of, I booked a mid-afternoon flight to San Francisco.

I called Paul and he confirmed the photo had arrived. I told him I was flying to San Francisco that day. He said they could strip the booking details from the picture and would print a three-by-five. I picked it up on my way to the airport.

During the flight, I formulated a plan of action, such as it was. Jacobson had told me about McNair's past occupations. It was unlikely he could land a bartender job with his conviction. Even if he used a new identity, I believed the California Department of Alcoholic Beverage Control would require fingerprints to process a would-be server's license application. Appliance repair and meat packing jobs might be easier for him to land. I might have to pursue that angle, but it was not where I wanted to start. What else did I have? An address; a nickname and a misshapened ear; a model-airplane hobby; a hot temper; a devoted fan of the New Jersey Devils. Somehow, in a metro area of over three million people, I had to align those puzzle pieces to point me to one man.

I would rent a car and check the San Leandro address as a first step. If McNair had wanted to hide, I was sure he would have moved as soon as his supervised release was finished. Still, it was low-hanging fruit so I would start there. I used my laptop to check the ownership of those premises. The owner's name was not McNair. That told me it was probably a rental. If I didn't find McNair at that address, it would be worth contacting the landlord to see what he knew.

The hobby was a little unusual so I decided that would be my second project. I googled "model airplane clubs San Francisco Bay" and found nine. But, on their respective web-sites, I learned that the organizations where they concentrated on actually flying the planes classified themselves as "RC" clubs, RC meaning "radio controlled". That cut the list to five. By then my plane was approaching the airport. Like a good passenger, I shut down my computer and buckled my seat belt.

The weather in northern California is generally good in April. During our descent, I could see some evening fog starting to form over the coastline but, above the Bay, it was clear and sunny. The pilot had evidently been assigned a northward landing so our plane made a lazy turn over the south end of the peninsula. Out the window, I could see the distinctive red tile roofs of the Stanford campus. Later, as the turn ended, I saw the serpentine, residence-lined canals of Foster City. Soon after, I heard the "clunk" of the gear being lowered and the whine of the flaps being extended. Then, the last drop, the gentle bump, and we were screaming down the runway alongside the water of the Bay.

My first stop the next morning was at a low frame building a block away from Bay Meadows Race Track in San Mateo. The RC Flying Club had one of the three small offices in the building. Fortunately, the club Secretary was in the office. He was a gray-haired gentleman in his late sixties. He told me that the club occasionally was allowed to use the race track's parking lot to fly planes.

My cover story was that I was an investigator working for an attorney in Oregon. I flashed my business card at him. I explained that there had been an accident several years ago at an Oregon RC flying event. The injured person had sued and I was tasked with locating an important eye-witness. I said no one at the event could remember the witness's name, but they thought he was visiting from the San Francisco area and was an ardent RC modeler and flier. The man wanted to be helpful, but I had not yet given him anything to work with.

Continuing with my cover story, I said a photographer at the event had taken some crowd shots of the persons attending. The litigants both agreed that the mystery witness's face was in one of those photos. I said we had cropped and enlarged the face of the man we were looking for and showed him the three-by-five. He studied it carefully, but shook his head.

"I know all our members personally and I can tell you this person is not a member. Of course, he might've shown up as a spectator or a kibitzer once or twice and I would not have noticed him. Sorry."

I put the photo back in my briefcase and thanked the man for speaking with me.

I drove across the flat, bluish-brown expanse of the south Bay on the San Mateo Bridge. I found the San Leandro address and saw a neighbor leaving her house with a plastic bag and a small dog on a leash.

"I'm looking for Sean McNair. Does he still live here?"

She looked up, a little startled. "No. He moved out about six months ago. I didn't much like the man. Hardly ever said hello and was kind of grumpy when he did talk."

I returned to the car and called the number of the landlord. He remembered McNair right away, but said he knew nothing about where he was now.

"Did you ever get any inquiries from new landlords checking his references?" I asked.

"No, nothing like that. Some people now days just get a credit check and don't bother with references. That's stupid in my opinion but, anyway, I had no contacts of that sort. He was an okay tenant ... never late with the rent, no damage. That's all I can tell you."

A dead end. From my research the day before, I saw the Bayside Radio Controlled Club seemed to have quite a large membership. It was headquartered in

Fremont on the east side of the Bay not far from where I was. Using the GPS in the rental car, I navigated to their little office. A smiling middle-aged man with a trim beard and a noticeable limp introduced himself as "Dennis" and welcomed me inside. I used the same cover story and emphasized that a lot was at stake in the litigation. Dennis nodded throughout and seemed both interested and willing to help if he could. When I got to the picture, Dennis's expression brightened even further.

"Yes, he flies here fairly often."

"That's great news! Do you have a name and address?"

"Well we're a pretty informal club. We don't do mailings and we don't require addresses. I'm a volunteer myself. Our calendar and our communications are relatively simple and our web-site seems quite sufficient. We collect dues once a year, but a lot of them just pay cash when they come by. Let me look and see if I happen to have his address" He opened a file cabinet and browsed a folder. "No. We have no address."

"But I'll bet you have a name."

"You know that's a funny thing. He's not too talkative and he just seems to go by his first name. He calls himself 'Marco'."

So McNair's using a different name and trying to keep a very low profile, I thought. My longshot idea had borne some fruit, but I still did not know how to find him. At least I knew he was living in the Bay Area.

That was consistent with his childhood, according to Jacobson, and it jibed with where he was during his supervised release.

In Bayside's small parking area, I sat in the car and fired up my laptop. Remembering that McNair had some commercial diving experience, I googled "diving San Francisco Bay". That produced numerous outfits connected to recreational scuba diving. I modified the search to add "salvage". That showed me three companies. A look at their websites indicated that most of them also did underwater inspection and construction work. I wrote the information in my notebook. The two with on-the-Bay addresses were near San Francisco. They would have to wait.

I thought some more about McNair and the New Jersey Devils. That looked to be a pretty large haystack. The only inspiration I had was to check out "sports memorabilia" stores. After googling those words, I was surprised to find twenty-two such stores from San Jose to San Rafael. I was already in the South Bay, so I looked over the list to see if any were nearby. I saw a store in Fremont and that was an easy choice. There were three more in San Jose and another in Palo Alto. I decided to work my way back to my San Francisco motel by curving around the south end of the Bay visiting the stores as I went.

I changed my story only a little. Instead of an accident at a model airplane event, I was now seeking a witness to a fatal auto accident. I would say the man was wearing a Devil's hat and had told someone else at the crash scene that he was visiting from the Bay Area. I struck out in the Fremont store. The mid-afternoon traffic in San Jose was brutal and my luck was no better. Ditto Palo Alto where the store featured countless items related to Stanford and the Forty-Niners. I was ready to call it a day when I came to the San Mateo exit off the Bayshore Freeway. I looked at my watch and thought "what the hell, I can hit one more store before business hours are over."

I took the exit and arrived at the store at a quarter to five. A man who appeared to be closing down asked me if he could be of help. As we chatted, he gestured toward a woman in a white sweater and burgundy slacks and said she was his wife and that they owned the place. I gave him my spiel about the witness being a Devils fan, and offered the picture. He studied it with a frown, but said he did not think he recognized the face. He called his wife over. I repeated the story and she stared at the photo.

"Why, yes. I think this man came in five or six weeks ago."

"Do you remember what he wanted to buy?" I thought her answer might substantiate her remembering his face.

"I do. He wanted a New Jersey Devils cap."

Bingo!

"Did he use a credit card?"

"I'm not sure, but I think he paid cash. It wasn't that expensive."

"That's terrific that you recognize him! Did you happen to get his address?"

"No. We don't collect addresses unless the customer wants to receive our annual cata --. Oh, wait! I *did* get an address. We get very little demand for things related to the Devils and we had none of those caps in stock. So I had to special-order it for him. I asked if he wanted us to mail it to him when the order filled. He was okay with that, especially since I said we wouldn't charge for our shipping and handling."

"Great! This should end what was turning into an expensive search."

She wrote the name and address on a slip of paper and handed it to me. Like a lot of folks in Portland, I follow the Seattle Seahawks football team as well as the Oregon Ducks. I was so glad to have this breakthrough that I bought a Seahawks cap from her. As she was processing the sale, I looked at the name she had written: Marco Quilington. Now I had him in my sights!

If I thought the mid-afternoon traffic in San Jose was bad, I had no clue what awaited me on Bayshore during rush hour. It took nearly an hour to drive the fifteen miles back to my motel. I checked in, took a steaming hot shower and called Angie. She could tell I was in a good mood and was excited that I had tracked down the elusive Mr. McNair.

"So you'll be on your way home tomorrow?"

"I'm not so sure about that, honey. The FBI guy hasn't fully signed on to my theory yet. I want to do some surveillance on McNair, learn more about where he works ... how he moves about. Remember, I still don't have any lock-down evidence ... what I have is pretty good, but it's still mostly circumstantial."

I could sense the disappointment and concern in her voice as she reacted to that. "Can't you just turn it over to Paul and the FBI? I don't want any chance you'll have to confront this guy!"

I already had a glimmer of a plan but, after what Angie said, I thought it best to keep it to myself. "Don't worry, I'll cover my bets!"

I told her to have a world-class interview tomorrow and said how much I loved her. After a pot-roast dinner at a Shari's, I cleaned my Baretta and tucked in early. I wanted to be at McNair/Quilington's house by a little before seven a.m..

16

Wednesday, April 29th early morning

The address for McNair was in San Bruno, a plain, small town about eight miles south of San Francisco's financial district. The town is known for many steel-making and fabricating businesses and, sadly, for the gas-pipeline explosion that killed eight people in 2010. I bought a small thermos at Starbuck's and filled it with coffee to keep me alert. McNair's house was faced with soot-darkened stucco and set on a narrow lot. I parked four houses down the street hoping that McNair was not so twitchy that he would notice an unfamiliar car.

I had brought my camera with a telephoto lens. McNair came out to fetch a newspaper on his front porch. I caught him in profile. I thought I could see the deformed ear. He left his house at ten after seven in a fairly old Volvo wagon. I followed at a discreet distance at first, then had to get closer as he took major streets. He finally got on Interstate Eighty northbound to cross the Bay Bridge. Twice I almost lost him. It didn't help that I was not used to the freeway layout. I found him again and was two cars behind when he took an exit signed Hercules/Rodeo. Rodeo is an industrial town on San Pablo Bay. I watched him pull into a pier area. I drove past and parked an eighth of a mile away. I walked back to the waterfront and surveyed the scene. I did not see McNair himself, but I could tell it was some sort of a project to rebuild a pier. I could not actually enter the construction area, but I saw two half-ton pickup trucks and one van all with "World-Wide Diving & Salvage" painted on their sides. I also saw what I assumed were employees' cars. Among them was McNair's Volvo.

So McNair was gainfully employed … and possibly working in his father's former profession as a diver or pump tender. I saw one of the World-Wide employees on a smoke break near the fence.

"Looks like a serious project," I said.

"Yeah. Replacing old wooden piles with concrete and that means new footings in the seabed."

"So long hours, I bet."

"Believe that," he answered. "Six days a week and we go 'til seven at night! The overtime's good though."

He finished his cigarette and we parted with a friendly wave.

I took this morning's discoveries as a good omen to take the next step in my evolving plan. I drove back to NcNair's home in San Bruno. As soon as I crossed the Bay Bridge, my phone chirped. It was Angie.

"Hey," I said. "Are you still on the plane?"

"No. That's why I called," she said with a cheerful, almost giddy, tone. "I called the station head in Denver this morning and told him I was withdrawing from consideration and would not be doing the interview."

"Wow! That's great ... I think."

Before I could express myself more eloquently, she continued.

"I could hardly sleep last night and before morning came, I knew I wanted to stay here in Portland ... close to you ... and to give us the best chance to move toward what we both want. And, before you ask, yes the station here came through with some good news too. They've given me a five-thousand dollar 'retention raise'. *And,* they told me I would be next in line if Sonja steps down or steps back."

"That's wonderful, Angie!"

"I'm happy too, Rick. I'm already looking forward to house hunting when you finish this darn Westlake case!"

"Deal! Was the guy in Denver upset?"

"Disappointed, yes. But this sort of thing happens in broadcasting. He'll move on to the next candidate, I'm sure. When do you expect to get back?"

"I can't be certain at this point. Possibly as soon as tomorrow. It kind of depends on what I find today. I'll call you tonight and let you know."

I was smiling as I drove and mentally turning cartwheels. I felt a tinge of guilt that my own professional situation might have forced Angie's hand, but I sensed some relief on her part that the "Denver opportunity" was behind us.

When I reached McNair's neighborhood, I again parked down the street. I would savor Angie's decision even more this evening, but today there was work to do. There was no one out and about. It was a working-class neighborhood and I concluded most were at their jobs. Making sure I had gloves, my smaller camera, some specimen bags, and my picklock, I walked confidently toward his house.

I had practiced enough with my picklock that I was confident I could get inside in under a minute. Once before, working a case, I had chosen the back door to do my B&E act. But there, I had a private back yard. Here, the houses were close, there were no high, dividing hedges, and – if any homemakers were at home in their kitchens – I could be quite visible. So, the front door it was.

McNair's door had a conventional lock and a bolt. It took me a few seconds more than a minute, but the picklock worked. I headed straight for the bathroom. I wanted some DNA to go with what was found on the threads taken from Wolfgang's mouth. I saw an electric razor next to the basin. I popped the head off and shook some of the shavings into the first specimen bag. Replacing the razor, I checked the bathroom waste basket. I got lucky. At the bottom, I found some nail clippings. They went into the second bag.

I moved to the bedroom where I looked for an accessory box ... none to be seen. I tried the drawers of the dresser. Same thing: no watch. Maybe the bastard was wearing it. Then I turned to the bedroom closet. I saw no tubs or containers, just a few pairs of shoes on the floor. Aside from the hanging clothes, there was only one garment bag and it had nothing but a fancy sport coat inside. On the closet shelf, I saw an extra pillow, three shoe boxes, a tote bag, and the New Jersey Devils cap.

I reached for the first shoe box. It appeared to be filled with tax returns for the last four years. The second contained an orange taser. I realized that could have been the orange object that Westlake had seen in Jumpsuit's hand. I snapped a picture of the taser. I brought the third shoe box down from the shelf. It seemed unusually heavy. Inside, I found a loaded Walther PP 380, a box of cartridges, and a silencer! DeNoli had found out from Niemus that ballistics had determined the lethal shots at Westlake were fired from a Walther PP 380 Auto. DeNoli had passed that on to me.

McNair might have been able to buy a gun with his new identity, but most states require finger prints.

Prints would have revealed he was an ex-felon. Similarly, to buy a silencer he would have to have filled out the ATF's Form 4. Since McNair had been a criminal and knew about guns, he surely had done none of those things. That meant he either bought the gun and the silencer illegally or had stolen them.

McNair was either more stupid than I had thought or else he was supremely confident he would never be caught. To keep a gun he had used to kill, was not a good move. I could see no serial number. I photographed the gun and returned the shoe box with the gun, silencer and ammo to the exact place where I had found it on the shelf.

I stepped quickly through the rest of the house. In the second bedroom, there was a worktable with model airplane parts and a couple of radio-control devices. Also in the room was a small desk. I went through the drawers and found a phone bill from the wireless carrier. I copied McNair's cell number into my note book. There was no conventional telephone so I figured he did not have a land line.

I had what I had come for and more besides. It was time to leave. Peering through the front curtains, I saw the street was empty. I exited the house and walked casually to my car.

I drove out of the neighborhood and pulled over at a small park about half-mile away. I was able to reach DeNoli on his cell and started to tell him the latest developments.

"Paul, I've learned the new name McNair is using! And I have his address. He's living in San Bruno under the name Marco Quilington."

"Fantastic, Rick! How'd you find that out?"

I gave him a short version of my visits to the RC club and the sports memorabilia store.

"You are the man!" he exclaimed.

"Not only that, I now have specimens from which you can get his DNA."

"Good Christ, Rick. How in hell did you get those?"

I ignored his question and continued. "Paul, I have a plan. We can have this son-of-a-bitch if we play our cards right and, in the process, get some more compelling evidence. If I can get a flight, I'll come back tonight; if not, tomorrow. Can you set up a meeting with us and Donaldson?"

There was a pause before DeNoli answered. "I'll try. He ought to be more interested now that you've located McNair."

"Tell him it will be well worth his coming, otherwise anything that happens will go down with the local police running the show."

"What's this about 'playing our cards'?"

"I'll fill you and Donaldson in when I get there, just trust me for now. I do need you or Donaldson to help with certain things. You know that PPB training center you told me about?"

"What about it?"

"You said they ran simulations that were very realistic ... they even had the good guys and bad guys firing at each other."

"Right. They use blanks of course, but there's stress nevertheless and that makes the exercises more meaningful."

"Exactly. I need you to get a dozen or so 380 auto blank cartridges.."

"Sheesh, Rick, how am I supposed to take ammo, even blank ammo, from the training center?"

"How about 'informally'? Can't you sweet talk some buddy over there to just let you take them without having to sign for 'em?"

"That would never fly for live rounds, but ... maybe someone would help me with that for blanks."

"It's important! Please give it a try, Paul. If you can't swing it, we can ask Donaldson, but let's wait on that."

"Alright. And I suppose you're not going to tell me why you need them?"

"Call it an experiment. We need to set a trap. If it works, we'll have McNair under arrest and ready for extradition!"

"I don't know why I listen to you, Rick, except that sometimes you pull friggin' rabbits out of hats."

"There's other stuff we'll need too but, if Donaldson will cooperate, it's better we get that stuff from the FBI. There's one more thing I need from you. It's about that video on Westlake's phone. Without screwing up its admissibility as evidence, can you make a copy and insert it on another cell phone? And throw in some credible call history?"

"Yeah, I'll check with the DA first, but I'm sure the lab people can do that."

"Thanks, Paul. You and Donaldson will get many kudos if this works out!"

"And if it doesn't?"

"There shouldn't be any repercussions other than justifying your expenses for going back with me to San Francisco ... hah, hah. In any case, we could at least keep an eye on McNair while all you law-enforcement types are busy looking for more suspects."

He told me not to be a wise-ass. Then he said to call when I got back. That's Paul. Sometimes my tactics make him cringe, but he's always got my back.

My next task was to call Cliff Gaston, Gary Stratley, Mel Westlake and Dr. Clark to find out if any of them knew anything about Brian getting dizzy in a tree. I called Gaston first.

"Cliff, it's Rick Conwright. Sorry to bother you, but I have one question to ask. Did Brian ever say anything to you about getting dizzy when he was up in a tree.?"

"Hi, Mr. Conwright. As a matter of fact, he did. I was with him that day and he climbed back down before we were finished. He looked kind of pale and I asked him if he was okay. He tried to shrug it off ... said he was just a little dizzy. It was almost quitting time, so we packed it in. The next day, he seemed fine and was back up in the tree. I kind of watched him and he picked up on that. He said not to worry about what happened the day before. And it never seemed to happen again, at least not when I was there."

"How long ago was that, Cliff?"

"Oh, seven or eight weeks before he was killed. Is the dizziness thing important?"

"Yes. It clears up something that was bothering me. Thanks, for the help! Have you been able to find work?"

"Yeah, Man. Another tree outfit had a guy leave and they knew about Brian so they gave me the job."

I thanked him and ended the call. I did not feel the need to call the other three. What Cliff told me was good enough to support Sandra Westlake's explanation.

I was unable to book a flight to Portland that afternoon, but succeeded in getting one early on Thursday. There was a man who lived in Oakland that I needed to interview regarding another of my cases. I made contact and set up a meeting that afternoon so the rest of the day was not a total waste. After the interview, I was looking forward to a great fish dinner at Tadich Grill in San Francisco.

The Tadich Grill is a place where the ambiance and location have not changed in forty-eight years, the waiters are sometimes surly, the lines to get in are long, and the seafood entrees are to die for. John Tadich bought the restaurant in 1887 and the bistro's lineage can be traced even further back to 1849. I guessed that hungry miners with their pokes full of gold dust might have had something to do with its opening. The Tadich Grill claims to be the third-longest continuously- operating restaurant in the United States.

17

Thursday, April 30th mid-day

The three of us met in Donaldson's office. He admitted that their questioning of the woman stalker had not produced any break-through. Her explanation of where she was and what she was doing the day Lunberg disappeared could not be corroborated. On the other hand, the FBI still could not put her on the scene. This was so even after canvassing neighbors and showing her photo in bookstores, drugstores and coffee shops in Multnomah Village.

I brought Donaldson up to speed on all that I had discovered in the Bay Area. I neglected to mention my entering McNair's home, but I think they had their suspicions when I produced the DNA samples. Donaldson asked for the specimen envelopes. DeNoli raised an eyebrow at me as if to say "there goes my control of this case." Donaldson said, probably correctly, that the FBI lab could process the samples much faster than the Oregon State Police forensic lab. We were not sure the lab analysis of those samples would be admissible in a criminal trial. But, if it matched the DNA on the threads from Wolfgang, it would give us confidence that McNair was our man. And we could always get his DNA in an admissible way if the FBI or Niemus were to arrest him. I gave Donaldson the envelopes.

I revealed almost all of my plan. They listened attentively. I told them there was one detail I would have to do alone and that they could not afford to know what I intended. DeNoli rolled his eyes, but said nothing. Donaldson asked if my "secret"actions would be illegal. I said, yes, but nothing injurious to anyone and they would not put anyone other than myself at risk. DeNoli spoke up and asked "how big a risk".

"If you guys tail McNair and call me should he leave work early, there should be almost no risk at all," I answered.

As for the rest of the plan, Donaldson insisted that I not play the part of "the tethered goat". He said that role would have to be played by one of his agents. I conceded that point, especially since there was *some* risk in that part of the plan.

We discussed whether McNair could claim "entrapment". Donaldson said he would have to run the question by the U.S. Attorney, even though the three of us doubted that defense would prevail. He was also nervous that McNair would contend that the agent had committed the crime of extortion and would check that with the U.S. Attorney as well.

I told them that a sharpshooter should be on hand on the night the plan went into action. We would also need someone with a sensitive directional microphone and an audio recording device. Donaldson was rightfully worried that McNair would come to the party armed. I said what I planned to do would hopefully eliminate that risk. I saw DeNoli give me a knowing look.

We spent another hour trouble shooting my plan and trying to envision what could go wrong. The sharpshooter was to be instructed to fire, aiming for McNair's leg if "Marco" acted too quickly and pulled a gun right away once the "meet" I was proposing began. The biggest obstacle would likely be that McNair would try to set the venue and the FBI team would not have enough time to get in place. If he read a lot of spy novels, we could have problems. He might give us time to reach the designated location and then, by a phone call to that location, send us to a different venue. He could even repeat that stunt a second time. Meanwhile, he would arrive at the ultimate location to make sure no third parties were lurking there. This would leave the FBI guys one jump behind instead of one jump ahead. I did not think he was that smart, but that *was* a weakness in the plan.

We concluded that the FBI agent playing the role would have to be adamant that he got to choose the place of the meet. He could credibly claim that he wanted to be sure that McNair did not have a bunch of his criminal buddies waiting to overpower him. The second thing we decided was that the FBI had to get an agent into the construction-zone parking lot where McNair worked. Using some pretext to walk around, the agent could put a GPS radio bug on McNair's car. Then, we could estimate when he would arrive at the meet. Finally, the FBI agent playing "the tethered goat" could claim he was coming to the meet from some northerly place like San Rafael to gain some extra time to get our team in place.

Donaldson and I drafted a "letter" that the agent meeting with McNair would claim was sent to him by his now-dead brother, Brian. It detailed how the brother had tailed McNair after he left Lunberg's house and, eventually, got the number of his car's California license. We had to be careful as we did not know all of the small details ourselves ... to some extent, the letter was a bluff. When we were satisfied with it, we printed it and faked Brian's signature. Then Donaldson had a postal-inspector pal dummy-up a postmark dated the day after Lunberg went missing and a canceled stamp for the envelope. The letter, in addition to raising McNair's temperature, would explain how the "brother" – we were calling him "Larry" – had located McNair.

I suggested a loose "script" for the agent to follow in contacting McNair to set up the sting and at their meet. Of course, he would very likely have to improvise at some point. But the script should not only give the agent some guidance, but should also help to shape the two men's interaction in the most productive fashion. We burnished and tightened the script a little and agreed to stay in touch. When Donaldson had made the necessary arrangements with the FBI's San Francisco office (and DeNoli had been able to get me the blanks), we would meet again to travel to San Francisco. DeNoli graciously found a way to expense my round trip to the Bay Area in recognition of the spade-work I had already done.

18

Monday, May 4th morning

Donaldson, DeNoli, and I had flown to San Francisco the evening before. We checked into a motel in the Marina District on Lombard Street. We arrived too late to see the kite fliers on the Marina Green, but in time for a filling dinner at always-colorful Tommy's Joynt on Geary just off of Van Ness Avenue. Back at the motel, we went over our plan for the last time.

Early Monday morning DeNoli staked out McNair/Quilington's house and tailed him to the diving site in Rodeo. Then, an FBI agent posing as a vendor delivering a hydraulic nozzle entered the construction zone long enough leave his "package" and to plant the bug on the Volvo chassis. Donaldson had arranged to borrow a sharpshooter, a sound man, and two more agents from the San Francisco office to fill out our team. He went to their office to begin reviewing everyone's respective role and to nail down our communication protocol. I went back to McNair's house, getting there at nine-forty-five. I had a different rental car than before and I parked on a side street this time.

A neighbor came out of her garage and drove away just as I rounded the corner. Other than that, the street was again empty. I worked my picklock even faster now that I understood the locks. Inside the house, I listened for a minute to be sure there were no sounds of anyone else present. It was absolutely quiet. Walking straight to the bedroom, I pulled on my gloves and activated one of the two-way radios Donaldson had loaned us. I retrieved the heavy shoebox from the closet shelf, removed the Walther, and ejected its magazine. I emptied the clip and extracted the bullet from the chamber. I put the nine bullets in the box with the other cartridges. Then I reloaded the gun with nine blanks and replaced everything as I had found it.

A garbage truck was rolling down the street picking up heavy vinyl garbage cans like a giant squid feeding its maw. This delayed my leaving the house by ten minutes. When the truck was out of sight and I could see no pedestrians through the curtains, I was out the door.

I met the others at the FBI's San Francisco office. Once DeNoli confirmed McNair had remained at the Rodeo job-site, he came back to join us. Donaldson introduced us to the rest of the team, including the AIC of the San Francisco office, Seth Hightower. Donaldson and Hightower told us that their respective U.S. Attorneys had cleared the plan and gave us a green light with no worries about the entrapment issue.

We started rehearsing the agent, Terry Lawson, who would be the "tethered goat". We worked hard to get him into the "loser of a cocaine-using brother" frame of mind. I explained how he would handle the first phone contact. We mooted a decent response if McNair demanded assurance that there were no copies of the video. Donaldson told him of the risk involved in his role and why he could not wear body armor or carry his gun. The man was a volunteer and did not back down. The sharpshooter and he knew each other and that seemed to give him confidence. If McNair turned out to be armed and fired at him, I told him to drop to the ground and play dead until the situation was resolved. By the time we broke for lunch, we all felt that Terry would carry off his role quite well enough.

At two o'clock, Lawson picked up the cell phone that the PPB techies had "seeded" with a copy of the video and some call history. He called Marco Quilington. Quilington did not answer and the call went to message. Lawson spoke his lines: "I know what happened to Lunberg and I have something you don't want to fall into the hands of the cops." He snuffled a little, gave Quilington a call-back number and ended the message.

It was three when Quilington called back.

"Who the fuck are you?" was his opening.

Lawson responded "I'm Larry. It's been on TV about this guy named Lunberg who's mysteriously gone missing. My brother, Brian, was an arborist. He was working up in that tree next door to Lunberg's place." He snuffled again. "My brother always has his cell phone with him, see? He saw you wearing some kind of a monkey suit and chasing Lunberg around his yard. So he videoed you with his phone. And he got a nice picture of your face!"

"I don't know what you're talking about. I'm Marco Quilington. You must have me confused with somebody else!"

Another snuffle from Lawson then, "My brother was a smart son-of-a-bitch. He followed you and saw you take the water heater to the scrap yard. Then he saw you ditch the van and strip the signs off and he tailed you to your motel. He got the license number on your car. He was a righteous prick, my brother was. I think he was getting ready to go to the police, but he waited a day too long! He was killed before he contacted the cops. I don't suppose you had anything to do with that, eh?" Another snuffle.

"And how do you think you know all this?"

"Old Brian may have been disgusted with me, but he did think to write his good old black-sheep brother a letter. The letter told me exactly what he saw and did and where he hid his cell phone. The letter said it was his "insurance policy" in case anything happened to him before he turned the video over to the cops. So now he's dead. And I figure the phone and that letter are my 'inheritance'." A short snuffle. "And it's time for you and me to make a deal!"

There were several seconds of silence, then "You sound like a two-bit bunco artist! I ought to report this to the cops."

"Sure, you do that, Marco! You bring the law into this and you're right in their cross-hairs for killing Lunberg!"

Another silence then, "I'll see what you're selling. What do you want from me, you turd?"

"Money. I'm proposing a sale, see? You want a phone and a letter and I have just what you're looking for! For ten thousand dollars I'll sell 'em to you. That's a small price I'm asking. ! Meet me at that Pulgas Water Temple place at eleven tonight."

"Wait a minute! I'll figure out where we'll meet and call you back!"

"No go, pal! I'm not going to some place you choose where you've got your thug friends all lined up to add me to your kill list! It's the Temple or no place." Another snuffle. "You want the goods, you be there."

"Okay, okay! But you come alone too and no weapons. How do you know about Pulgas if you're from Portland?"

"Took a tour of the Peninsula like a good tourist. The guide said it's not lit at night. I figure there won't be any traffic on that side road. Makes it a nice private place ... neutral ground you might say ... to do our business." We were giving Lawson the "cut it off" signal. He finished with "Be there and bring the money. I'll meet you at that pool."

Pulgas Water Temple is located on Canada Road, a short paved road that parallels Interstate 280 running north and south on the spine of the San Francisco peninsula. It was commissioned by the San Francisco Public Utilities Commission to mark and commemorate the western end of San Francisco's water-supply pipeline. That line transports water one-hundred-sixty miles from the Hetch Hetchy reservoir high in the Sierra Nevada mountains. The Temple itself was completed in 1934 and designed by architect William Merchant. Although his design was derivative, the original concept was based on the ancient Temple of Vesta in Tivoli near Rome. The Temple sits eight-hundred feet above the Crystal Springs Reservoir, the last stop before the water is processed and distributed to thirsty San Franciscans.

Today, the pipeline's water no longer gushes visibly through the Temple. The pipe now bypasses the Temple and delivers the water directly to the reservoir below. The setting is nevertheless quite beautiful with a reflecting pool and ornamental shrubbery fronting the white-columned dome of the Temple, and evergreen trees in the surrounding area. Consequently, today, the grounds can still be visited and are even a popular place for weddings.

Donaldson and Hightower had their team concealed in their places soon after dark. A cold breeze coursed across the ridge. Fog was starting to form, but we could still see stars in the dark sky. Cars occasionally shot past up-slope from us on 280 but, other than their muffled noise, all was quiet. Terry Lawson got a first-hand look at the layout and it was decided where he would attempt to stage the meet. DeNoli and I were stationed on a rise a good third of a mile away from the action. We had been given night-vision binoculars and we were patched into the communications net.

Marco's Volvo pulled close to the flagstone decking of the pool at ten-twenty-five. He got out, walked around the pool, made a cursory look behind a few shrubs, and returned to his car. Lawson drove in at ten minutes before eleven and he too made a show of looking over the pool area. At eleven, Marco got out of his car and the men cautiously approached each other. McNair/Marco was the first to speak.

"Come closer. I'm going to pat you down. Got to be sure you're not wearing a wire or carrying."

"Fair enough. I'll do the same to you," said Lawson/Larry as he walked up and subjected himself to the pat-down. He reciprocated. When both men were satisfied, Marco said, "So show me this *video* you've been talking about!"

Lawson kept hold of the phone as he initiated the video. He turned it so Marco had a clear view. The video lasted eighteen seconds.

"That looks like you, Marco," Lawson said.

"So you say! It could be anybody."

"Look closely when the left side of your face is shown. I noticed when you checked me for a weapon that your ear is kind of different. I'm guessing if the cops ever got a hold of this, they could make it larger and there you are, ear and all!"

"What a bunch of crap!"

"You may say it's crap, but it's worth ten-K. Plus, you get my brother's letter."

"And how do I know you haven't made a copy of the video?"

"I need the money! You think I'd show my little prize to the cops or some nosy guy at Fry's! Besides, I don't even know how to *take* videos with these fucking smart phones!"

Marco stared into Lawson's eyes. "Anyway, I need to see that letter."

Lawson handed him the envelope. Marco extracted the letter and read it. "I see. Same question. How do I know you haven't made a copy of this letter?"

"I'll tell you. After I read it, I copied off your name and address so I'd know how to find you. Then I put the letter back in its envelope. I don't want any copy to ever be found in my possession! That way, this whole thing stays just between us. And my brother must've deleted it from his computer because I looked and it wasn't there. Now show me the money!"

Marco had come out carrying a small briefcase that he had placed at his feet during the pat-downs. He picked it up, moved the dials on a combination lock and started to open the case. Lawson tensed. If Marco had a gun in the case, his odds would change for the worse. Marco raised the lid and Lawson saw bundles of bills inside. Lawson relaxed a bit.

"I want to count it."

Marco shrugged his shoulders and handed "Larry" one of the packets. Lawson saw all the bills were fifties. He counted two thousand in the first packet. He flipped the bills in the other packets and saw they were also all fifties. Looking again at the packets, he counted only four bundles.

Lawson did a loud snuffle and dabbed a tissue to his nose. "You asshole! There's only eight thousand here!"

"What? You think I'm rich! That's everything in my account and there's nothing under my mattress either. It's take it or leave it. And don't get any ideas about coming back for the rest. I know you're a shit-eating coke-head, but you better not be lying about no copies of the video! If we do this, it's a 'one and done' deal!"

Lawson muttered under his breath and snuffled once more.

"Alright, alright! Here's how we do it. You take the briefcase with the cash and carry it another thirty feet in the direction I came from. At the same time, I'll take the phone and the letter thirty feet toward your car. You lay the briefcase down, turn around and head back to pick up the phone and the letter. I do the same thing. We each end up with what we want and we're then safely sixty feet apart. Then we split and won't ever see each other again!"

Marco thought about it for a few seconds, then nodded. They each walked their respective thirty feet. Marco did a U-turn and went to pick up the envelope and the phone and put them in his car. At the same time, with his back to Lawson, he retrieved the silenced Walther from under the seat and slid it into the front of his windbreaker.

Lawson simultaneously walked the reverse pattern to pick up the briefcase, then he yelled across to Marco, "So I think I know how you did my Goddamned brother, but how'd you get rid of Lunberg's body?"

Marco laughed softly. "I *didn't* do your brother, shithead`! As for Lunberg, after he stopped breathing, I stuffed his body inside a hollowed-out water heater and simply drove it off to that scrap yard. Pretty slick, huh?"

"Well aren't you the genius!"

As they finished the exchange, Lawson thought he saw one of the agents starting to come out from behind a tree, but the man was still shrouded in darkness. Marco had not noticed the agent and he took a few steps forward.

"You don't really think I'm going to let you walk away from this do you!"

With that, Marco pulled the gun from his jacket and leveled it at Lawson. Almost instantly, the sharpshooter fired. Marco was knocked backwards, but got off two shots in Lawson's direction before he fell clutching his left leg. The FBI team, wearing their Kevlar vests, rushed from the trees and pinned Marco where he lay. He fired one more wild shot before they disarmed and cuffed him. Following his instructions, Lawson had collapsed to the pool deck as if mortally wounded. He arose with a whoop when he saw Marco was overwhelmed. He was unharmed.

The radios came alive as everyone on the team confirmed they were unhurt and accounted for. DeNoli and I gave each other high-fives and started running toward Pulgas Temple. When we got to the scene, we were told that Donaldson had called for an ambulance. He had arranged to have one on stand-by in San Mateo. The bullet had missed Marco's artery and his femur. The agents applied first aid awaiting the arrival of the ambulance. A few minutes later, we heard the distant blasts of the approaching ambulance. Marco's gun was bagged as evidence as was the briefcase with the packets of bills. Donaldson said that, after Marco was sentenced and any appeals were concluded, the briefcase and money would be returned to him. The sharpshooter and Hightower were already filling out the paperwork for the agent-involved shooting. The sound man reported that he got the entire conversation between Lawson and Marco.

One agent was to ride in the ambulance with Marco. The rest of us were to assemble for a debriefing in Seth Hightower's office. Even Paul and I were somewhat adrenalized after the evening's action and, despite the late hour, the whole team was ready for the debriefing. We were back in San Francisco by a quarter to one. One of the agents had been detailed to stop by an all-night Dunkin Donuts to bring us coffee and, yes, doughnuts.

Donaldson and Hightower called us to order and gave everyone a shout-out for a tricky job very well done. Lawson got a round of applause for his bravery and his acting. And I got some nice attention for tracking down McNair and designing "the plan". The Walther had been sent to the criminalists who would first lift the fingerprints and then test fire some rounds to establish the ballistics.

DeNoli whispered in my ear, "I wonder what they'll find in the magazine?"

Since I could not know for sure that Marco had not reloaded the gun and I still did not want DeNoli burdened with guilty knowledge, I whispered back, "No comment."

I was pretty confident Marco had not reloaded because, if he had found the blanks, I did not think he would have showed up at the meet.

Hightower continued, saying that the hospital would get a DNA sample before Quilington was released. He also assigned one of their rookie agents to canvas all the commercial sign shops from San Jose to Oakland and San Francisco. His task would be to see which shop had produced the "Armstrong Appliances" sign. The feds were hunting for more evidence to tighten the noose around McNair's neck.

I asked Donaldson if Marco was wearing a watch when they arrested him. Having already checked his bathroom and bedroom dresser and not found a Rolex, I was disappointed when Donaldson answered, "no, he was not".

The sound technician asked what charges Quilington/McNair would face. Donaldson said, for starters, he would be charged with being an ex-felon in possession of a firearm and an unregistered silencer and as a person in possession of a firearm with an obliterated serial number. Then there would be assault with a deadly weapon and attempted homicide.

DeNoli and I had discussed the possibility of that last charge among ourselves. If the gun was shown to have been loaded with blanks, we felt the charge would nevertheless stand since the defense of impossibility was trumped by the belief and intent of the shooter.

Donaldson said he could not go into detail since the matter might go to trial, but told the group that there was more compelling evidence in Portland. He said the original cell phone video had been enlarged and clearly showed Quilington/McNair's deformed ear. The FBI folks had some more internal details to cover and DeNoli and I were excused. At the motel, I was asleep a few seconds after my head hit the pillow.

The next morning, I called Mel Westlake to report what had happened in San Francisco. The good news was that the FBI had used my information to smoke out Sean McNair and capture him. The not so good news was that we had not recovered Brian's Rolex watch, that McNair's body showed no signs of a healed dog-bite, and that he denied even knowing that Brian had been up in the tree, let alone killing him. And although McNair had wanted the incriminating video, he had not indicated any pre-awareness of who took it or how it was taken. I told Mel we were awaiting a DNA analysis to see if McNair's DNA matched that found on the threads in Wolfgang's teeth. If that came up positive, McNair would still be the leading suspect in Brian

Westlake's murder. If there was not a DNA match, we would be back at square one.

Mel sounded discouraged. "'Square one' would mean we're back to the homeless-person-in-the-park theory?"

"I can't rule that out, but I don't have much reason to believe that's how Brian died. Has Detective Niemus developed any more suspects?"

"No. At least none that he's let me know about. His partner told me that robbery is still their idea of the most likely motive. That makes me think they have no real leads. A random robbery – if that's what it was – would have no logical connection to my brother and would not give them any clues as to who did it. I guess they're talking to persons in the city that have been suspected of violent robberies in the past, but that could take a while. It seems that, so far, no one has emerged as … what do they say? 'A person of interest?'"

"I want to keep working on this! I'm not at all convinced it was just a robbery gone bad."

"I agree. And I want you to keep going. Just send me your bill for work to date."

"Listen, Mel. I've run up a big bill for you with no results in terms of Brian's death. Here's what I propose. I'll eat my time and expenses for the trips to Phoenix and San Francisco. I'll bill you for my early work and my work going forward. Or, if you'd rather,

I can submit a bill for everything to date and then go forward on my own nickel."

There was a pause and then Westlake said, "Let's reach a compromise. I appreciate your generosity in being willing to eat the out-of-state trips. Seems like the feds should pay you for that! What if you simply suspend billing for that period and I'll pay your full rates for your work before then and going forward. If you succeed in identifying the snake who murdered my brother, I'll also pay you for your work that led to McNair. You had good intentions and both of us thought that he had killed Lunberg *and* my brother. If you don't get anywhere in your new search for my brother's murderer, I'll still pay you for your work going forward."

"I can live with that. What if I work with the police and make a real contribution, but identifying the killer is a joint effort?"

"Why don't we negotiate that later? I can tell you now that any real contribution from you would count as 'success' as far as I'm concerned."

That informal arrangement was fine with me and I told him so. I also said that I needed a week or so to catch up once I got back to Portland. My plan was to return to the hunt after two or three weeks. I told him that, in the meantime, the FBI's lab at Quantico should have given us the results of the DNA test. On that note, we ended the call.

I had a ten-thirty appointment to be interviewed by an FBI agent. I had enough time to walk up Powell Street from Union Square to Sears Restaurant for one of their famous breakfasts. It was late enough that I hoped to avoid a long wait. It was still crowded with people waiting, but I lucked out with a table for one. I enjoyed a mouth-watering breakfast of their Swedish pancakes topped with lingonberries, turkey sausage, and fresh orange juice.

The agent was a woman in her thirties with rimless glasses and black hair pulled into a pony tail. I was not told how the jurisdictional issues were to be sorted out. My best guess was that McNair's trial for the murder of the retired ATF agent would be held in Portland, but the firearms charge and the attempted murder of the FBI agent, Lawson, would be tried in San Francisco. In any case, she wanted to hear about everything I did in working on the Lunberg case. We talked for an hour and a half with her recorder running. She said she would send me a transcript of my interview and a summarizing statement for me to read, correct if necessary, and sign.

I grabbed a tuna melt in the federal building cafeteria and used my phone to book a ticket on the late-afternoon Alaska Airlines flight to Portland. That taken care of, I called Angie to give her the information about apprehending McNair. There would be details to follow up on: why had he done it? Where did he get the water heater and the stick-on signs for the van? I omitted my substitution of blanks for live ammunition in McNair's pistol. I did give Angie most of the other details as to how I located McNair. Given the possibility of a trial, Hightower would not allow me to disclose how we set up the actual confrontation and how his agents made the arrest. Basically all I could tell her – and all the Bay Area media would be told – was that there was an exchange of shots in an area south of San Francisco and the suspect was then taken into custody.

Angie was thrilled to have the scoop. There was no time for her to get to San Francisco with a camera person in tow, but there would still be plenty of things to delve into and cover at the Portland end. I urged her to not over-emphasize my role in all that happened to avoid any possible conflict of interest. The call took a while and, when it was over, I had to hustle to the airport to get my plane.

19

Friday, May 15th afternoon

Angie's news story on the Lunberg murder and the arrest of McNair broke the day I arrived back in Portland. To protect her exclusive and stay ahead of the Bay Area reporters, she had had to do an "all-nighter" gathering background information and confirming many local details. The result was excellent coverage and her segment led off that evening's local news. The story had legs and Angie continued to develop it in the following days.

Ten days later, the report on the DNA samples arrived on DeNoli's desk. The samples did not match the DNA from the bloody threads in Wolfgang's teeth. Detective Niemus had never been invested in my theory about McNair so his position was to keep plugging away interviewing known criminals and drug addicts. For me, however, this was quite a setback.

But McNair's DNA did match that from the hair found on the headrest in the stolen van. That added another brick in the wall of circumstantial evidence against McNair in the Lunberg prosecution.

I also heard from Donaldson that McNair had admitted to blackmailing Fulton to get Lunberg's true identity and his current address. Through his underworld connections, he had known of Fulton's cocaine habit and his use of prostitutes and used that as his leverage.

Angie and I had found a house on Alameda that met all our requirements and would become a very attractive home once we did some remodeling and otherwise spruced it up. We were dancing in the streets when our bid was accepted, especially since we knew another couple wanted it too. We got the good news Friday at two-thirty. Angie was up for more sculling so I borrowed a neighbor's boat for her to use. We rowed north to the downtown area. Coming home against the current was a little more work, but we made it back tired, happy, and ready for an early supper.

I had cleared up another pending investigation since returning from California. My brother-in-law, Vince Langlow, had offered us their second home at Black Butte Ranch for the weekend so Angie and I had a wonderful Saturday and Sunday reading, loafing, and riding bikes around the resort-development's hundreds of acres. From the house, we gazed across the tree-framed meadow at that famous triplet of Cascade peaks, The Three Sisters.

Monday, May 18th morning
Aside from working out the home-inspection process with our realtor, my upcoming week was relatively free. I was intrigued by Hefty Fulton's statement – even though I now knew for sure that it was not the true reason for his snooping into Lunberg's file – about the unrecovered money.

I called Stan Madruga and he had interesting things to tell me. He grudgingly admitted that ATF never recovered the payment made by the gun-runners. With one-hundred-fifty some guns involved, the sellers' take would have been around two-hundred-twenty-five thousand dollars. Madruga said Jacobson had twenty-five thousand with him when he was caught. That left two-hundred thousand unaccounted for. He said McNair and his pals had never revealed to Lunberg, in his role as Jeb Furman, where they hid the money from their "deals".

Madruga said they had thoroughly searched the building. They found a secret room. A smart agent sensed that the interior of their workroom somehow seemed smaller than it should have been. The agent used a surveyor's tape to measure the outside "depth" of the structure going back away from the road. Then he went inside and measured the same dimension. It was almost five feet shorter. Anyone inside the workroom saw only a solid rear wall with no windows or doors. Likewise, the exterior of the rear side also had no windows or doors. On a closer inspection of the interior, they saw a drain grate, roughly twenty inches square, in the concrete floor near the apparent rear wall.

They lifted the grate. It was covered with black synthetic mesh on its underside to block anyone from seeing anything below. Beneath the grate was a shaft going down six feet with ladder rungs embedded in one side wall. The shaft opened into a narrow tunnel that had another set of rungs embedded in the wall six feet further along. Climbing that set of rungs, they pushed on an overhead square of flooring and found themselves in a secret room. That room was in the unaccounted-for space between the false inner wall and the true outer wall. They determined it was in this room that the guns were stored before they were ready for crating and delivery.

They also discovered that the tunnel continued a short way and ended at a small wooden door. When they opened that, they were looking into a thirty-inch diameter corrugated vinyl pipe. They crawled through the pipe some twenty-five feet. At its end, it intersected the grade on a down slope covered by wild undergrowth, juniper and deadfall from pinon pines. Its opening was concealed by a camouflaged, hinged lid and some dead boughs.

Madruga said they thought that was how whoever took the money got it out of the building. I asked if ATF knew the identity of the "mule" who carried it out. Madruga said Lunberg had identified the four men involved and the only one they did not arrest on the scene was Mike Jacobson. They arrested him that same night as he was hastily packing some belongings at his apartment. Madruga said Jacobson admitted to using the tunnel to escape, but consistently denied taking the money with him. He had claimed that he last saw the money, in an aluminum briefcase, in the parking lot in front of their building. That was where the exchange had taken place after the pre-purchase inspection was done inside. It was also where the ATF team descended upon the buyers and the sellers and arrested everyone other than Jacobson.

Lunberg had at least learned that the place where the gang stashed their gun-sale proceeds was off premises. All the members except Lunberg seemed to know the location, but none of them had ever revealed it despite repeated questioning. Madruga said this was surprising as he expected someone would spill the beans trying for a lighter sentence. This led ATF to conclude that the group had sworn to keep the secret so they would have a "nest egg" awaiting upon their release from prison. By the time that happened, however, ATF had different national and regional directors and its zeal to pursue forfeiture of the ill-gotten gains had waned. In any case, it did not have the budget for 24/7 surveillance on those who were released.

When Madruga had finished that summary, he said he had a proposal to make.

"You know, I've always been real disappointed that the money was never recovered. Of course, we liened their building and took it through forfeiture and eventually sold it. But we could've gone the same route with the cash. The years went by and there was no follow up! Now, no one is much interested.

"Right now, we have more funds than operatives. What I'm proposing," he continued, "is that we hire you as a private contractor to find who has the money and where it is. Or, if it's already been spent, to do some rudimentary tracing for us. You should collect any hard evidence you find along the way and develop a time-line of how it all transpired. I talked it over with the AIC of our unit and he's okay with the concept. He sent it upstairs. Washington came back with approval for a five-thousand dollar budget. Would you be interested?"

I did a fast guestimate of the time and effort required in my head.

"Okay, I'm in. Of course, if additional people were involved and/or if they were clever about laundering the money, I might have only scratched the surface. But I'm certainly willing to try."

"We understand. If you're truly on the trail but need more hours, we can see if Washington will goose the budget a little. This might be a little bit of a longshot but, if you hit pay dirt, it would be an inexpensive way of getting the process started. We know we'd have further expenses to grab the cash and/or liquidate the assets but, even so, if you and we succeed, the forfeiture should net well over a hundred thousand."

"When do you want me to start?"

"That's the only catch. Now that the new managers are finally interested, they'd like you to begin ASAP. Ironic, huh?"

Since my work on Westlake was at a temporary hiatus, I figured I might be able to shoehorn it in before the closing of our escrow and before I resumed digging into Brian's murder. We worked out an hourly rate and some upper bounds on expenses.

"Alright, I'll get started today. I'll probably have to call you back later this morning."

Madruga said they would fax a contract within the hour.

So slippery old Fulton was not blowing smoke on the missing money issue after all. The possibilities of who took the money from the crime scene were pretty limited. The exchange with the gun runners was done late at night and the building was on a county road with very few homes on it. So the odds of a third-party stumbling onto the briefcase during the confusion were infinitesimally small. Equally unlikely was the chance that it had been left unnoticed in the heat of the arrests and was found by a third party the next day.

One of the ATF agents could have scooped up the briefcase. But, with an inventory surely taking place as soon as the perps were safely cuffed, he or she would have to have found a place to ditch it immediately. And the agent would have to have done so without anyone else noticing. While bad cops have been known to lift a portion of confiscated drugs or bank-robbery money, that happened very rarely and seemed even less likely here.

That left Mr. Jacobson. The fact that he possessed twenty-five K when they nabbed him suggested to me that he had had the stash and "skimmed" it for some get-away dough. Despite his disclaimers, I believed he took the briefcase with him through that tunnel. I called Madruga back.

"I think you said you were with the field agents the night of the arrests. Can you remember how long it took you guys to get Jacobson after you crashed the party at their building?"

"Yeah, I've got a good memory for past events. It took us about forty-five minutes to transport all the guys we arrested at the building to holding cells downtown. Then forty-five minutes or so to figure out where Jacobson lived and get a few of us there on a stake out.

Soon after we got there, he arrived and went inside. We waited for maybe five minutes, then followed him inside and made the collar."

"Stan, I need to know the addresses for the building and Jacobson's house and how long a drive it would be directly from the crime scene to his house."

"Well, he lived on the northern edge of the metro area. I'll have our archivist find the address in the case file. Their building was in the same general area, but a little further north and east, beyond Scottsdale. So, probably a twenty minute drive. I don't have time to drive it for you, but get yourself a good street map from Triple A. With the map, you should be able to estimate it pretty closely. I'll call you back when I have those addresses."

"I don't want this to sound insulting, but I'd be right to think your team gave his house a good going over looking for the money, wouldn't I?"

"Damn right! You'd better believe we searched the house ... top to bottom .. looking for secret panels, loose floorboards ... the works! Nada!"

An hour later, I had the map and Madruga called back with the addresses of the building and the house. I pin-pointed each of them on the map. Obviously, Jacobson had taken the long way home and had hidden most of the money somewhere along the way. I estimated a county road speed limit of fifty miles per hour. Jacobson still hoped to get out of town, so he was probably speeding. Did he pick a place opportunistically or did the group have a pre-agreed place to hide their loot that they used every time? Madruga thought it was the latter. I assumed Jacobson was doing sixty miles an hour. If it took him five to ten minutes to get out of the building and run to his car and another ninety minutes to get to his house, I could plot a "boundary envelope". I added ten minutes more as a margin of error. The stash would have to be somewhere within those bounds. I could rule out places that could not be reached by road. That reduced the area a bit, but there still could be hundreds of houses. And, if they were simply using a hole in the ground "in front of that old Oak tree just past milepost eleven", there were an infinite number of places.

I needed a better way to narrow the focus. I would try to learn if any of the group owned property within that envelope. This meant another trip to Phoenix. It was unclear how long my skulking around would take and Angie had a busy week on her broadcast schedule. She decided to scout some furniture stores in her spare time. I landed a seat on a late-morning Alaska Airlines flight. By two o'clock Mountain Time, I was through Sky Harbor Airport and driving a rental car. I snagged a motel room and planned my moves for the rest of the day.

My first stop was the Pima County Assessor's Office. I checked to see if Garcia or any of the still-living three, Roberts, Jacobson, and McNair, owned property there. The answer was no. I had to have one of the clerks show me how to research past records since I wanted to look back fifteen years. The information was a matter of public record, but he seemed irritated that I did not understand his explanation the first time around. The "tax parcel" denomination did not help much either. Survey meets and bounds would be precise, but using those would take me far too long. I started looking for family names. Jacobson and Garcia were more common so I started with McNair and Roberts. There were a few dozens of Roberts, but only ten McNairs. I called the clerk back and convinced him to work the software to show how many of the McNairs owned property in the sector I was concentrating on. That produced only two: Donald and Ian. Similarly, we narrowed the Roberts families down to three. I copied their addresses into my notebook, thanked the clerk effusively, and set out to cast my line in a very large lake.

The nearest address was for Cecil Roberts in a little community called Carefree. Cecil and his wife were a pleasant couple in their seventies. They both suffered from rheumatism and they told me the hot weather helped. But, no, they had no relations, close or otherwise, named Darius or Sean or Michael. Next up were Ian and Shirley McNair. As we sat on their canopy-shaded patio, they told me of Shirley's career designing greeting cards and his as a civil engineer. They too had no relatives named Sean or Darius or Michael.

The sun was getting lower, but I figured I could cover at least one of the last three names before sunset. Donald McNair lived in a modest, adobe-style home in the desert a little beyond the community of Cave Creek. I saw a pair of spinning whirligigs and a comical pottery bullfrog accenting his front yard. The man who answered the door had several days of white stubble on a rather expressionless face. He wore faded yellow shorts and his scrawny legs ended with feet in sandals. A slightly soiled Mexican wedding shirt completed his attire. His face and arms were a deep bronze corduroy of wrinkles and blemishes. I guessed he was well into his eighties.

He stared at me for several seconds. "Yes?"

I showed him my business card and said I was trying to sort out some property issues involving the estate of someone who had recently passed away. He nodded his head rather vacantly.

"Do you have any relative named Sean McNair?"

That brought some spark to his eyes. "Sean has died?"

"No. Sean may be a beneficiary, but he's not the one who died. What relation is Sean to you?"

"Well, he's my grand nephew."

"Do you see him often?"

"No, not for a while. He used to live around here, but he moved. To California, I think."

"But you used to see him when he lived in the Phoenix area?"

"Yes. He and his buddy used to come around once in a while. They'd have a beer with me and shoot the breeze. They were very interested in my old well."

"Your old well?"

"That's what I said. Are you hard of hearing?" This with an impish grin.

As we talked, he led me to a couple of lawn chairs on a small wooden deck on the shady side of his house. He seemed a little weary so I joined him in the chairs.

"No, I'm not. Sorry. But tell me about the well."

"Oh, I have a new one with a pump and all now. But the old one was possibly from pioneer days. The county wanted me to seal it off, but I just had a wooden cover put over the top. The old bucket windlass is still there. Sean and his buddy made the cover for me."

"I wonder why Sean and his friend were so interested in the well."

"I don't know myself. They seemed to like to fuss with it. I think once I even saw them looking down inside."

"I can see why it might be interesting. My! From pioneer days! Would you mind showing it to me?"

"No, I suppose not. Does this have anything to do with the inheritance?"

"No, not really, but you pricked my curiosity!"

"Okay then." He heaved himself out of the chair. "Follow me."

We walked past a small patch of juniper and my nose caught the distinctive scent. Then we cleared a low rise and I could see the well. It had a mortised stone exterior rising about three feet above the sand with the windlass above. The shaft was circular, perhaps four feet in diameter.

"Do you mind if I remove the cover and look inside?"

"Sure, go ahead."

I wrestled the cover off and could see down about fifteen feet before dark shadows took over. I could make out the coarse surface of the stones. Ten feet down there was something I had missed at first glance. In the concave face of the shaft I saw a small inset area with metal door, a hasp and a padlock.

"Wow, there's even some hardware down there ... looks like a little door!"

"There is? News to me!"

"Is there anything around here to lower me down a few feet? I can study it up close and tell you what it is."

The old man was probably glad for the company and the conversation. He said he thought Sean had rigged a painter's seat on a sling and that he might have left it in a little shed behind the house. We walked over there together and I found the seat, some lengths of nylon rope, and a rappel brake. I carried the ropes and the seat back to the well. Donald watched as I tied one end of a rope to the chair bridle, slid on the brake, looped the rope around the windlass and inserted its free end back into the brake. I took a second length of rope, tied a bowline knot around my waist, measured out fifteen feet and secured the other end to one of the vertical posts supporting the windlass. The ropes looked okay, but I knew they could be over ten years old. I gave Donald my cell phone and said if I were to fall in, he should call 911. With more than a little trepidation, I eased myself over the rim and lowered myself to the level of the little door.

Up close, I saw the padlock I had seen from above and could see that the hasp had been cut through. Someone had used bolt cutters and had been there before me! I gingerly swung the door open. Behind the door was a dug-out cavity about twenty inches wide, sixteen high, and going inward another twenty or so inches. It was empty. I used my phone to take a picture. Climbing out took all my energy. I wasn't a mountain climber and that failing extended to getting up ten vertical feet to exit that well. After one pulse-elevating slip, I finally got my hands on the top rim. Pushing with my feet on tiny nubbins of stone and pulling with my arms, I made it to the top.

Donald gave a cheer and went to produce cold beers for us. I hauled the painter's chair and ropes back to the shed. Donald returned with the beers and asked me what was behind the door. I told him what

I had seen, but did not indicate my disappointment. He was bemused, but untroubled by my find. With a cold Tecate in hand, I had one more question for him.

"Tell me, did you know Sean's friend's name?"

"Aw, that was a while ago. Maybe it was Mickey." He scrunched his eyes shut and thought for a few seconds. "No. I think it was Mike. Yeah, Mike. Never did hear a last name. "

"Did those two come back often?"

"Oh, say twice a year. I liked my nephew. They both acted nice to an old codger like me. About the time they first started visiting, I was in the hospital for almost a month. I suppose they could've come out then too, but I wouldn't have been around."

"Did Sean visit you in the hospital?"

"I can't remember for sure, but I don't think so. He probably didn't know."

The afternoon sun was closing in on the horizon setting the cactus and sagebrush aflame with a vermilion glow. I felt confident the nice old gent did not know his grand nephew was using his property to hide the group's ill-gotten gains. And now, he seemed to have forgotten about the "inheritance" I had mentioned. I gave Donald a man hug and headed for my car.

20

Tuesday, May 19th morning

Last night in the motel, I considered the possibilities. Had an opportunistic intruder come onto Donald's property and discovered the compartment inside the old well? There seemed no chance of anyone getting that lucky. Besides, such a person could not get down in the well without help and equipment. For the same reason, I ruled out a rogue ATF agent on his own private treasure hunt. That left Jacobson, Sean McNair, and Darius Roberts; or, any combination of those guys.

Having myself entered the well in broad daylight, I thought it highly unlikely that Jacobson would have had time, working alone and in the dark, to have left the cash in the well. That meant that he hid it somewhere else while he was on the fly. I had gone to a lot of trouble to find what probably *had* been the secret place they used. They must have stopped using the old hiding place – or at least emptied out whatever was left there – at some time before they were arrested. Then who cut the hasp? And when? I would have to puzzle that out later. For now, I wanted to concentrate on the one man who escaped the raid and very probably took the money with him.

Jacobson had moved to Oregon and done his supervised release there. He could have taken the money with him when he moved. Or, if the heat was still on and he thought he was being watched, he could have been patient and returned to Arizona later to retrieve it. I called DeNoli to see if he could learn whether Jacobson had ever flown from Portland to Phoenix since he moved to Oregon. Then I headed for the airport to start my own flight home.

Throughout the flight, I was bothered by something that would not quite enter my consciousness. I was sure it was something about Jacobson but, whatever it was, I had not captured it in my notebook. On my way to the houseboat from PDX, it hit me. When Jacobson was telling me about his new occupation, he said, "with this kind of business, I can make an honest living." He *did not* say "with this job I've landed, …." or "with the work I'm doing now, …." Was this just a sloppy choice of words or was it some kind of a slip?

After the refractory heat of Arizona, the high cirrus clouds and moderate temperatures of Oregon's spring were welcome. As soon as I was on board, I looked in my notebook for the name of the company that did the landscaping job for McMeniman's Edgefield. It was Green Valley Landscaping.

I got on the phone to the Secretary of State's Office and asked a clerk the name of the person shown as the incorporator of Green Valley. Her answer was Ronald Mathieson. I asked if she could tell me when the company was incorporated. This took her a little longer, but the answer was late 2012.

I hopped in my Acura and drove to the Clackamas County Building in Oregon City. The County's modern offices are sited on a plateau well above the Willamette River and the huge boiling cauldron that was the horseshoe-shaped waterfall named after the city. I quickly located the Assessor's Office and, for the second time in two days, started checking property-tax records. Ownership of the company's yard and office had changed to Green Valley in 2012. The previous owner was a sole proprietorship with the owner's name being Peter Danarian. The property tax had been late one time during Green Valley's ownership and the delinquency notice was sent to none other than Ronald Mathieson. The arrearage was paid up quickly thereafter.

I wanted to keep a low profile on this for the time being so I searched the phone book for Mr. Mathieson. He most likely would be at work on a Tuesday afternoon, but I tried the home number anyway. After five rings, a man answered. I told him I was a PI working for an attorney who was handling a property-line dispute and needed to ask him a few questions. He sounded slightly confused by that, but said I could come over. When I got to the address in the phone book, I saw I had arrived at a retirement facility in the small southeast suburb of Canby. I reported at the desk in the gracious lobby saying I had an appointment with Mr. Mathieson. The young man at the desk made a call and told me Mathieson would soon be there. Moments later, a chubby man with gray hair and a goatee shook my hand. He led me into a pleasant alcove lined with bookshelves.

"I'm sorry to bother you, sir. I wanted to check something with one of the company officers and yours was the name of record."

"Oh that. Yes. You must mean Green Valley Landscaping. I think the lawyer put my name on the original document."

"So you're not the officer I should be talking to?"

"No, no. My half-sister's son runs the company."

"And that would be?" I prompted.

"That would be Michael Jacobson."

I gave myself a mental pat on the back. "So you're merely a silent partner or the principal investor?"

"No, not at all. It was Michael's money ... at least for the down payment. I think he financed the rest, but I didn't get involved in that part of it."

"Alright then. I'm sorry to have troubled you and I'll make an appointment to see him."

I considered asking him why they used that particular arrangement, but I doubted Mathieson knew all the facts. I settled instead for saying, "he sounds like quite an entrepreneur, your Michael."

Mathieson paused and seemed to look me over for the first time. Perhaps he realized he had been talking a little too freely.

"Well, this was a bit of a new area for him, but he has done very well with it."

I shook his hand and took my leave.

My next effort was to contact Peter Danarian. He too was retired and, after I introduced myself over the phone, he invited me to his home in Lake Oswego. To live there, he must have done well with the landscaping business, I thought. I approached an older, but handsomely designed two-story house. I did not know if Danarian was a golfer but, if he was, he was only a short walk away from the immaculate grounds of the Oswego Lake Country Club.

Danarian, wearing a brown cashmere cardigan, welcomed me inside. He was tall, well over six feet, but getting a little stooped. I declined his offer of a "refresher" and asked my first question as we stood in front of the fireplace.

"This little fuss over the property taxes should not involve you, but I am trying to get the succession of title straight in my mind. When you sold the business and its property, do you remember who was calling the shots on the other side?"

"Well I used a commercial broker, of course. But yes, I do remember the other party's name. As I recall, he wanted me to carry the paper ... make it an installment sale. I wasn't too keen on that. I felt, since I was retiring, it was time to cash out and put the business completely behind me. He must have found other financing and I did get my cash-out. But you asked his name. It was Jacobson. Michael Jacobson."

This had been quite an afternoon. I now thought I knew where the missing money had gone: into a down payment that helped Jacobson get his "normal life". How did I feel about that? A criminal had seemingly been rehabilitated with a solid income from a legitimate enterprise. On the other hand, he had scammed his partners-in-crime and hogged the stash. And, he had taken the government's money. But where was the moral high ground on that issue? It wasn't *taxpayers'* money. It was money the gun-runners had earned by selling guns to God knows which criminal or terrorist organizations. I wondered if the money had not, after all, been put to a productive, socially acceptable use. On top of all that, what was my responsibility? In any case, I had to report my conclusion to Madruga. Under the Racketeer Influenced and Corrupt Organizations Act – with a handle like that, no wonder they called it RICO for short – the feds could confiscate the money or the assets it had been spent to acquire.

Angie was coming over for dinner. She arrived at the boat just minutes after I did. I had just turned the barbeque on when she ran onto the now-varnished aft deck and into my arms.

"Welcome back, lover!" she said after we finished our embrace. "I have lots of things to tell you about my scouting for furniture! I'm so glad you measured the rooms and drew that little house plan. It helped me get ideas. So, first chance we get, we can go looking *together!*"

"I'm on! I've forgotten the exact date we close. Is it June fourth?"

"Right. A little more than two weeks from today!"

"Let me get the meat on and make us drinks and then you can give me the full run-down."

I had left a tri-tip in a teriyaki marinade all afternoon. I speared the meat out of its bowl and laid it on the grill. I poured myself a Bushmills and Angie asked for a Rob Roy. She told me about the furniture she had seen. We entertained ourselves placing imaginary furniture into the rooms of the home that would soon be ours. The evening was warm so we ate outside off of individual folding tables. The river was still and we watched a few powerboats making their ways back to their berths. As the temperature started dropping, we went inside. We snuggled on the couch, Angie with her head on my shoulder. She told me again that she was very content with the decision to back out of the Denver interview. That led to another kiss. We snacked on Edam cheese and flame grapes for dessert.

I told Angie about the missing money and what I thought had happened to it.

"I'm not too impressed with Jacobson's 'rehabilitation'," she said.

"I agree he's not a saint, but he does seem to be going straight now."

"But think about it this way. If the feds confiscate the landscaping business, they don't want to run it. So they'll sell it either directly or by means of a court order. So 'honest citizen Jones' buys it. The feds get their money, Jacobson's lender gets paid back and the assets return to productivity under new owner, Honest Jones. The only loser is Jacobson and he's a sneaky two-face anyway."

I thought I'd play a little Devil's Advocate, just for fun. "What about the fact that the money itself was dirty? It wasn't the taxpayers' money."

She wasn't buying it. "But everything that gets forfeited under RICO is ostensibly dirty anyway, isn't it? Crime fighting is expensive. What could be more reasonable than having money from crimes used to lighten the taxpayers' budget for fighting crime?"

"How about this?" I countered. "An acknowledged societal goal is to rehabilitate criminals and assimilate them back into the productive mainstream. It'll cost the taxpayers more than two-hundred thousand to keep Jacobson in prison for more jail time!"

"Well, first I'd argue that his post-release action in greedily deceiving the others about the whereabouts of the money doesn't demonstrate much rehabilitation. Second, if he'd been content just to get a job as a landscaper and work his way up from there, that would have just as well met that 'acknowledged societal goal'."

"Okay, Angie, you win. Of course, the FBI will have to dive into the escrow records and Jacobson's bank records to try to trace the down-payment money back to the gun deal. But I bet Jacobson was smart enough to never deposit that money in a bank. He would have to come up with a damn good explanation of how he had that much moola, though. I mean: he'd been in prison for over eight years, he hadn't inherited it, he doesn't have a rich wife, he didn't win the lottery …"

"Yeah", Angie agreed. "He'll have to do some fast talking!"

Angie had a report on bicycle-car collisions in Portland she wanted to study. I had a few bills to pay for maintenance on the apartment complex so I retreated to my little on-board office. I also had to write my report to Madruga and detail my invoice. After that, it would be time to turn my full attention to Brian Westlake's murder.

21

Wednesday, May 20th morning

I set up a conference call with Stan Madruga in Phoenix and Agent Donaldson in Portland. When everyone was on the line, I told them I thought I knew who had taken the money and where it had gone. I said my report would follow, but gave them an oral account of to whom I had spoken, what records I had checked, and how I believed it had gone down. They were surprised and pleased. Donaldson or his Phoenix-based counterpart might re-enter the picture later but, in the near-term, it was a management decision at ATF on how to proceed. I felt sure the agency would contact the U.S. Attorney's office for legal advice if they decided to go after Jacobson's company.

I was ready to regain my focus on Brian Westlake's murder. I needed to meet again with Sandra Westlake.

And I wanted to have a further conversation with Mel Westlake to see if anything else he could tell me would spark an idea. Brian's laptop had never turned up and Niemus's neighborhood burglar still maintained he had never been inside the house. I wondered if the computer's hard drive had any incriminating content. I convinced Sandra to take a long break and I met her in a coffee shop a block from the office where she worked.

"Have you thought of anything else that might help me or the police?"

"No. I *have* tried, but nothing has come to mind."

"How about any other friends or contacts, any relationships that had become strained, business deals that fell through? Things of that sort?"

"No, as I told you before, Brian didn't have a lot of close friends and he always ran his own business."

"Does the name 'Carolyn' mean anything to you?"

"Not really. Why?"

"There was a matchbook found on his person. It was from that cocktail lounge down the road, The Skyliner. On the inside of the cover, the name 'Carolyn' was printed."

"I know the place. Brian and I had been there a few times, but Brian wasn't a guy to hang out in bars or cocktail lounges. And I already told you that there wasn't another woman in the picture."

"Okay. I've asked this question of everyone I've talked to and I suppose that should include you as well. Can you tell me what you were doing and where you were on the late afternoon and evening of Thursday, April ninth?"

"The police asked the same question. I picked up a pizza at Papa Murphy's around 5:30 after work. You have to bake them within an hour after you pick them up so I came home and stuck it in the oven. It takes about half-an-hour to bake and when it was ready, I ate it ... alone in my apartment."

I asked her which Papa Murphy's and she gave me the street intersection nearest the store.

"Did you pay for it with your credit card?"

"Yes," she answered with a little bit of an irritated sigh. "Do you want to see my card statement for last month?"

"I hope you understand a good investigator has to check everything. That would be very helpful."

She left the room and came back several minutes later with the credit-card statement. Her purchase was confirmed. I thanked her for producing the statement and hoped to steer the discussion back to a more comfortable subject.

"I saw that you told Detective Niemus that Brian's laptop was missing after that break-in. How did you know that?"

"Well, Brian told me a window had been broken in the back of the house. When he looked things over, he saw that his laptop was missing. Besides business stuff, he was working on a novel. The novel manuscript was also on the computer."

"Did he report the theft to the police?"

"I don't know that for a fact, but I would assume so. Brian was a law-and-order person. Do you think that could be important?"

That meant that Property Crimes would have a record of the report and probably details like brand, model and serial number. I could ask Niemus to get those details for me so I could check pawn shops.

"Do you happen to know the e-mail address Brian used?"

"I think I can remember the one he was using before I moved out. It was 'treetopper75@comcast.net'. Of course, he may've changed it since then."

"And the laptop was his only computer?"

"Yes, unless he bought another one after I moved out. Of course he may've bought a new one to replace the one that was stolen, but he mentioned the break-in to me just a day or two before he was killed.

"What was this manuscript about?"

"I never read any of it. He had just started it a little before I left. He said it was going to be a crime story."

"I think most people who keyboard lengthy documents, back them up somehow. You know, either a copy under a different name on the hard drive or on an external drive or even a thumb drive. Do you know if Brian made a back-up of his manuscript?"

"It sounds reasonable that he would have, but he never mentioned it to me."

"Is there any place on the property where he might have stashed something like that if he wanted to be protective of it? Some sort of secret closet or a strongbox in the attic?"

"Well, you're welcome to look in the attic. I haven't made the final choice of a realtor to sell the place, so I can give you some extra keys. The place is pretty much empty except for the workshop in back. Brian *did* store odds and ends out there and I suppose he could've put a digital copy there for safe-keeping. I've asked Gary Stratley to help me dispose of the stuff in the workshop, but we haven't done that yet. But, to answer your question, no, we or he did not have a 'secret' place."

She again offered to lend me the keys to the house, but I said Mel had already given me a set. When I got to Brian's house, I could see it was empty of furniture. I checked on top of cupboards, in the far reaches of shelves and closets, under sinks, behind the washer and dryer … even looked for loose floorboards. Nada. There was a pull-down ladder to reach the attic. It swayed and creaked under my weight. I opened the hatch and stepped into a dark, musty space. I turned on my mini maglight. The usable space was bounded by rib-high plywood. There were no tubs or containers and a stack of plastic shelving was empty. As I peered over the plywood to look for anything taped to the other side, a spider web clung to my face. I brushed it off and continued checking the back side as I proceeded around the perimeter. Again, nada.

I couldn't be sure Brian had made a back-up, but something told me this writing project was more than just a new hobby. If it was important to him, the odds were he would have backed it up. And, if the content were inflammatory or threatening to someone else, he would have kept that back-up hidden. I locked the house door behind me and entered the workshop. It wasn't exactly cluttered, but there were lots of items ranging from paint cans and gas cans to tools to spray tanks. I tried to think where I would hide a small item like a thumb drive. The floor was concrete and the interior walls were solid. I overturned an old coffee can full of screws and bolts. Nada. I opened a small metal box and found only assorted drill bits. I looked at the underside of the shelving. Nada. I shook the paint cans; nothing rattled. I spent over an hour opening, peering, thumping all to no avail. I was about to give up when I spotted a step ladder. I looked upward. There was no ceiling, only rafters and a few simple trusses supporting the roof. I positioned the ladder at the end furthest from the door and looked at and behind each two-by-four in the truss system. There were four trusses in all and I moved the ladder as I worked my way back toward the door. The last truss was close enough to the outer wall that I could not get my head in position to see the back side of the truss. I reached my hand up and ran it along the two-by-four. There it was. A small zip-lock bag stapled to the wood. I tore it off. I was ready to climb down the ladder when my hand felt something else. It too was sealed in a zip-lock bag and stapled to the truss. I yanked it off and descended. Each bag contained a thumb drive.

By lunchtime, I had glanced at what was on the first thumb drive. There were no threatening e-mails, no spread sheets, and no extortion letters. The only item was an apparently unfinished draft of a novel with a working title of "The Past Perfect Murder". This did not look like the clue-laden content I was hoping for. But I had gone to enough trouble to get my hands on it that I decided to invest the afternoon in reading Brian's novel-in-process.

It was not a bad effort, especially for a wannabe author's first attempt, but it had plenty of rough edges. I'm certainly no literary critic, yet even I noticed that the plot and descriptions were fairly good while dialogue and characterization were pretty weak. Was this disparity merely the result of Brian's unevenly honed skills as a novice author or did it suggest that his 'novel' was more of a documentary disguised as fiction?

After six hours of reading off the computer monitor, my eyes were weary. The plot involved an attractive coed who went missing and whose body was found two days later on an unnamed pastoral island near the Columbia River. The protagonist, who had dated the woman months earlier, was finishing an early-evening run. His route took him along her street. As he passed her house, he thought he saw one of her instructors get out of a Saab SUV and walk to her door carrying a bottle of wine. The police had no leads as to the killer. The story continued with the hero investigating on his own and uncovering more and more facts that pointed to the instructor as the murderer.

I was surprised that Brian, with his unassuming and non-violent personality, would choose such a dark topic for his first foray into creative writing. But what did I know about where an author's imagination might touch down in the search for an engaging plot? I printed out the manuscript.

The second thumb-drive held a video that was something of an enigma. It seemed to show a small parking area, perhaps off a county road. It looked to be taken from early evening through early morning of the following day. The parking area and a short stretch of the road were lit from an unseen source. Beyond that, it was pretty dark. There was almost no activity recorded. After eight p.m., only two vehicles passed. One was a pick-up truck moving from the camera's right to left. The other, some kind of a small SUV, first moved from left to right and then, nearly an hour later, from right to left.

Tomorrow, I wanted to dig a little into that storyline. I needed to check known facts, search for as-yet-unknown connections between the fictional characters and real people, and dig deeper into Brian's past relationships.

22

Thursday, May 21st morning

Mel Westlake agreed to see me at his office a few blocks from Lloyd Center on Holladay Street. His office suite on the fifth floor of a boxy, mid-rise building was comfortably – not extravagantly – decorated. There was one framed poster from an early Burgerville promotional campaign but, otherwise, nothing to suggest Mel was in the fast-food business.

We settled into chairs and I let him know that McNair was still denying ever confronting Brian. I said the fact that McNair did not have the Rolex in his possession was a setback. There were many untraceable ways he could have disposed of it. Thus, its absence was not conclusive of his innocence, but it did eliminate what I had expected to be more evidence of guilt. The biggest blow to the circumstantial case against McNair, we both agreed, was the lack of DNA or a bite wound linking him to Brian's dog attacking the killer. I also reminded Mel that DeNoli had learned that the ballistics from McNair's Walther did not match the markings on the bullets recovered from Brian's body. Having closed the book on that avenue of enquiry, I turned our conversation back to Brian.

"Mel, I want to go back to Brian's acquaintances, his peers, maybe even his past life. Can you add anything to what you've already told me?"

"Not much, I'm afraid. He used to have a fishing buddy, but that man died of cancer a couple of years ago. Brian wasn't a 'joiner' so I don't know of any club memberships. He didn't get involved in partisan politics either. Like I said before, he wasn't dating to my knowledge. I'm sure he knew people in the arborist and nursery businesses, but I wouldn't know any names. You could ask his buddy Gary Stratley about that."

"How about military service?"

"Brian was in the Army as an enlisted man, but he was never stationed overseas. I think he was in some kind of a logistical unit. After he finished active duty, he had to be in the reserves for a few years. I had the feeling it was all pretty uneventful."

"Was fishing his only hobby?"

"He enjoyed fishing, but I wouldn't even call that a 'hobby'. I suppose the closest thing to a hobby was his fairly recent interest in writing."

"Sandra mentioned something about that, but it sounded like he was just getting started when they split up. His writing sounded rather secretive the way she described it. Did he tell you anything about it?"

"No. I never knew how he was going about it or what he was going to write about. I do remember he once said to me that he was joining a writing group. It sounded like the members met periodically to critique each other's work."

"Did he name the group or any of the persons in the group?"

"Uh, uh. It sounded like they had a schedule and someone in the group sent out e-mails telling where they would meet, who's turn it was to present a chapter sample, stuff like that. But I never heard Brian mention any names."

"I've come across a partially finished manuscript of his. It's a crime story. About a coed having an affair with a faculty member and then going missing."

"A crime story, eh? I wouldn't have thought that would be his subject, but I guess everyone wants to be a Michael Connelly!"

A buzzer on his desk indicated that he had a phone call. I had some new things to mull over and probably had exhausted Mel's ideas about his brother's interests and relationships. I shook his hand and left him to answer the phone.

Sitting in my Acura in the parking lot, I called DeNoli. "Hi, Paul. How's the hottest detective in PPB this morning?"

"Har, har. I have to admit the Lunberg case didn't do my reputation any harm! And I put in a big plug for you as the guy who did all the heavy lifting. Now if you'd just stop getting parking tickets, you might even get back in the good graces of the suits on the top floor!"

It is true that not too long ago I had quite a backlog of unpaid parking tickets. The higher-ups in the Bureau could not help knowing who I was since I'd been involved in some pretty prominent cases over the last few years. But some of them still felt I was too independent and unpredictable to be associated with their investigations. One guy in particular had discovered the unpaid tickets and argued I was a scofflaw on top of my other failings. I eventually paid the fines and penalties, but Paul still rides me about it now and then.

"Listen, I called because I need a favor. Despite the fact I seem to have struck out liking McNair for Westlake's murder, I'm back in the hunt looking for new suspects. Could you convince Niemus to get a printout of Brian Westlake's e-mail sends and receives? Say over the last four months of his life? I'd like to see if that shows any patterns or new connections."

"I'll certainly ask Niemus. I talked to him a couple of days ago. He seems to have more respect for you after the Lunberg thing. If he's already got that listing, he'll probably share it. If he hasn't thought of asking for it, his ego might get in the way. In any case, I'll ask."

Two hours later, DeNoli called me back. "Niemus said he already had what you want going back six months. I kidded him about having a high-level contact at NSA. Don't repeat this, but he said he didn't need one. Seems he has a guy at Westlake's internet service provider that owes him and that resulted in a quiet hand-off. Of course neither the dead Westlake nor his living brother would care, but I guess it's the privacy of the folks on the other end that makes it so dicey. Anyway, he'll make a copy for you. But, it's on the condition that if you want to contact anyone whose name you see there, you have to invent some other way you learned about their relationship with Westlake."

"No problem. It may not lead anywhere in any case. Did Niemus say it gave him any ideas?"

"He didn't say, but his readiness to share might mean he didn't find it interesting."

DeNoli told me to come by his office to pick up the print-out. Half an hour later, I had the listing. I was already downtown so I just walked over to the nearest Starbucks. I ordered a cappuccino and plopped down with the list in one of the easy chairs. There was the usual profusion of messages that I guessed would be spam. Those I ignored on my first pass. I still had

Brian's business journal and I cross-checked to see if any e-mail addresses in that matched the actual traffic. A few did, but they were either for Home Depot or nurseries which suggested routine business communications. I could return to them later if nothing interesting turned up in my first screening.

I started looking for repeats in personal communications and for messages to or from entities whose purposes I could not infer from their addresses. Starting about three months before Brian's death, I saw a fairly consistent pattern toward the middle of each month with the prefix of "bestseller" in the address.

My next thought was to send an e-mail to "bestseller". I sent a straightforward message saying that Brian had been murdered and that I was a PI working for his family and starting to investigate the killing. I asked that the recipient get in touch with me. I suppose that was a slightly risky move. If "Bestseller" turned out to be Westlake's killer, I had identified myself up front as someone digging into the death. But, even in that case, I figured kicking the hornets' nest would likely give me some useful clues. And I used the word "starting" deliberately to suggest I was not presently any kind of a threat. Less than an hour later, I had a response.

"Bestseller" turned out to be the tongue-in-cheek handle for a man named Geoff Dillard. He was a member of the writing group that Brian had joined just months before his death. He lived in Tigard, a few miles south on the freeways from downtown Portland.

He said he was somewhat disabled and wheelchair-bound and he worked "his real job" out of his home. He told me I was welcome to visit him there. I asked if I could come right away and he was agreeable.

Mr. Dillard was a cheerful fifty-something with a bushy mustache and greying hair. He appeared to live alone. He pivoted his chair and asked me to follow him to his living room. He had a real fire going in the stone fireplace and I inhaled the scent of the pine logs. He motioned me to sit in a leather recliner. He worked as an insurance underwriter and we chatted briefly about our respective professions. I said that Brian's brother had told me about their writing group. Then I got to my questions.

"I found a manuscript that Brian was working on. Did he discuss that with members of your group?"

"Well, it was unfinished. We couldn't get much out of him about what inspired him or about the plot trajectory, but he did offer a couple of chapters for us to critique. We knew it was a story about a tragedy on a college campus, maybe a murder."

"Did you think his reticence was just being a little bashful as he adjusted to a new circle of friends? Maybe a little insecure in the presence of more experienced writers?"

"He *was* kind of quiet. But I sensed it was more than being shy. His writing project had a kind of personal intensity to it. We all need lots of drive and determination to attempt writing a novel, but his work seemed very important to him personally. And he *was* pretty cautious about disclosing details."

"Could he have been afraid someone would steal his idea?"

"I doubt it. That may happen sometimes in Hollywood, but we wannabe authors are pretty darn supportive of each other. Besides, we all have our own premises and plot ideas by the time we join a group like this."

"Did you ever think or did he ever hint that it was autobiographical? Or a slightly dramatized version of a true story?"

"I don't think we suspected it was his story. Though, as I said, there was a certain personal intensity about his desire to publish a novel."

"Did he ever seem stressed to you? Or even concerned about his own well-being?"

"No. I wouldn't say that. He seemed healthy and pretty calm to me. I did have a hunch that when he'd learned a little of the craft from us and improved his own skills, he'd drop out of our group. But that was just a guess."

"Do you mean it seemed like a one-book project for him?"

"Oh, I wouldn't speculate that far. But, yes I *did* see a slight sense of urgency for him to complete his novel."

"How about others in the group? Any friction with Brian? Animosities?"

"Generally, no. Terry Mendenhall seemed to rile him a couple of times, but Terry can be a little pushy sometimes."

"Can you elaborate?"

"Terry several times wanted to know more about the story-line. A little more than just 'how does it end?' He wanted to know if there were 'villains' in the plot. Stuff like that. After the second time Terry pressed him, Brian got a little heated – just for a few minutes – and said he didn't join our group to be interrogated, that the story wasn't ready to be published yet."

"Is that unusual for a rookie author?"

"Yes and no. Some of us are ready to bounce lots of details off our peers in the group. Others are more protective of the characters and plot development, at least until the manuscript is in third draft."

"And Brian had not even finished his first draft?"

"So he told us. I had a feeling he had the whole story in his head. Maybe he wasn't ready to produce a completed draft, but my guess was that he had a good fix on how the story would play out."

"So, again, that 'urgency' thing?"

"Yeah, I suppose that's part of why I got that feeling."

"Anything else between Mendenhall and Brian?"

"I think they had some history. I believe they were both in Portland Community College at the same time. I partially overheard a crack Terry made about some woman that was a fellow student. I could tell

Brian didn't appreciate it. Terry is a pretty fair writer, but he could be a little aggressive at times."

"You mean physically?"

"No. But, you know, he might make jokes at the other person's expense just to make himself the top dog. He was too smart to do that all the time, but it would come out from time to time."

"I'd think that personality trait would not be a good fit in a writing group where all your members had egos to protect."

"I didn't mean to overstate Terry's occasional lapses. Maybe he just had a sixth sense about people who were a little sensitive and how to get under their skins."

Dillard wheeled over to the fireplace to stoke his fire. His body language told me that was all he had to say. I handed him one of my cards and thanked him for talking with me.

I had enough time left in the day to go by the Papa Murphy's where Sandra said she had picked up the pizza. The store manager was a little spooked by my question, but when I suggested she call Sandra Westlake to confirm her willingness to have me check, she agreed. Sandra gave the manager the credit card number and the date. There was only one customer in the store and the manager soon had the information for me. Yes, the holder of that card had bought a pizza in the afternoon on that day. I knew that a clever killer could have set up the pizza purchase as the framework of an alibi but, on the face of it, Sandra's story held together.

Soon after I got back on the houseboat, DeNoli called to update me on the Lunberg case. He told me that McNair was still in California, but they hoped he would soon be extradited. The booking photo was shown to the young man, Mark, at Scrappy Jack's. He was able to positively identify McNair as the man who brought in the water heater. And a clerk at the auto parts store looked at the photo and identified McNair as the person who bought the replacement head lamp.

DeNoli continued, "the most interesting thing McNair's told Hightower recently is that Jacobson and he went to that old codger, Donald McNair's, place and checked the old water well. He said they opened that compartment you found and it was empty. No stash. Jacobson acted as if he were astounded. He told McNair that was where he had hidden the cash. They concluded that their partner in crime, Ignacio Garcia, must have told the feds about the well hoping to get out of prison early in return for cooperating. Then the feds went there and scooped it up. Hightower asked McNair why he didn't just ask his great uncle if the feds had come and taken something. McNair answered that the old man was in the hospital at the time they went back there and the old man's memory was shot anyway so he never bothered."

"That was pretty clever on Jacobson's part, Paul. He never had time to put the money there – probably never even *intended* to hide it there. But, by taking McNair back to the well, he threw him off the scent and convinced him that Garcia had squealed before he died. And remember, Jacobson got out of prison ten days before the other two. He probably went back to the well and cut the hasp to make his explanation more convincing. McNair had no way of checking whether the money had been recovered and that deflected suspicion away from Jacobson."

"Did you learn whether Jacobson ever flew back to Phoenix?"

"Donaldson checked and said he never did. Of course, he could've driven back there."

We ended the call. Angie was working the six o'clock news and I was alone and hungry. I decided to treat myself to a nice restaurant meal. I drove to Lake Oswego and headed for Gubanks. This great, family-owned place is always full, but it is never noisy and offers a gracious setting for diners. I had visions of their mouth-watering bacon-wrapped meatloaf as I settled into my chair.

23

Friday, May 22nd morning

Angie and I spent most of the forenoon going to furniture stores to see what we might like for our new home. We still needed to be budget-conscious so we passed on a couple of pieces we were drooling over. Still, we found a dining table that we could afford and would look great. The new dining room was larger and more gracious than the ones in our present places so the table was a priority. Angie was anchoring the mid-day news so we called it quits at eleven. She invited me to her apartment for dinner and an overnight.

I talked Terry Mendenhall into speaking with me. He was an assistant sales manager at a large car dealership. Friday afternoons were busy for him so our meeting had to be during his sixty-minute lunch break. We met at a Denny's and both chose half-sandwiches with cups of clam chowder. When the waiter left, I started with my questions.

"As I said on the phone, the reason Brian missed your writing-group sessions recently is that he was dead. In fact, he was murdered."

"I couldn't believe it! Brian murdered?"

"Yes, it's true. The police haven't gotten any closer to knowing how it happened so Brian's brother hired me. He knew about Brian joining your writing group. Tell me how Brian acted with you guys. Did he ever seem stressed or sound fearful?"

"Not that I could see. He seemed a little on the serious side … that's all."

"Did he talk at all about his time in the service?"

"No. He kept to himself, pretty much."

"But you knew he had served?"

"Yes, I knew that."

"Have you served?"

"Yeah, I was a Marine."

"In Afghanistan?"

"No. Before then. Before I went to PCC. I never was deployed to any war zone. The Corps was good for me and I believed in what it stood for but, when my enlistment was up, I got out. So are you thinking Brian's being in the army had something to do with his death?"

"I certainly can't say that at this point, but I'm looking carefully at his life, now and in the past. I'm trying to see if there's anything or anybody that could somehow be connected to his death. Did you know the setting for his story?"

"Well, he only shared a few chapters. It wasn't clear from what we read, but I could tell it was on some college campus."

"Did you know him from any time before the writing group?"

"As a matter of fact, I did. We were both at the Sylvania campus of Portland Community College at the same time years ago."

"Friends? Roommates? Classmates?"

"You really are nosing into things, aren't you? No, not friends or buddies especially. We chased the same girl at one point."

I chuckled to soften my next question. "How did that work out?"

"I'd been dating the chick. Our relationship was starting to cool off. Then Brian started taking an interest in her. I didn't really know him at that point, but we met on her driveway one day. A week later she and I broke up. A little after that, she was dating Brian pretty steadily."

"Did you have hard feelings?"

"Maybe … for a few weeks. You know how it is when you're young. I quickly lost touch with her and by the next year, I had a new girl."

"Referring to the first woman you just used the phrase 'broke up'. So your dating her had turned into some sort of a deeper relationship?"

"Yeah. We never lived together, but it was kind of hot and heavy for a little while."

"Did she stay dating Brian?"

"For a while, I think. That was his last year at PCC, then I believe he transferred to Oregon State. After that, I don't know."

"What was her name?"

"Why in hell do you need to know that?"

"Well, she'd be another person I could talk to about Brian."

"You really do dig into the distant past, don't you?"

"I don't know if I will in this case, but you never know where your investigation will lead you. This way, I won't have to bother you later for her name."

"Her name was Mary Aparicio. But she was killed."

"What!"

"Yeah. I think it was at the end of spring term. She disappeared and a few days later some hikers found her body on Sauvie Island out by the river."

It took me a minute to absorb that. So many deaths: Lunberg, then Brian, and now I learn about his former girlfriend. "I see. When was the last time you saw this woman?"

"Hey, man! *I* didn't do it!"

"Okay, but can you answer my question?"

"I think I ran into her a couple times on purpose after we broke up. Not at her house or anything, just on the campus. But she was pretty definite about us being over. Anyway, those 'chance' meetings were just during the two weeks or so after we broke up."

"Thank you. Let me come back to the present. Did you know Brian was going to join your writing group?"

"Not at all. I think somebody he knew, knew someone else in our group and that's how he connected."

"Were you surprised?"

"Yeah, a little. I hadn't seen him for years and then he pops up with the same interest in the same group. That's life, I guess."

"When you say 'the same interest', do you mean you both intended to write college-life stories?"

"No, I just meant writing fiction. I like American history. I'm trying to write about a family during The Great Depression."

"And, other than college days and more recently in your writing group, did you ever run into Brian?"

"No, I never did."

Mendenhall looked at his watch and said he had to go. It was unlikely he had anything more to tell me, so we shook hands and left the restaurant. I decided that I had seen the car-salesman pleasant version rather than the verbal-bully version Dillard had mentioned. In any case, he didn't seem to know anything useful about Brian's service years or any details about his manuscript. Mendenhall might have blamed the end of his affair with Mary Aparicio on Brian, but that was relatively small potatoes and quite a few years in the past. He would remain on my person-of-interest list but, at the moment, I thought him unlikely to be the killer. But now I wanted to learn more about the Aparicio murder.

I found a Monica Aparicio in the phone book and tried that number on the off chance she was a relative. A woman with an older, raspy voice answered and said she was Mary's mother. When I said I was a private investigator and asked if she would talk to me about Mary, there was a long silence followed by a sigh.

"Well, Mary died eight years ago. She was murdered. Who are you again?"

I offered my belated condolences and said I was working on a case involving Brian Westlake who was also murdered.

"Brian? Brian Westlake dated my daughter for a while!"

"That I knew and, again, I'm so sorry about your daughter's death! Could you give me the names of any of her close friends or other men she may have been dating?"

"I remember Terry Mendenhall. He seemed to be fun, but he was a little 'macho' at times. I remember Brian as a decent, responsible guy. They had dated for a while, but not too seriously and – in the end – Mary said Brian turned out to be a little boring."

"When Mary and Terry broke up and she started dating Brian, did she ever tell you Terry was angry?"

"She *did* say she thought Terry was unhappy about her breaking-up with him. And I suppose he could've been aware that she had started dating Brian. But I could not see Terry having any violent intent toward Brian. How he felt about Mary, I'm less sure."

"How about close friends? Girlfriends or roommates?"

"Well, Mary was renting a small house at the time. She wasn't interested in living at home with me; wanted to start being independent. The house had just room enough for her so there were no roommates. I can only remember two of her friends. There was Bella Frickerson. I remember she came here for Thanksgiving dinner. She and Mary studied together for some of their classes. And there was Deanna Teal? No. Tielson? Ah, maybe it was Theilman. Something like that, anyway. I think Mary and Deanna were quite close."

"That's helpful. Was her murder ever solved?"

"No. I don't think they even had any suspects."

Mrs. Aparicio started to weep.

"I am very sorry I had to bring this up. Thank you again for talking with me."

Learning that the young woman Brian had dated had been murdered suggested a whole new line of inquiry. It was time to talk with Niemus. He was on the phone when I called, but he returned my call very quickly. I told him I had some ideas about the Westlake case and he agreed to meet me at the Justice Center in an hour. His attitude seemed noticeably more respectful.

A man with a dark-blond mop of hair and a frame like a welterweight rose as he saw me enter the homicide detectives' squad room. He did not shake my hand, but gave me a reasonably friendly "hello". His tie was loosened and his sleeves were rolled up. Remembering the roofing-tar coffee DeNoli usually got me from the squad-room pot, I almost turned down Niemus's offer of a mug. But it felt like a little gesture of fellowship so I accepted. His cubicle was relatively uncluttered with a few police documents tacked to one of the fabric walls and some family photos on the other.

I informed him that my suspicions about McNair being Westlake's killer had not held up. Then I told him about Brian's new interest in writing crime fiction, that his manuscript involved a professor dating a coed, about the theft of his laptop, and how I'd found the hiding place for the thumb drives. I concluded by bringing up Mary Aparicio's murder and the eight-year-old connection to Brian. I said there might well be parallels to the "story" he had almost finished and the unsolved Aparicio case.

Niemus scrunched his eyes almost shut, then gave me a thoughtful look. "I can see where you're going with this. I'll need to look at the manuscript and the video."

"I'm fine with that. I'll make copies for myself and bring them to you today. Or would you rather make the copies to keep the chain of custody cleaner?"

"Not a bad idea. I'll make you copies at this end so our techies can certify how it was done and that nothing was edited in or out."

"Did you by any chance handle the Aparicio case?"

"No, before my time. But I can access the file."

"Yeah. If the detective had checked her course schedule, we should look at that. If he or she did not, I would like to see it. There probably will be some kind of a FERPA issue. Do you think you have enough for a subpoena duces tecum?"

"Let's wait to see what the old file contains … I'll cross that bridge when we get to it. What's this FERPA?"

"The Federal Educational Rights and Privacy Act. I ran into it last year. It basically puts restrictions on schools releasing student records."

"Got it. You're thinking you'd like some way to identify the professor?"

"*Exactly*. And another idea: we can look to see if she and Brian Westlake took any of the same classes. In Brian's manuscript, the male student knew the instructor by sight. I'm thinking maybe Brian and Mary both took a course from the same person. I can get Sandra or his brother, Mel, to make the request as next-of-kin.

That might circumvent FERPA restrictions. Or not. But it's worth a try. And I'll ask Mary's mother, Monica, to request Mary's transcript."

"Okay. You work on that," Niemus said.

" I'd also like to know what the autopsy report showed."

"That will be in the file. I'll summarize it for you when I get it. Right now, I want to read this manuscript. You're thinking the killer got Westlake because of something in the story?"

"That's certainly what I'm wondering. From the date-and-time overlays, I'm guessing the video is from a security camera. Check out one-twenty-three a.m. and two-fourteen a.m. You'll see a small SUV, maybe a Chevy Blazer, pass by. If the manuscript were purely fiction, why would Westlake have hidden the thumb drive with the video alongside it? That suggests he was memorializing things that really happened and the SUV must have some real-world significance."

"Oka-a-ay." Niemus leaned back in his chair and fiddled with a paperweight on his desk. "And you figure the villain in the story might actually be the person who murdered Ms. Aparicio. And, if that's true, that person had a big motive for killing Westlake before he 'published' his story."

"That's my thinking, yes. Westlake's wife told me that Brian's laptop was stolen from his house shortly before his death. That was reported, so Property

Crimes should have a file. Maybe those two things are completely unrelated. But I can imagine a scenario where the killer heard rumors that Westlake was digging into Aparicio's death and wanted to see what Brian had uncovered without openly confronting him."

"That's possible, I suppose. Anyway, I'll round up the file."

"Great! I've got a line on a couple of Aparicio's girlfriends from her Portland Community College days. I'm going to contact them. I'll let you know if I turn up anything useful."

"Okay, but either way I'll want their names."

"No problem." I wrote down the names of the two women and added Terry Mendenhall, the man who had dated Aparicio before Brian.

As soon as I was back in the Acura, I used my phone to go to the web-site of an internet tracing service I sometimes use. I searched for Bella Frickerson, hoping she was not now married with a new last name. I got a hit. I keyed in her phone number. A woman answered, obviously looking at caller ID and speaking cautiously to a stranger calling from an unfamiliar number. I stated my profession and said I was working on a case that could be related to Mary Aparicio's murder. She said she was then at a New Seasons store in Beaverton just starting her grocery shopping. She agreed to meet me in the coffee-and-pastry café that was part of the store. I told her I could be there in twenty minutes max. I got there in eighteen. I found a nicely dressed, very slender, and somewhat nervous woman at a table with a cup of hot chocolate. I smelled the rich chocolate wafting out of her mug and was tempted to also order one. Instead, I reintroduced myself and showed her my PI license. She studied it and that seemed to make her more at ease.

She told me she had divorced and returned to using her maiden name. She wanted to know how my case tied into what had happened to Mary.

"I'm really not at liberty to say. It's early days and there may be no connection at all. That's sort of the way it goes for we private investigators. You explore lots of dead-ends before something meaningful turns up."

"Alright. What would you like to know about poor Mary?"

"Did she share any fears with you? Or hint that she was under stress for any reason? Was she in a relationship that was going sour?"

"No I didn't ever sense she was fearful. It did seem like she was getting a little wild. I even wondered if maybe she was using drugs. She denied it, of course. As for a relationship, there must have been one because she confided in me that she had just missed her period."

"Did she tell you whom she thought was the father?"

"No. I pushed our friendship a little by asking that question, but she definitely wasn't going to tell me."

"Had she been tested?"

"I don't know for sure, but the way she stated it made me think she hadn't. You might say it was 'breaking news'."

"Did you know whom she was seeing?"

"I think she had been pretty involved with a guy named Terry, but they had broken up by the time she and I became close. Then she dated a man named Brian and I had met him a few times. I think he was kind of sweet on her, but I don't think she felt that deeply for him. They broke up too. After that, I think she *was* seeing someone else, but she was very secretive about it."

"Was that the time when you said she seemed kind of 'wild'?"

"Yes. And we sort of drifted apart a little bit, because of that and her preoccupation with whatever she was into or whoever she was into it with."

"Had you spoken with her in the days right before she disappeared?"

"Yes. We were studying together for a mid-term exam. I thought she seemed a little distant and not too focused, but – on the other hand – quite happy … almost maniacally happy."

"Mary's mother told me Mary had another friend, Deanna Thielman. Did you know her?"

"Oh, yes. She and I bump into each other now and then. Our friendship was mainly through Mary so we didn't keep up after college. She's married now. I believe her married name is Browder. She and Mary were very tight and she took Mary's murder pretty hard. I'll bet she will be willing to talk to you."

I wrote Deanna's new last name in my notebook and thanked Bella for meeting with me. I handed her my card in case she thought of anything else. By then, it was five o'clock and I was ready to fight the eastbound traffic and get back to the houseboat.

24

Sunday, May 24th morning

I could not reach Deanna Browder on Saturday. Angie was anchoring the Saturday evening news so we had the earlier part of the day to ourselves. On a frivolous impulse, we walked along the bike path from the marina to the Oaks Bottom Amusement Park and took a ride on the roller coaster. There was another crazy ride that revolved in a vertical plane and pressed you – standing up -- into the back-rest by centrifugal force. I can handle roller coasters, but no way was I going to ride that puppy!

Sunday, I was back in the hunt. Not knowing where Deanna Browder worked and being a weekend, I called her home number. She answered and I explained why I had contacted her. She said her grade-schooler son was in bed with a nasty cold. I realized it would be a bad time for a home visit, but we agreed that I could ask her questions over the phone.

"Ms. Browder, I understand you were a close friend of Mary's. Can you tell me anything about how she seemed in the days and weeks before she was killed?"

"Mary was vivacious, into living life to the fullest. She would try new things, was always ready to meet new people. She wasn't a great student, but she once told me that you could learn lessons about how to live your life every single day."

"Alright. How about her attitude in those last weeks?"

"Yes. Sorry about running off like that! She seemed very happy, but I thought it was kind of an edgy happiness."

"What made you think that?"

"She was just going full-throttle. Sort of amped up, I guess."

"Could she have been using drugs?"

There was a pause on the phone line. "Maybe. She never used anything around me. But she was a little more driven, more secretive ... even from me and we usually shared everything in our lives. But she never talked about drugs and I never saw that she possessed any."

"I'm told she was quite social. Did you know the guys she was dating?"

"Mary was plenty social, but she didn't play the field. If she was seeing someone, it would just be one fellow."

"Okay. One at a time. Did you get to know them?"

Again, the pause. "I knew Terry Mendenhall. He was kind of a jock type. Good looking, self-confident. They certainly had a relationship ... and it started up pretty quick that first quarter."

"Did it develop in sexual ways?"

"Well, I think they fooled around some. But, she implied he pushed too hard ... kind of wanted to take over her life. That wasn't Mary at all. She was very independent. By mid-winter she had broken it off."

"How did Terry take that?"

"Mary said he wouldn't let it go at first, and she had to tell him unequivocally that it was over. After that, I guess he left her alone."

"Other men?"

"There was a student named Brian ... Brian Westman? Something like that. Like Terry, he was a little older than most of us. He was quiet, steady. She liked him – a change from Terry, I think – and they dated for almost two months. I double-dated with them a couple of times. Brian was not the Big-Man-on-Campus type, just a very decent guy. But, after a while, Mary broke that off."

"Did she say they were intimate?"

"She didn't say, but it didn't feel that way to me."

"Anyone else?"

"Just as she was dumping Brian – maybe even the *reason* she dropped him – she had met someone. Someone that seemed to totally entrance her."

"Did you meet this new person?"

"No, never. That was when she became sort of secretive."

"Did she ever allude to who this person was? Tell you his or her name?"

"There wouldn't have been a 'her' …. Tommy I'll be there in a minute! … Sorry, my son wants some cough medicine. Early on, she told me this much: she said she had really 'fallen for' one of her instructors. That was Mary: something different, something a little risky, something with excitement and she might very well get involved. And, once she started, she'd be in all the way."

"I see. Did she tell you what class he was teaching? Where they would meet? Whether he was a married man?"

"She did say he was unmarried. But that was all she would tell me."

"And sex with him?"

"She never said, but I do think it led to their having an affair. … I'm coming, honey."

I could tell she needed to tend to her son. "I'll let you go, but I may need to contact you again, if that's okay?"

"That would be okay. They never found out who did that to her. And that instructor never stepped forward. I never said anything, because I didn't want to hurt her reputation and break her mom's heart. Do you think the *instructor* could have been her murderer?"

"I can't say. I can see why he would be extremely reluctant to admit to an affair with one of his students. But, at the very least, he was probably the one person who knew the most about what was going on in her life in those last months."

I gave her my phone number and encouraged her to call me if she remembered anything further.

I called Mel and asked him to write out a request for Brian's PCC transcript. I said he should include a photocopy of the death certificate so it was evident that Brian was no longer alive and that Mel was the next of kin. He said he would do that and that his printer had a fax feature. I gave him my fax number.

Almost immediately, Niemus called. He came right to the point.

"That video you gave me? On Friday, I had our techies run it and then I brought in a guy in Traffic who's a vehicle-identification whiz. He's sure that car was a Saab 9 - 7. He says they were made in the good old U S of A by GM on a Chevy Blazer chassis. So you weren't far off. I'm not sure what that gets us, but at least it's one detail clarified."

It was my day to get phone calls. Paul called and asked if Niemus had been more cooperative.

"Yes, he seems quite willing for us to collaborate a little ... at least up to a point. In fact, he just called me with some new information a few minutes ago."

I gave Paul a fast run-down on the "manuscript" that I found in Brian's workshop, the fact that his one-time girlfriend had been murdered, and the cryptic video.

"Have you considered," he asked "that Westlake could have killed her over the break-up and his own death was a revenge murder? She had a Mediterranean name. Maybe some kind of vendetta?"

"That crossed my mind for all of about two minutes, Paul. Nothing about him suggests he could murder someone. Yes, she broke up with him, but he was a mature man with absolutely no signs of instability or violent behavior."

"Just sayin'."

"Listen, there may be a way you can help. In Brian's manuscript, the 'hero' sees a faculty member pull into the hero's ex-girlfriend's driveway carrying a bottle of wine. And he notices the guy's car is a Saab SUV. The 'new information' I said Niemus gave me was that the car on the surveillance video was a Saab SUV! I want to follow that lead. Do you still know that Chief of Campus Security at Portland Community College?"

"Oh, Jerry. Yeah, he's at the Sylvania campus. I don't see him too often anymore, but he used to sky-dive with us. He and I still grab a beer together every once in a while."

"I want to check the parking permits, especially for faculty, from eight years ago. Could you sweet-talk him into helping me?"

"I can try. Do you think they'll have records that old?"

"I'm not sure, but it's worth a try. Thanks. I'm going to grab some lunch. Let me know if you have worked your magic on the parking thing."

I was finishing off a home-made chocolate malt when my phone chimed. It was Paul telling me to contact Jerry Sanderson. I called Sanderson's home phone number. Paul must have been a good buddy, because he offered to come to his office on a weekend to meet with me. When I got to the PCC campus, the man who greeted me was of medium height with a trim mustache and close-cropped brown hair. He looked so fit that I guessed he worked out with weights.

"So Paul said you wanted to look at old parking permits from eight or nine years ago," Sanderson said. "They wouldn't be in this office, but our liability insurance company insists we keep records like that for ten years. We started digitizing the records six years ago, but the older ones -- hard-copy ones -- should be in the basement of the Library."

"Could you approve me looking them over?"

"Possibly, but I'd have to say you were helping me. Paul says you're a good guy. What's your angle?" He added with a grin, "You'd better not be working for someone who's going to file a claim!"

"I think the statute of limitations ran out on fender-benders a long time ago," I countered, with a grin of my own. "If this ever amounts to anything, it'll be a criminal action. If it got that far, there'd be subpoenas and conceivably even a civil suit, but I'm not working for anyone who could file or would want to file a civil claim."

That brought a frown to Sanderson's face. The frown held for a few seconds, then he seemed to shake off his concerns. "I'll call the records librarian tomorrow and tell her you're coming over. I'll leave it at that"

He gave me a campus map and showed me how to get to the library. Then he handed me a document to place on the Acura's dashboard. "Here's a guest-parking permit. Don't want to have to give you a ticket!"

25

Monday, May 25th morning

The Records Librarian asked me if it was a parking permit for a student I was interested in. I said "no, it was a faculty person". That seemed to satisfy her and she showed me to a worktable. Minutes later, she brought me the file boxes containing the old permit information. I asked her if the forms could be sorted by vehicle type or make. She shook her head.

"Now they could, but we didn't have digitized records in those days. They're separated into calendar years, but that's all. And the staff and faculty permits are all mixed together. I've already removed the information pertaining to student permits. Looks like you may be here a while. There's a coffee urn just outside my office. You can help yourself."

I blew dust off the box for the two years I was interested in. I studied the forms to find the "vehicle make" and "year" fields. Another field contained a code for faculty, staff, or student: I saw the code for faculty was a "1". Still another field displayed the car's license number. I started flipping through hundreds of forms. About two-thirds of the way through the stack, I saw it. "Blue 2004 Saab 9-7X". I checked the "owner" field. It read "Cameron Lentier". I asked the librarian if there was a copier in the building. She pointed me to an alcove on the far wall where I saw a coin-operated machine. I copied the page and inserted the form back in the file box. I returned to her office and asked if she had a current faculty directory I could borrow. She handed me the booklet and I quickly saw there was no longer a Cameron Lentier on the faculty.

"I hope I'm not becoming a pest," I said. "But do you have old time schedules for courses here as well?"

"We do, although at PCC we call them 'credit schedules'. Follow me."

She led me to some shelving and left me to find what I needed. The credit schedules were printed on inexpensive paper and the archival copies had a protective plastic cover. I returned to the work table and settled down for another tedious job of flipping pages and searching for a particular instructor's name.

It took me almost an hour before I found it. Lentier taught courses in Business Administration and I wrote the course names in my notebook. I asked the librarian if she could direct me to the office of the Business Department. She produced a campus map and pointed to the Social Science and Technology building. When I got to the office, a bald, middle-aged man with a bit of a pot belly was on his feet with a laptop in hand heading for the door.

He looked at me with a frown. "Yes, I'm the Department Head, but it's time for my class. Don't want to be late. What do you need?"

"I'll try to be quick," I said. "I'm trying to locate Cameron Lentier. It looks like he no longer works here. Do you happen to know where he is now?"

He gestured for me to follow him quick-stepping down the worn pattern of vinyl flooring in the hallway. "I do. He moved up in the world," he said with a flicker of a smile. "He's now an Assistant Professor at the University of Portland. ... left here three or four years ago. Smart guy ... and ambitious."

"Any residence address?"

"We don't usually know that even when people are on our faculty and certainly not after they leave. Maybe Payroll would have it or, maybe not after several years."

"Is there anyone else on your faculty who would know him fairly well?'

"Try Jeff Mortinson. I think they shared a house at one time."

With that, he sprinted out the door and headed for a nearby building. I waved my thanks to his back and walked back to the departmental office. I asked the secretary for Mortinson's office number. I knocked on a door that had two names, one of which was Mortinson's. A man with sandy-red hair and an easy smile answered my knock. He confirmed he was Jeff Mortinson and I gave him my card and asked if we could talk. He looked puzzled, but shrugged his shoulders and showed me inside a small office crammed with students' papers and books. He said his office-mate had left for the day and I should use his chair. I told him I was doing a character investigation on Cameron Lentier.

"I understand you were house-mates at one time so, if it's okay with you, I like to get some background."

A little flush of alarm crossed his face and then he relaxed. "Oh, yeah. He's up for promotion and tenure at UP. I get it."

I did not know that myself, but if Mortinson wanted to think I was working for the University of Portland, I wasn't going to disabuse him of that idea.

"Well, go ahead," he continued. "I'll see if I can help."

"When did you share that house with Mister Lentier?"

"That was before I married so it was at least six years ago. Let me think. We shared the place for two years ... it would've been eight or nine years ago."

"Were you two close friends?"

"Not especially. It was more a matter of convenience to keep our living costs down. I mean Cam was an okay guy. We were both instructors here and both of us fresh out of graduate school."

"You said he was an 'okay guy'. Did you have some reservations about his attitude or his character?"

"Well I suspected he might've been using marijuana at one point. Even in this day and age, that's never been my thing."

"Did you call him on it?"

"I thought about it, but I never saw any evidence of it being in the house. What he did for recreation was none of my business anyway. We were both going to move to separate places when our lease was up in three more months so, no, I never talked to him about it."

"What else?"

"Oh, I don't know ... he wasn't very sensitive about some things. Once we were in his car and he hit a cat that was crossing the street. He didn't stop ... didn't even seem to care. I suppose the poor critter died instantly, but it didn't seem to bother him one way or the other."

"Any other reservations or things that made you uneasy?"

"Mr. Conwright, I'm starting to get uneasy right now. Getting past P and T is a big hurdle in an academic's life. I'm not sure I want my opinions on the record."

"That's quite understandable. Let me say two things. First, I'm a private investigator and things I discover stay private. Even if I learned of something embarrassing like his using marijuana or something harder, it would have to be verified. And, even then, it wouldn't necessarily make it into any report I wrote. Second, I can tell you this much: the investigation I'm doing involves something far more important and serious than getting or not getting tenure. I only have a couple of more questions and I'd really appreciate it if you could help me here."

I could see he was getting nervous and ready to shut down. I shifted to a less direct question.

"How about Lentier's social life. Was he dating anyone?"

"Ah, well … that's kind of what I was uncomfortable about."

I nodded and used the old wait-him-out-and-he'll-probably-cave-in-and-give-you-an-answer tactic. I sat expectantly, but silently. He shifted in his chair, studied the floor and –after many seconds – answered.

"I think he was shagging one of his students."

"I can see why that made you uncomfortable. I'm not in academia, but I'm pretty sure that's a big no-no."

"Yes, it definitely is."

"Did you know her name?"

"He was kind of cocky about his conquest, but he wouldn't go into details. One night he came in late and was pretty looped. He let slip that her first name was Mary. That's all I knew. He never brought her around the house or introduced her. Nothing like that."

"Let me ask you something else. Do you remember what kind of car he drove?"

"I do. I had an old junker and it was in the shop half the time so I'd occasionally borrow his car. It was a Saab. Kind of a smaller SUV."

"Did this dalliance with the student last?"

"No, not for long. After eight weeks or so, he seemed to just drop her cold. He never even talked about her after that. I never knew what went wrong, but that's the sort of thing I did not want to know."

"Did he seem upset or tense or nervous about ending the relationship? Did he say which of them wanted to end it?"

"As a matter of fact, he *did* seem a little strung out. But I suppose that could be natural right after a breakup. As to who broke it up, my guess would be him. He inferred she had fallen pretty hard. Even knowing Cam the little that I did, I don't think he was thinking marriage or anything permanent."

"Do you think he was supplying her with marijuana or any other drugs?"

"Look, I don't even know for sure *he* was using marijuana! That was only a supposition on my part. I shouldn't have even mentioned it. So no, I don't have any idea if he was giving anything to her."

"Tell me, did Lentier ever have any firearms in the house?"

Mortinson gave a little shudder. "Damn! You *are* making this sound serious! I never saw a gun, but one evening there was the odor of oil or solvent in the house. I asked him if he smelled something also. He said 'oh, I was just cleaning something'. Two days later, I was in the basement hunting for my bicycle pump and I saw a little can of gun oil. I was curious enough to put a drop on my palm and it smelled exactly like what I had smelled before. So, yeah, maybe he did have a gun."

"What about his recreational reading?"

"We were both new at our jobs. No time for pleasure reading!"

"How about movies? Did he own any movie discs?"

"Yeah, he really liked caper movies, James Bond movies, stuff like that. I think he had a DVD of every Bond film ever made!"

Mortinson looked at his watch and rose from his chair. "My wife is expecting me home for an early dinner. I need to get out of here!"

The poor man had given me a lot of sensitive information, not the least of which was the first name "Mary". His face had reddened and his shirt at the underarms was visibly damp. I had put him through enough for today.

"I don't want to get you in the dog-house on the home front, so get going. I appreciate your time and cooperation. One last thing though: please treat my contacting you and our conversation as confidential. Believe me, that will be better for all concerned."

As I was heading north on I-5, my phone chimed. I put it on Blue Tooth and kept driving. It was Detective Niemus.

"Hey, Conwright, I got the old murder file on Mary Aparicio. Three things got my attention right away. She had been using marijuana right before she died, she was six weeks pregnant, and the cause of death was strangulation."

"Holy crap! Those are more pieces to the puzzle. I just talked to the guy who shared a house with the instructor who owned a Saab SUV. His name is Cameron Lentier. The former housemate thinks Lentier may've been a bit of a pot head and he heard him say he was screwing a student named 'Mary'."

"Jesus Christ, Conway, how'd you find *that* out!"

"Remember in Westlake's manuscript where his hero sees this instructor at the victim's house with a bottle of wine? It also said he saw him get out of a blue Saab SUV. Well, I checked old parking permits at PCC's Sylvania campus for those years and found one for a blue Saab owned by Lentier."

"Great work! But if this 'manuscript' for a 'novel' is really Westlake's recording of a real happening, why didn't Westlake go to the police?"

"I've been asking myself the same question, especially if Westlake was sweet on this girl. He was a cautious guy. Determined maybe, but not a big social-risk-taker. I can think of a few reasons why he might've held back. First, he could've been afraid, as a former boyfriend who was dumped by the victim, that he might become the lead suspect. Second, in his story, the man with the wine turns away and looks down so that the hero, as he continues with his evening run, can only see a partial profile of the guy's face. So no for-sure identification. Third, he may've thought even if the man he saw *was* the instructor, just coming for dinner on the night Mary disappeared does not make him her murderer. And exposing that the man was dating a student would ruin the instructor's career."

I could hear doubt in Niemus's response. "So he writes a story about it instead? To salve his conscience?"

"Don't laugh. He somehow gets hold of the video of a car that we now know was a Saab and thinks it's significant in some way. The case is never solved. The years go by. Westlake gets married and gets on with his life. But guilt is gnawing at him. He couldn't have stopped the killing, but maybe he could've provided information to identify the killer. Now he and his wife have separated. He has more time to stew about it. He resumes his own personal investigation. He probably knew Mary's best friends and he questions them. He forms a hunch about who did it. Somehow Lentier finds out that Westlake is on his trail. And remember, he probably knew Westlake even back in the day and that's why – in the story – the villain turns his head away so he won't be recognized! And suppose that

Westlake now feels he has enough that he *can* go to the police. He's almost there. A few more facts and his 'manuscript' is complete. But before he can, Lentier gets him."

"I don't know. That certainly could be the way it was with Aparicio, but we still don't have evidence to tie him to Westlake's murder."

"I agree."

"One more thing in the old file. They checked her cell – she didn't have a land line – and contacted everyone on her call list or her phone book. None of them were plausible suspects."

"Interesting. I wonder if she and her new boyfriend were using pre-paid, throw-away phones. So where did they end up?"

"Yeah. If the killer was the new boyfriend, he'd know to get rid of hers as well as his own."

"True. There's another thing that would be nice to nail down. I told you I had the license number of the Saab from the parking permit archive. Just to be sure it really *was* owned by Lentier, could you call DMV and check the ownership from eight years ago? They may not have it at their fingertips, but I'm guessing it'll be in their files somewhere. I doubt they'd do it for me, but they would for you."

"Okay, I'll find out."

I read him the license number. He sounded just a touch irritated. Either he was embarrassed that he had lost a little of the initiative or he was irritated with me for asking him to take care of that ownership detail. Oh well.

"There're a few more things I want to check on the Aparicio side of this problem. And could you please have your man check that video again. If we could figure out where it was shot, I think it would open things up on Aparicio."

By the time we ended the call, I was crossing the Sellwood Bridge and almost home. As soon as I cleared up a couple of those loose ends, I wanted to confront Lentier.

26

Tuesday, May 26th morning

Angie had spent the night and, over breakfast, I filled her in on the investigation. The frustrating thing, I said, was that while I was making progress on the Aparicio killing, I still didn't have conclusive evidence that Lentier had killed Brian Westlake. And that was the case I was being paid to solve!

"You need more evidence that this instructor was at Brian's house for the break-in and again when he ambushed him. He probably didn't take a cab ... too risky that the cabby could identify him as the fare he took to Forest Lane. So maybe someone in Brian's neighborhood saw Lentier's car."

"You're so right, Angie. I hadn't thought of that."

"If you can find out what he is driving, I'll do some legwork up in that neighborhood. Your case has pushed my investigative-journalist buttons! Besides, I smell a good story once you and the police figure it out. I've got a pretty light schedule this week. Tell me the kind of a car and I'll get on it!"

"We can probably find that out from here before you leave. The police almost certainly did a door-to-door right after the murder. But Niemus didn't tell me anything about a strange car in the neighborhood so maybe they didn't come at it from that angle."

I went to the internet and came up with two cars, jointly owned by Lentier and his wife. A 2011 maroon Buick crossover and a 2010 black Ford Fusion. Angie gave me a kiss and said she had to get going.

After Angie left to get ready for her mid-day newscast, I went to the office to think about my next moves. I had only been there a few minutes when the phone chirped. It was Jeff Mortinson.

"Mr. Conwright, I remembered something last night. When you and I were talking I had totally forgotten about it. It was a stupid thing I did, I guess, but it didn't seem important at the time."

"Alright. What happened?"

"In the first place, I didn't think to tell you that a man named Brian Westlake called me about a month ago and asked some of the same questions you did. I asked him why he was dredging up old things like that so many years later. His response was evasive to say the least. But I did answer his questions. The stupid thing I did was to tell my wife about his strange visit and his questions."

"Well, I suppose it's natural enough for a man to share an unusual experience with his wife."

"But, you see, it didn't end there. Cam is now married. Judith told one of her friends, forgetting that that friend was also a good friend of Cam's wife. I don't know for sure that the friend passed it on, but it's quite possible she did."

"Can you tell me your wife's friend's name?"

"It Susan Williamson."

"Well, thanks very much for remembering that and letting me know."

I found a listing for Dick and Susan Williamson and called the number. The person who answered said she was Susan's sister and looked after their children on Tuesdays and Thursdays. She gave me Susan's work phone. Ten minutes later, I had her on the line. She unapologetically admitted to telling Lentier's wife.

"Well why wouldn't I?" she demanded. "I was single then and I was a year ahead of Brian Westlake, but I remembered him. But why was he asking questions about Cam? And why now! I thought it was kind of spooky, so I passed it on. That's what friends do!"

"You said you 'remembered' Brian. Did you keep up with him after he left PCC?"

"No. I have a faint memory that he went on to a university, but I didn't even know if it was U of O or

OSU or someplace else. I never saw him after community college days."

So that was how Lentier could very well have found out that Brian was digging into his activities and relationships all those years before.

I had a good description of Brian's stolen laptop from his estranged wife. I found a link to abbreviated bios and thumbnail photos of its professors on the U.P. College of Business's home page. I took a screen-shot of that faculty bio page and printed that. Then I took my own digital photo of Lentier's picture. I digitally enlarged it and printed three copies of the result. Now I had passable visages of my person of interest. I called Julio and asked if a couple of his people could contact all the pawn shops in town to see if anyone had brought in the laptop. If they got a hit, I asked them to show the picture and see if anyone in the shop recognized Lentier. Julio agreed to get a couple of his people on it and said he would tell them not to volunteer Lentier's name. My guess was that Lentier was smart enough to remove and destroy the hard drive rather than taking the laptop to a pawn shop, but you never know.

I had just finished talking with Julio when Niemus called.

"I had our guy take another look at that video," he began. "He thought there was a sign visible closer to the roadside. It was positioned almost perpendicular to the flow of traffic – probably had the same message on both sides. Anyway, its face was at a pretty oblique angle to the camera so it was hard for us to read. He fiddled with the video, found the best frame and sharpened the resolution. Lo and behold, we now think we can read the sign! It seems to say 'FRESH BAIT' and, under that, 'Night Crawlers'."

"Hey, tell your guy that was nice work! That sounds like a tackle shop or a sporting goods store close to the coast or a river *or close to Sauvie Island!* I'm going to run out there and see if I can spot that sign."

"That's a good place to begin since that's where they found Aparicio's body. Let me know if you find where the video was taken."

"Will do."

I was still in the office when Mel Westlake called.

"Rick, like you asked, I went over to PCC this morning and managed to get Brian's transcript. Luckily, I thought to call Sandra last night and she loaned me the death certificate and co-signed the request. They asked to see it as well as my own ID. They weren't too keen on giving me a copy, but they finally came around. I can drop it off at your houseboat this afternoon if you wish."

"That'd be great because I'm going on the road in just a few minutes and I can't tell how long I'll be. The marina gate is usually open until six o'clock. If it happens to be locked when you get there, call Arkady Turkiev. He's the on-site manager. He's a little hard of hearing, so you might have to raise your voice, but he'll let you in the gate. Do you remember my slip?

I'm moored at number thirteen. Just tape the envelope with the transcript to my door."

I gave him Turkiev's phone number. His call reminded me to call Monica Aparicio whom I had asked to get Mary's transcript. Monica said she had telephoned first and was told to bring the death certificate. With that in hand, she got the transcript yesterday afternoon. I told her I would swing by her house in late afternoon to pick it up.

It was a nice day for a drive, but the only kinds of scenery I was looking for were signs along the roadside and tackle shops. After all those years, the sign may have been taken down. It was even possible the store had gone out of business. And the video could have been taken at a place nowhere near Sauvie Island. Nevertheless, I wanted to give it a shot.

Sauvie Island lies near the south bank of the Columbia River. It is roughly five miles long and two miles at its widest. It is very flat and has little timber. There are a few farms growing hay and one growing flowers. There is also a sizable lake and some marshy areas near the river.

I cut through downtown Portland on our open-trenched freeway, 405, and turned off that onto Highway 30 just before 405 spanned the Willamette River on the impressive arc of the Fremont Bridge. The first couple of miles on 30 were very industrial with factories, warehouses, and tank farms so I sped along confident I would not see any small businesses.

About a mile past the graceful St. John's suspension bridge, I slowed down. There were a couple of small boat-works and a tavern, but no tackle shops. I took the turnoff and crossed the little bridge over Multnomah Channel to reach Sauvie Island. There were four buildings right there on the island side of the bridge. One of them looked like a general store: the kind you see at country cross-roads. There was no sign near the roadside but, in a window next to the entrance, I saw a sign advertising bait for sale. Over the door, a larger sign read "Island Store". I pulled to a stop and went inside. A man in his late fifties wearing a canvas apron and a cap that said "Cat Dozers" was placing some two-gallon plastic gas cans on a shelf. They also seemed to sell everything from canned food and soup to fishing tackle and garden tools.

"Excuse me, sir. Are there any more stores on the island?"

"No. Just these four small buildings. The fellow next door repairs cars and tractors and lawn mowers. The other two places are empty."

"I see. Was your store here eight years ago?"

He laughed. "Son, I've been here fourteen years and the store has been here thirty-five years!"

"Then I have a question for you. I see you sell fishing bait. Did you, in the past, have a sign out near the road that said 'fresh bait, night crawlers'?"

"Damned if we didn't! It got hit by cars a couple of times so we moved it away from the road and just tacked it on to the front of the building. But eventually it got so weathered we had to throw it away. About then, I was having several plastic signs commercially printed so I also had them make a 'bait' sign and there it is…" he pointed toward the door, "taped to the window facing out."

"Was the old one a two-line sign with 'fresh bait' on the top line and 'night crawlers' on the line underneath?"

"Yes, I think that *was* the way it was. Why in the world are you asking about that old sign!"

"I'm a private investigator working on an old case. Did you have surveillance cameras in those days?"

"Yes we did. Kind of fancy for a little country store, but we'd had two break-ins. Our insurance company more or less insisted on the cameras so we had one inside and one facing the area outside in front."

"Were you a full-time employee in those days?"

"You could say that. My partner and I owned the place. He died of a heart attack four years after we partnered up and I bought his half from his estate. Not sure why. Some of the farms on the island are unproductive and none of them brought us much business. The customers are mostly from Highway 30 plus the odd hiker or bicyclist or fisherman. The store keeps me in food and covers the mortgage on my little house, but that's about it."

My professional side was frustrated by his rambling answers but, at the same time, I thought here's a hard-working man who's making the best of the hand he was dealt. "Think back to that time, if you would, sir. Did anyone ever ask you for the recording from your outside camera? Ask you if they could have it?"

"Why yes! A man in his late twenties came by one day and noticed the camera. He asked me if it operated at night. I said yes, because that's when the break-ins occurred. Our camera had a motion detector so it wouldn't clog up the hard drive of the recorder with useless information. He wanted the coverage for the most current week. I hesitated and he finally offered to buy it from me. Gave me twenty-five dollars. He came back the next day with one of those little plug-in storage things and copied it off. How'd you know about that?"

"Tell me what the man looked like and I'll tell you why I knew to ask that question."

He gave me a general description that would fit a younger Brian Westlake. Mel had given me a photo of his brother and that picture was in my briefcase. I fetched the photo from my car and showed it to him. "Do you think this was the man?"

"It was, like you said, eight years ago, but his request was so unusual it made quite an impression on me. Yeah, I'd say that was the man."

I asked him for his name and phone number and wrote them in my notebook. I bought a stick of beef jerky from him. Then I told him that the man in the photo had been murdered and, working for his family, I had found the thumb drive in his house.

Driving back to the city, I knew I had already done a good day's work. I now had Lentier's car on a thinly populated island and not far from where the body was found. And the video was taken on the same night that Mary Aparicio was murdered.

27

Wednesday, May 27th morning

Yesterday, after I left Sauvie Island, I swung by Monica Aparicio's home and picked up Mary's PCC transcript. When I boarded my houseboat, I found the envelope with Brian's transcript taped to my door.

This morning, I brewed a pot of coffee and took a thermos-full into the office. I spread the two transcripts side-by-side on my desk and started looking for any courses they had each taken. Mary seemed to have been floating between Business Administration courses like Social Media Marketing and Advertising, and introductory courses in Multimedia. Brian was taking mostly Business Administration courses and dabbling in some Philosophy courses like Ethics and Environmental Ethics.

I eventually found three overlaps. They had each taken a course in Western Civilization: Medieval to Modern, a course in Business Communication, and a course in using Microsoft Office. I went back to the PCC records center in the basement of the Library, hoping I would not need to bother Jerry Sanderson to smooth the way again. The librarian recognized me from Monday and, without any formalities, reminded me where the old credit schedules were filed. I found the appropriate two years and looked for the three "overlap" courses. I already knew from my previous research that Lentier was one of the instructors for the Business Communications course. I saw that the Instructor for the Business Communications course taken by Brian and Mary was, indeed, Lentier. To be extra careful, I wanted to check the other two instructors. With the help of the Campus Telephone Directory, I called the Computer Applications and Office Systems Department and asked if the instructor who taught the Microsoft Office course was still teaching. The answer was no. He was already retired when he became a PCC instructor as a "second career" job and he retired for good in his late sixties three years ago. I struck him off the list. The History Department office told me that the person who had taught the Western Civilization course was a woman. I struck her off my list.

Brian had taken the Business Communications course a year earlier than Mary, but all I needed to know was that he would have recognized Lentier as the instructor. And that Mary, as a student, would have fallen under Lentier's gaze. When Brian and Mary were dating, I thought it likely that they talked with each other about their courses and instructors. I called Niemus and told him we had another nail in Lentier's coffin, at least as to Aparicio. Niemus said he had reached DOT's Motor Vehicles Division and got official confirmation that Lentier was the owner of the Saab at that time.

I sliced some cold corned beef and had a sandwich and an icy Stella for lunch. Before I finished, Julio called to say Miguel and Theresa had covered the pawn shops and none of the shops had received Brian's laptop in the last two months. I told Julio to send me their hours and said I would cut the checks.

It was time to pay a visit to Cameron Lentier. I arrived on the UP campus in mid-afternoon and parked in a big lot behind the Clark Library. From there, I walked to Franz Hall, the stately building that housed the Pamplin College of Business. The bulletin board beside his office door indicated that Lentier was holding office hours this afternoon. I could hear no voices through the door so I assumed no student was with him. I knocked and he said to come in. Lentier was almost six feet, but not especially muscular. He was a handsome devil though, and I could see that coeds would find him attractive. He brushed a lock of dark brown hair from his brow and looked up at me from behind his desk.

"Oh, you're not one of my students. How may I help you?"

"I'm a private investigator. I've been talking to Mary Aparicio's mother. I'm looking into her daughter's death."

I looked him straight in the eye as I said that and, to his credit, he kept his composure. He moistened his lips before he spoke and splayed his fingers out on his desk blotter, but his face neither paled nor reddened.

At that point, I almost tuned out his response as I shifted my focus to his left wrist. He was wearing an expensive watch that looked, to me, like a Rolex!

He answered in a calm voice. "Oh, yes at PCC. That was an awful thing. Mary took a class from me. I don't remember her very distinctly …" his speech was interrupted by a head-snapping sneeze and he grabbed a tissue just in the nick of time. Then he continued, "Sorry, my allergies are bad right now. Like I was saying, I can't remember her very well from all those years ago, but when one of your students is murdered you certainly don't forget the name."

"Well, I've been told that you were seeing each other and yet you say you don't have a distinct memory of her?"

"Who told you that! That's untrue!"

"I can't reveal that." Now I could see beads of perspiration forming below his sideburns.

"It's true that she came on to me a couple of times during office hours, but nothing happened. I knew better than that! She shut the door behind her when she entered so, of course, no one else was in the room. She must have fantasized an entire romance and then told someone it really happened!"

I made a showing of writing that in my notebook.

"Why would her mother want to pursue an investigation *now*?"

I did not want to clarify for whom I was working, so I deflected his question. "I couldn't tell you exactly what her reasons would be, but she seems never to have stopped grieving."

"That's too bad," he said non-committedly.

I leaned toward him hoping to lock in eye contact. "I've also uncovered a surveillance camera record from a facility on Sauvie Island close to where her body was found. The camera shows you driving by at one-twenty-three a.m. on the night she died."

"That's bullshit! I've heard the name 'Sauvie Island', but I don't even know where it is!"

"But video cameras don't lie."

"You say it was the middle of the night. If a car passed at that time no camera could see me or anyone else inside the car!"

"So who was driving your Saab SUV then?"

The DVD did not capture a license plate, but Lentier did not know that. I hoped my bluff would push him into a reckless answer.

"Wait a minute! What day of the week was this video taken?"

"Mary was last seen on Wednesday and her body was found on Friday. The video tape was for early morning on Thursday.

"Oh, that explains it! My car was stolen on Wednesday night. There were two of us sharing a one-garage house. I was parked on the street that night."

"Did you report it to the police or your insurance company?"

"I didn't discover it was gone until the next morning. I had to hurriedly walk to campus to get to the classroom in time to meet my class. I was going to call the police as soon as I got back home. After my class, I headed home to make the call and fix my lunch. Before I got there, I saw my car at the curb a block from my house. It looked like it had been hot-wired, but otherwise nothing was damaged and I had left nothing inside that could have been stolen. I figured some kids must have been joyriding in it and the cops never catch car thieves anyway, so I didn't bother reporting it."

The man could think on his feet! I gave him a skeptical look. "I see. You were quite fortunate."

He glared at me. "I think we're finished here! It's sad what happened to Ms. Aparicio and I'm sorry for her mother, but I'm through answering your impertinent questions!"

I stood and turned toward the door, then stopped and asked, "have you ever used a throw-away phone, Professor Lentier?"

The glare turned to rage. "Get out!"

After his hellacious sneeze, I noticed Lentier dropped the tissue in his waste basket. It was almost four o'clock and I guessed that custodial staff probably worked the swing shift from four to midnight. I had an idea. I returned to the first floor where I had noticed a door with a sign saying "custodial closet". I found a chair near the outside entrance and sat where I could keep an eye on that closet. My luck held and, at four-oh-five, an older man wearing blue pants and a blue shirt unlocked the closet. I walked over to him.

"Are you responsible for this whole building?"

"Yeah, it's all mine to 'clean and polish' as they say."

I looked at the cart he pulled from the closet. It had brooms, a mop and mop bucket, a small vacuum, a large black garden bag on a frame and, folded up, some smaller, white bags like kitchen garbage bags.

"When you empty waste baskets from the offices, I bet you carry them out into the hall where your cart is and then return them empty to the office. Is that right?"

"Yeah, that's the way we do it."

"I have an odd, but very important request to make. Can you do the top floor first? And when you empty the waste basket from Professor Lentier's office, would you please empty it -- and *only* it -- into one of those white bags? And then come downstairs and hand that bag to me?"

"Uh, I don't know ... are you the fuzz?"

"No, I'm not the police. I'll make it worth your while." I pulled two twenties from my wallet.

His hand was reaching for the bills even before I could put the wallet back in my pocket.

"I guess I could do what you asked."

I shook his hand and gave him the money. I saw the name on the white oval stitched on his shirt was "Grant". "Thank you, Grant. I'll be right outside that main door. How long will it take?"

"I should do all the offices on that floor on the same pass. I'll meet you in twenty-five minutes."

I went outside and moved away from the building. I did not want Lentier to leave and find me still hanging around. In any case, I had to trot back to the parking lot and get gloves, tweezers, a sharpie, and an evidence bag from the kit in my trunk. I made it back a little before the agreed time. I was standing about thirty feet from the entrance when Grant came out and handed me a white bag.

I handed him the little evidence bag and the tweezers and we moved out of sight behind a large shrub. "What I want you to do now, is use the tweezers to pick up any tissues in there and transfer them to that small bag."

He nodded and did as I asked. I sealed the bag and showed him the pen. "Now would you please write on the bag today's date and 'facial tissue from waste basket in Prof. Lentier's office' and sign your full name."

"Whoa, man! That's more than you said I had to do. I don't want my name on this thing!"

I reached for my wallet and pulled out two more twenties. "Look, Grant, here's the deal. If the tissue in the bag is what I think it is, you won't get into any trouble. If the bag contains nothing important, it will just remain between us and you'll be eighty dollars richer."

He thought about it for a few seconds, then sighed, took the money, and reached for the pen.

As I drove downtown, I called Niemus on my cell. I told him I had a specimen of our subject's DNA. He had the good sense not to ask me, over the cellular airways, how I got it. We agreed to meet at the Starbucks down the street from the Justice Center.

It was after five when we sat down at a table in an unoccupied corner. I told him the details of my visit to Lentier and handed him the evidence bag with Grant's writing.

"Christ on a crutch, Conwright! I never would have approved your going on your own to see Lentier!"

"But look at it this way. My visit wasn't official PPB business. The investigating detective – you – knew nothing about it and weren't involved. So what, if a conscientious citizen found some useful evidence and gave it to you?"

He calmed down a bit. "Okay, you might have a point there. But you just got lucky. If he hadn't sneezed and given you that opportunity, you would've just been out in front of my investigation … tipping our hand to Lentier and giving him time to think through his excuses!"

It did not escape me that he said "tipping *our* hand …." That sounded like our collaboration was still on.

I said, "Lentier's smart and quick thinking. I believe he would've given the same answers no matter when you were to interview him. And I think it never hurts to make a suspect jumpy. Sometimes the smarter they are, the quicker they panic."

"Yeah, yeah. Maybe so. I'll send the Kleenex to the lab to see if they can get some of his DNA from it. That will probably take at least a week so you stay the hell away from him!"

"I will. There's one other thing you should know. When I was talking with Jeff Mortinson, his former housemate, I quizzed him about Lentier's hobbies and taste in movies. He said the guy owned DVDs of every James Bond movie ever made. Said Lentier thought Bond was the coolest hero ever. Now think about that. What was the gun Bond used?"

Niemus gave me an admiring grin. "A Walther PPK!"

"Right! Unless he's a bigger fool than I think, he will have ditched the gun right after he killed Brian. But, if you can check the gun registration records, we can at least find out if he owned a Walther. I don't see him having connections to the underworld so that he could have obtained an untraceable weapon. Of course, he could've bought the Walther privately or at a gun show and never registered it."

"Sure," Niemus replied, "but if he *did* register it, that's an additional argument for me to get a search warrant." Then he added, with an unhappy look, "If there's anything left to find."

Despite his inferred rebuke of my confronting Lentier, Niemus said he would stay in touch. I took that as an implicit get-out-of-jail-free card. It looked like the next move would have to await the forensic report on the DNA.

Angie cruised the length of Forest Lane to get the general lay of the land. She found the Westlake house and saw that it now had a "For Sale" sign in front. She then walked the lane in both directions from Brian's place noting the locations of the other homes on her hand-drawn map. Starting at the south end of that range she approached the first house. If she were recognized or if people asked why she was questioning them, she had an answer ready. She would say she was doing background for a possible feature on car thefts in somewhat isolated neighborhoods. Her pretext was that there had been reports that either a Ford Fusion or a Buick crossover had been noticed in other neighborhoods at the time of the thefts. The supposition was that the thieves worked in pairs and used one of those cars to get to their target area.

Only two residents were at home in the five houses to the south. None of them had had noticed any unfamiliar cars in the last weeks. Angie entered the portion of her range to the north. A young mother in the first house had not seen any strange cars. The residents of the next two homes must have been at work or out doing errands. A man in his seventies answered the bell at the fourth, and last, house. Angie gave him her pitch.

"I did not know of any cars being stolen here but, yes, I did see that little Ford. You said it was black didn't you?"

"Yes. Black"

"We saw it twice as a matter of fact." He turned around and raised his voice a little. "Betsy, you remember we saw that car parked just down from here where the shoulder widens out?"

A white-haired woman wearing house slippers joined him at the door. "Yes, I do. Two days in a row! It seemed like a funny place for someone's guest to park since everyone up here has nice long driveways."

The man picked up the narrative. "And, a third time, I'm pretty sure I saw it where the hikers leave their cars when they enter the park. I'm a little less certain about that one because I never got closer than thirty or forty yards. I was just taking a late-afternoon stroll."

"Did you ever see the owner of the car?"

"No. Never did."

"Do you remember what days you saw that car?"

"Let me think. It must have been in early April. We left for ten days down south toward the end of March. We didn't get home until the sixth of April. And I think it was the very next day when we first saw it."

"And when was that last day you saw it?"

"The last time, I was alone. If it was the Ford I saw, that would've been the ninth, I guess."

"How about the license plate?"

"Well, I'm sure I must have seen it, but the car being there was just more of a curiosity. I didn't think about it in terms of a crime. So, no, I didn't memorize it or write it down. Do you think the thieves are casing our road?"

"I can't say, but I wouldn't worry too much. The spate of thefts seemed to peak almost three months ago. Things have quieted down now."

Angie asked them their names in case she "needed to check other details" and they readily identified themselves.

She told Rick what she had learned that evening. They agreed that there was probably more than one black Ford Fusion in the greater Portland area. But, at the very least, Angie had added yet another piece of circumstantial evidence against Lentier.

28

Friday, May 29th morning

More than a week had gone by since Lentier threw me out of his office. I read his righteous indignation as bluster designed to make me question my suspicions. But his explanations had been way too "convenient" and unverifiable to change my belief in his guilt regarding Mary Aparicio. What I really needed now was better evidence that he did or did not kill Brian Westlake.

Angie and I had used the intervening week to resolve issues with our seller over the house inspection, to buy a new refrigerator, and to set some priorities for painting and remodeling. We continued to believe that, if we were patient, we could do a fair amount of the work ourselves. I also had time to investigate a plaintiff's claim in a civil action for a defense-attorney client and to finish the last of the reports I owed other clients. I was getting ready to deliver that last report when Niemus called and asked me to come to the Justice Center.

I could sense he was energized as he waved me toward his cubicle.

"Okay, here's where we are," he began. "Your crazy movie hunch paid off! Lentier *is* a registered owner of a Walther PP 380. If we can find it – preferably in his possession – we can see if the ballistics are the same as for the bullets they took out of Westlake's body. Second, and you're going to like this, there was DNA on that tissue. The lab says it's a match for what the vet got from the threads in the dog's mouth."

"All *right!* If he hasn't disposed of that Rolex I saw, we'll have two or three compelling pieces of evidence. I haven't told you yet, but Angie Richards has been interviewing folks on Westlake's street. On Monday, she found a man who saw an unfamiliar black Ford Fusion in the neighborhood on Tuesday, Wednesday, and possibly on Thursday of the week Brian was killed. Lentier owns a black Ford Fusion."

"Angie Richards the newscaster? What was she doing up there!"

"She's also an investigative reporter. She can read the obituaries or the police blotter like anybody else. She's probably sniffing around for a story since it's an unsolved crime at this point."

Niemus put his head in his hands and groaned. "Jeez, we don't need the media on it at this point! I got to admit though that what she learned is helpful. I looked at the date of the laptop theft on the report from Property Crimes. That would've been the same day this man first saw the car."

"*Yes!* And the second time the car was up there, either other people were around and he had to postpone the killing or else he just needed to observe Westlake to figure out his late-afternoon routine."

"That makes sense. In the time in between, he's reading the manuscript and assessing how big a threat Westlake could be."

Niemus walked over to a pump thermos and filled his mug with coffee. He actually brought me a cup as well. Was this another peace offering?

"Speaking of cars, I found out in the course of my car-ownership search, that Lentier's married now. Could his wife have been involved also?"

"Hm..m..m. Possible, I suppose. I'll look into it. In any case, we're going to get Mr. Professor down to PPB and give him the grilling of his life!"

"Not going to use an arrest warrant?" I asked.

"I have one, but I'll keep it in my pocket. I'm not crazy about arresting him on the campus. All those students around and he might still have the Walther."

"I want to be there."

"I guess you deserve to be there when we pick him up, but you'll have to stay outside the building. My partner's been on loan to two of our colleagues who needed a third person for a 24/7 stakeout. But that's finished and she's back so she and I will go to the campus this afternoon. I'll also have two uniforms, one out in the hallway and the other watching the back of the building. You can pick your location so long as it's outside."

"I'm okay with that arrangement."

"We called the Public Safety Office out of courtesy. Told them where we would be and asked them to let us know if he had any afternoon classes. They got back to us and said he has a one-thirty class that lasts seventy-five minutes. So we'll be watching for when he gets back to his office. That's when we pay our little visit."

We agreed to meet at the campus book store, The Pilot House. I guessed the place was named after the University's varsity sports teams, The Pilots, one of which was a damn fine women's soccer team.

I doubted that Lentier would be carrying on the campus but, with a guy who has killed twice already, you can never be sure of anything. My brother-in-law, Vince Langlow – mindful that, two years ago, I had been shot at twice as I worked to rescue him from his abductor – had bought me a Kevlar vest. I drove back home to put on that vest and to strap on my Baretta.

Niemus waved me over to a corner of the bookstore behind the "Geography" section. He said they had entered the campus off of Portsmouth Street and parked behind the Physical Plant. That location was the farthest from the city streets, but their idea was that it was close to the College of Business and would also make their vehicles less obtrusive. He introduced me to his regular partner, Linda Rollins. Rollins had been surveilling Lentier and reported the professor left his office and got to his classroom on schedule.

One student followed Lentier to his office from the classroom. Rollins was loitering down the hall. When the student left, Rollins spoke softly into a mike under the lapel of her pantsuit. Niemus and Rollins knocked on Lentier's door a minute later. They were told to enter.

"What can I do for you two," Lentier asked warily.

Niemus flipped open his wallet to show his badge. "I'm Portland Police Detective Dan Niemus and this is Detective Linda Rollins. We'd like you to accompany us downtown to answer a few questions."

"Questions? What kind of questions?"

"We're looking for information about two murders. One eight years ago and one last month."

"Murders! I don't know how I could help you there. And even if I could help, I don't want to get involved! I believe in minding my own business."

Niemus put on his game face. "Professor Lentier, when there's a homicide, no one has a choice." Then

Niemus smiled and spread his palms in a more sympathetic manner. "Even honest citizens have to assist the police. And if they won't, they might be accused of obstructing justice." Neimus's smile faded. "We might have to arrest such a person just to be able to interview him."

"Who *were* these people who were killed?"

Niemus gave Rollins a glance, but did not miss a beat. "Mary Aparicio and Brian Westlake."

Lentier swallowed and said, "I see. Well, Mary was a student of mine but, like I said, I can't imagine how I can be of help."

The two detectives were silent, unflinching.

"Okay, okay! I'll go with you," he said.

Lentier grabbed his windbreaker from the back of a chair and shut his door behind them. As he walked toward the elevator, he noticed that Niemus was a little in front of him and Rollins a little behind. On the main floor, they went through the impressive exterior doors and descended the steps that faced the long, grassy quadrangle with the chapel and bell tower at the far end. Niemus pointed to the right, the direction of the physical plant and the lot with their cars. It was then that all hell broke loose.

I was sitting on a bench in front of the Library. I had a good view of the broad staircase leading up to the entrance of Franz Hall. I watched them descend and do a "column right" at the bottom. Two women were coming toward them on bicycles. As they passed, Lentier wrenched the bike from under one woman. She crashed to the ground shrieking. In a flash, he was on the bike and peddling furiously down the sidewalk crisscrossing the lawn of the quadrangle. Even though final exams would begin next week, there were several dozen students strolling or lying on the grass in that open space. I saw Rollins start to reach for her gun and saw Niemus lay his hand on Rollins' arm to restrain her from drawing her weapon.

I launched off the bench and gave chase on foot. I was a little closer to Lentier than the detectives and they seemed momentarily transfixed. Lentier now had a good fifty-yard lead, but I was in full sprint mode. He was gradually lengthening his lead, but he was not leaving me hopelessly behind. He peddled southeast toward the river. It wasn't easy sprinting while wearing an armored vest, but I hadn't lost sight of him. The detectives had now joined the chase and were yelling in an effort to disburse the students. The students were not really disbursing, but were all watching intently. No one seemed willing to intercept the speeding bike rider.

At the end of the quadrangle, Lentier veered left onto a sidewalk diagonally crossing a smaller quadrangle. Thirty seconds later, I too veered left. I was starting to feel the exertion. I wasn't quite gasping, but my breathing was one notch short of a dog pant. Lentier left the last quadrangle and raced through a small parking lot. The campus ended in a high bluff overlooking the shipyard on Swan Island. I thought I would soon have him trapped. He could continue down the paved road that led to Willamette Boulevard, but I was fairly sure that the police would, by now, have blocked that campus exit.

By the time I made it through the parking lot, I saw a single-file of parked cars on that road, but no one on a bike. Beyond the cars to the right was a forty-foot-wide strip of lawn before the bluff peeled off. I ran in that direction and saw the bike lying on the grass. I went to the edge and looked down the precipitous slope. There he was running, jumping, tumbling down the bluff. I could see railroad tracks at the bottom, right next to the dredged lagoon on the landward side of the peninsula that was, in a classic misnomer, called "Swan Island".

This creep had heartlessly killed two human beings while keeping up the façade of a law-abiding academic! I wasn't going to let him get away. I heard some shouting and realized Niemus and Rollins must be approaching. I had only seconds to decide. I lunged off the grass and fought to retain my balance. As I leaped and tumbled down the brush-and-vine-covered slope, I could see that Lentier had almost reached the bottom. I heard the rumble of a deep-throated engine. Then I saw a slow-moving freight train easing around the curve at the bottom of the bluff. I narrowly missed running into a fir tree, but was able to brace a hand on its trunk to slow my descent a little. I tripped on a blackberry vine near the bottom, but managed to stagger back to my feet. The train was now in front of me screeching its way around that lazy S-curve. I watched Lentier jump for a ladder at the end of one of the boxcars. He got one hand on a rung and his legs were flailing near the wheels. Then he got a grip with his other hand and pulled himself onto the ladder. By then, I had reached the bottom. The graffiti besmirched boxcars passed in front of me. I had a choice: wait there and use my cell phone to report to Niemus or try to get on the train myself. There was hardly any time to consider it. I ran alongside the train for a few yards to come abreast of a ladder and jumped.

Despite my racing heart and my heaving breathing, I managed to grab on. It was the devil to hold my weight with my hands. I had to get my feet on a rung. My legs were penduluming too close to the turning wheels. I pulled myself up a rung, then two. It was like doing chin-ups except falling would be far worse than landing on a gym mat! I finally got my feet on the ladder. The vibrations of the cars passing over the rail splicings jolted me, and I clenched the rungs even tighter. Once I felt more secure, I looked ahead for Lentier. The train was still in that left curve and I could see him four cars ahead of me. He was still clinging to the ladder.

The train was now in a slow curve to the right. The wind changed and I could smell diesel fumes from the locomotive. The shipyard had been left behind. The bluff was further away and we were passing an area of warehouses and machine shops squatting on barren fields of dirt and crushed gravel. The locomotive sounded the hoarse bark of its whistle. The train gained a little speed as the track straightened. I wanted to call Niemus, but I could not risk holding on with one hand. The train passed a pair of buildings on the bluff above displaying the name "Adidas". I assumed that to be the American headquarters of the German athletic shoe company. But this was no time to be looking for landmarks!

I thought I could hear the wail of sirens from the direction of the campus. Niemus had called in reinforcements. The rise to the left of the tracks was closer again. Four cars ahead, Lentier jumped off the train and started running up the wooded slope. I had never jumped off a moving train in my life, but there's a first time for everything. I turned to face forward and told myself to hit the ground running. As soon as the car I was on reached the point where Lentier had bailed, I jumped.

My left foot landed on packed dirt, but my right foot dug into the broken rock that bedded the track.

I felt a shooting pain, and pitched forward. It was the same ankle that I had so badly sprained two years ago. The sprain had healed, but the ankle must have been vulnerable to new twists. I galloped the thirty yards to the base of the slope. Lentier had nearly reached the top. My ankle hurt like hell, but I could put weight on it. I started climbing. The underbrush was less dense and the slope not as steep as back on the bluff. Ahead, the slope eased further and I could begin to see lawn.

I staggered onto the grass. I had to catch my breath. If I could reach Niemus, he could set up some kind of a cordon. I stupidly had not put Niemus in my "phone book" or on speed-dial. I called DeNoli as I trotted across the mini-park toward a residential neighborhood. I crossed a street that I thought was probably Greeley Avenue. DeNoli picked up.

"Paul, it's Rick. I was with Niemus when he went to bring in Cameron Lentier from the UP campus. I guess he was coming voluntarily … in any case, they didn't arrest or cuff him. He broke away when they got outside. I chased him and now he's on the loose. You've got to reach Niemus and tell him Lentier is on foot heading East on … stay there …"

I started running again and the mini-park gave way to homes. I could make out a running figure more than two blocks ahead. I had entered a dead-end street heading off to the East. I kept running. In another half-block, I hit an intersection and read the street sign. "... Paul, I'm back. I just crossed Greeley and now I'm running East on Wygant Street. Lentier is ahead of me two or three blocks. Tell Niemus!"

"Got it. You crossed Greeley and Lentier's ahead of you running East on Wygant."

I had regained my wind and started running again. I could no longer see Lentier. I hoped he had not gotten inside a home. Better to think he had just taken a side street. My ankle was starting to be damn painful, but I was on an adrenalin-fueled crusade. I was not stopping.

Wygant stopped at a school yard. Did Lentier turn right or left or – God forbid – did he try to enter the school? It was now after three-forty and I hoped classes were over for the day. There were a few youngsters playing on the swings. I stopped to catch my breath and leaned on the cyclone fence. A boy -- he looked like a second or third grader -- watched me curiously.

"Did you see a man run by here just now," I called to him.

"Yeah. He was really running!"

"Which way did he go?"

The child pointed to my right.

"Thanks, son."

I ran to the next intersection. No sign of Lentier. To my left, I saw an acre of open space that served as a community garden. It was bordered on the south by a thick hedge of old mugho pines. Straight ahead and to my right were homes. I called DeNoli again and asked him to tell Niemus that I had lost Lentier just south of a grade school on Blandena Street. I said I felt he had gone to ground and I was going to search a community garden nearby.

There were houses on Blandena across the street from the school and the garden was behind and a little below them. The vegetables and melons had barely started growing. There were two sheds where I imagined the gardeners stored fertilizer and wheelbarrows. The first shed was padlocked. I stopped at the door and listened. Nothing. I trod quietly to the second shed and saw it had no lock. I listened again and heard nothing. I unholstered the Baretta. I eased the door open and got a good whiff of chicken manure. I peered through the darkness. There was a shovel, an opened bag of manure and a wheelbarrow. In the corner, I could make out a slat lattice leaning on the wall and the handle of a piece of equipment – perhaps a rototiller? – poking out from under a sheet of black visqueen.

I was ready to leave the shed and continue my search in those mugho pines. I had started to turn back toward the door when I looked again at the black sheeting. Something more bulky than a rototiller was under there. I yanked the sheeting away.

Lentier sprung up from his crouch armed with a long-handled, three-pronged cultivator. I jerked myself backwards and the deadly spear points missed my head by inches. Lentier's momentum carried him past me. I got my foot out in time to trip him. Instead of flying out the door, he crashed head first into the door jam. He collapsed onto the cement floor. I could not see the cultivator. He lay still, but made a wheezing sound.

I started to roll him over and saw two of the prongs of the cultivator sticking into his abdomen near the bottom of his ribs. There was very little blood, but I did not dare to remove the tool. I heard sirens coming down the street. I ran out of the garden and waved my arms as the first patrol car swept past me. The second one slammed to a stop and a third, unmarked, car screamed in behind it. Niemus and Rollins jumped out of the unmarked car and yelled at me.

"Do you know where he is!"

I pointed back to the shed. "He's in there. He's pretty badly hurt, but he's alive. He came at me with a cultivator. I tripped him and he fell on top of it!"

They ran down the gentle slope to the shed. As he ran, Niemus yelled to the uniforms "call for an ambulance!"

I followed them back to the shed. I was starting to shiver. I wondered if I was going into shock. Lentier had not injured me, but when somebody attacks you with a lethal weapon, it probably does mess around with your blood pressure. I noticed that the right sleeve of my sweater was torn and there was a small blood stain. I must have picked up an abrasion on my forearm jumping off the train.

I went back to join Niemus and Rollins at the shed because there was one thing I wanted to check. I looked at Lentier's left wrist. It was still there: a handsome Rolex.

29

Saturday, May 30th morning

I had iced my ankle the night before, but it was so tender and painful that it was affecting my balance. Today, my doctor agreed to squeeze me into his morning-only schedule for a quick exam. He determined nothing was broken or torn despite the swelling. I left his office heavily taped and walking gingerly.

I drove to Mel Westlake's home and gave him a detailed summary of how we confronted Lentier and eventually captured him. I told him I had not yet heard from Niemus about when Lentier would get out of the hospital or whether he had confessed to anything.

"He sounds like an all-around evil prick," he said.

"For sure. Maybe he's a psychopath or maybe, like you said, just a violent, self-centered guy. Either way, he should get the needle!"

"How strong is the evidence?"

"Detective Niemus told me to expect an interview with the Deputy District Attorney first thing next week. I'll probably be able to get a sense then of how strong they think it is. They aren't likely to go for the death penalty unless it's pretty solid. My guess is that they will have a tough time showing premeditation on the student's death. They might convince a jury if she had previously told him about her pregnancy, but we do not know that. Otherwise, he'll most likely claim it was just a spontaneous rage brought on by being high on marijuana. Or, he may even claim they drank their wine and he left her that evening alive and well. That's the old 'mysterious third party' defense."

"But the prosecution would have the video of his car!"

"Yes. That's a strong point but still, it's circumstantial and he has that 'my-car-was-joy-ridden' story. And he may even deny having sex with her. Again, the third-party idea."

"But didn't her girlfriends say she was having sex with her instructor and that she had missed her period?"

"They did, but neither of them heard her explicitly say Lentier was the father or the sex partner."

"That's discouraging. Is the prosecution on stronger footing regarding my brother's death?"

"Even there, the evidence is circumstantial. There were no eye-witnesses to the shooting on that trail inside the park. There's the Rolex if its serial number does match the number for the watch Sandra gave Brian. But he'll probably say he just bought it off some guy on the street. The DNA samples *do* match although Lentier could say he was out walking and this unleashed German shepherd just came up and attacked him for no reason. The police are going to try to tie him to the break-in and the computer theft. But the thief must have worn gloves because there were no unaccounted-for prints in Brian's house. I'm sure they'll be able to get a search warrant to search Lentier's house, but he may well have disposed of the laptop and the pistol by now."

"What about this manuscript you found on Brian's thumb-drive?"

"There are even ways that can be challenged. Lentier might claim that the prosecution can't prove that was Brian's manuscript. Neither his wife nor his writing group had seen the whole draft,"

"I see what you mean … if he gets a clever defense attorney …"

"Yes. That's the name of the game. They'll try to create 'reasonable doubt'. That said, there are too many connections to be coincidental. Brian's writing group can testify he was writing some kind of a thriller set on a college campus. Brian took a class from Lentier and so did Mary. So their lives intersected with Lentier. And Brian was sweet on Mary and saw himself, to some extent, as a 'righter of wrongs'. Why would Lentier be out walking way up near Forest Park? Wolfgang, on the other hand, was a close-to-home dog. Will the jury believe Lentier was just incredibly unlucky to have been bitten by a dog owned by the very man who suspected him of murder and was starting to document his reasons?"

We kicked it around for another half hour and I was getting ready to leave when my cell chimed. It was Niemus.

"I looked to see if Lentier's wife was on Facebook. She is and it turns out she works swing shift as a nurse at Good Samaritan Hospital. So the chances of her helping with Westlake's killing or even knowing what her husband was up to on those afternoons is not very good. I'm sure the trial investigator will follow up on that issue, in any case."

"Well, at least you looked into it and, I agree, it doesn't seem likely."

Niemus continued, "Another small victory. One of our forensics guys went back to that trail in Forest Park with a metal detector. Pressed down out of sight into the dirt and needles, he found the second shell casing. They examined it back at the lab and the mark left by the firing pin shows it was fired from a Walther.

Doesn't prove Lentier pulled the trigger, of course, but it's another circumstantial tie to him as a Walther owner."

"And," Niemus added, "the criminalist searched the underbrush for twenty feet on either side of the trail going back from where he found that casing toward the road. Behind a fallen tree and under some salal, he found a raffle stub from the Outdoor Show on April fourth. We traced the stub number and matched it to a ticket where Lentier had filled in his name and phone number! It must've fallen out of his pocket when he hid there!"

"So he was 'lying in wait'," I said. "Isn't that enough to charge …"

"… first degree murder," Niemus finished.

"As long as we're talking good news", Niemus said, "there's more. The hospital doctor said he *did* find scarring on Lentier's lower thigh that could've been from a dog bite."

"Fantastic! The DA will nail the bastard for sure."

We ended the call and I relayed to Mel that more circumstantial evidence had just been found in Forest Park.

"The way you all keep adding to the stack of evidence, I'm hoping the jury will *have* to find there is no reasonable doubt," he said.

Then he stood and walked toward me. "Rick, I haven't forgotten our deal about fees. I'm convinced you found the right man. And along the way, you solved the Lunberg murder *and* the Aparicio murder. I'm ready to pay you for *all* your work!"

"That's very generous of you, Mel. It was like finding our way through a maze, but in the end we found the exit. Thank you for your decision on the fee!"

"You're welcome, Rick. One more thing. You told me about your friend Julio Mendez and his foundation."

"Yes, I did. And they helped with the Lunberg case by finding where McNair bought that replacement headlamp and by checking pawnshops for Brian's stolen laptop."

"That's nice to know and, in any case, I very much approve of what your friend is doing for those young men and women. I'm going to write a five hundred dollar check to his foundation."

"Terrific!"

"I have another idea, too. I use punch cards for the most regular customers at my Burgervilles. Find out how many employees Julio has and let me know. I'll give each of them a card that is good for ten cheeseburgers."

"That's great, Mel. They'll appreciate that! And, it'll bring traffic into your places. Plus, they have friends and they'll tell them how good your cheeseburgers are!"

I shook hands with my client. Before I had even reached the parking garage, Niemus called again.

"Rick, I have more news. First, Lentier's wound was not fatal. It damaged his spleen and the doctors removed it last night. He'll recover. I told you the Deputy D.A. will want to talk with you. But you need to understand, she'll also have to cover herself as to your fight with Lentier ... to be comfortable that you weren't the one who used that cultivator on him. I'm sure you didn't and equally sure that during the struggle in that shed, you were defending yourself from a killer."

"That's exactly right. I shouldn't have any trouble telling my story."

"The next piece of news is that the Rolex *did* have a serial number that matched up! And Rollins and our criminalists got that search warrant and are in Lentier's house as we speak".

I had a few more bases to touch. With the cops and I chasing Lentier across the campus in broad daylight, the media were already on it. But Angie was going to get the story directly from me. She and I had to be careful not to disclose evidentiary issues or anything that would prejudice a future trial if there was to be one. But she was a pro and I knew she would handle it with care. And, what happened after I dove over the edge of the bluff was fair game for an Angie scoop.

I also wanted to fill in DeNoli. He already knew much of it and could find out more from Niemus. Nevertheless, he deserved to hear how the final act played out straight from me.

30

Saturday, June 6th morning

Two days after we ran Lentier to ground, Niemus told me they did not find the Walther in or around Lentier's home. But, he added, they had found a single page from a notebook behind a shredder during their search of Lentier's home office. It measured four-by-six and had been torn from a notebook with a spiral binding. The handwriting on the page started in mid-sentence, but went on to record someone stating that "Mary" had missed her period. A new entry at the bottom of the page began with a notation "3/22/15" and referenced "Deanna Browder". Niemus said they had shown the page to Sandra Westlake and she positively identified the handwriting as Brian's. The police then turned it over to a handwriting expert who said the same thing. Sandra also said her husband had favored small, spiral-bound notebooks. Niemus speculated that Lentier had been shredding the notebook and did not notice one page slipping off and falling between the wall and his shredder. They also found Lentier's fingerprints on the page. More nails in his coffin!

Donaldson told me confidentially that the Assistant U.S. Attorney handling the McNair prosecution wanted a tighter foundation for the video Westlake shot. He said they rented a cherry picker and, with the permission of Lunberg's neighbor, positioned it in her backyard. Then, with the bucket some forty-five feet in the air, they used Brian's cell phone to video an agent standing in the Lunberg back yard. It wasn't Columbia Pictures quality, but it was plenty enough to rebut any argument that the Westlake video was staged or was taken somewhere else.

In the week following Lentier's capture, Angie produced and aired three excellent television news segments on the Portland Community College murder and it's link to the tragic death of Brian Westlake. The station was enthused about the broadcast and about Angie's role in helping solve the case. Although Angie was careful not to favor me or focus on me, I inevitably got some nice publicity. The community college undoubtedly hated the public disclosure that its former instructor was now an alleged double murderer even though it had no way of knowing of his actions.

I'm sure the University of Portland also cringed as the media spotlights shined on one of their assistant professors and his dramatic attempted escape. I hoped UP took solace in the fact that its vetting of Lentier could never have revealed his true character and that the murders he committed had no connection to its campus.

DeNoli and Niemus treated Angie and I to a jolly, top-shelf dinner at The Beast. A night to remember for any carnivore! Even Jim Sanderson, the Campus Security Chief at Portland Community College sent me a congratulatory e-mail.

My meeting with the Deputy DA had gone well. Naturally, my prints could not be found on the cultivator and Lentier's were. And the medical examiner and the trauma surgeon both agreed that the angle the prongs entered his body was consistent with his falling on top of it. The long-and-short of it was that the DA's office had no interest in me as a culpable party. The rest of the time was spent on my explaining how my investigation developed and where it led.

Angie and I closed on the new house last Thursday and all went smoothly. We bought a bottle of champagne and had invited my sister, Debra, and her husband, Vince, to help us celebrate at Angie's apartment.

Angie had only six weeks left to go on the lease for her apartment. Her landlord had a waiting list for his first vacancy so he waived the last month's rent. I'm near to finalizing a private sale of my houseboat. The would-be buyer is one of our best tenants in the twelve-unit apartment building. He and his wife are responsible people and I know they will be good neighbors to the other folks at the marina. My partner and I will have to find a new tenant, but we're hopeful that won't take long in this improving economy. So, real-estate-wise, things have worked out very well.

I will miss the houseboat and will have to find a place to store my scull, but the prospect of sharing a roomy house in a nice neighborhood with Angie trumps everything!

Today is moving day. We have rented a truck. We will start with emptying Angie's place and try to get most of her things over to the new place and put away before the day is over. Angie's friend, Charlene, will help us today. My friend from our volleyball team, Doug Wilkerson, will pitch in tomorrow when we'll repeat the process with my stuff. Angie knows how much I like the old brass enunciator and has agreed it can have a place in one of the extra bedrooms that will become an office for both of us.

This morning, before we start the move, we are eating a celebratory breakfast at Mothers. As is usual on weekends, the place is mobbed. We lingered over our last cups of coffee. Then it was time to get started with the weekend's project. We walked out of the restaurant with my arm around her waist and hers around mine. The sun was shining and the sky was blue. It was a great day.

ACKNOWLEDGEMENTS

Thanks to Del Thomas, Kathy Brault, and Nolan Gardner for their careful proofreading of the manuscript and for their most helpful critiques of the story. Jennifer Hudson at Schnitzer Steel Industries educated me about the recycling of scrap metal. Brian Ostrom at the Oregon State Crime Laboratory gave me useful information about magnifying images from cell-phone cameras. John Siebenaler helped me to understand the federal sentencing and parole provisions. Wayne and the rest of the staff at Cabella's as well as the owner at J&B Firearms Sales guided me on some of the finer points involving firearms. And Randy Lapp at Supreme Comfort explained the internals of water heaters to me.

Made in the USA
Charleston, SC
11 June 2016